"What do you think you are doing with our chattel?"

"After I fix them up? By the looks, I'd say hitting the food court," said Gani.

"*Come out here!*" Heston ordered triggering the mind control. Four of them started to move.

"*Be still,*" ordered Gani. The four froze. While her brother sleeps, she is able to tap into some of his power and Merlin is a magí same as Hex. They are both supposed to be in the same power category. Gani knows more than either of them, which makes her as effective, if not as powerful. The snow-haired mage waved as the doors closed. Heston charged and pounded on them. A few seconds later they glowed and vanished, but Heston was still pounding so hard he put a hole in the wall.

"Don't you hate it when someone won't hold the elevator door for you?" I said.

"You will bring our property back," shouted Heston. The dance floor had pretty much cleared by this point and his four vamp friends had moved in a semi-circle around me.

"Not going to happen," I said.

"Then you will replace them yourself," he said.

"So are all Dubbelsuckers…" I intentionally mispronounced the name assuming Gani had correctly ID'ed the breed. "Delusional or is it just you?"

"You think one lone woman can beat five Dubbelsuger vampyres?"

"You're right. It is unfair. Do you have any other friends who'd be willing to help you out?" I said.

"I'm going to enjoy feeding on you. The things I'm going to make you do will make you beg me to let you meet Death," ranted Heston.

Layla had moved to watch. I looked at her and she nodded. Heston was about to violate both the no fighting and feeding rules. I was doing this anyway, but it was nice to know I had the management's blessing.

I pulled out the two-way radio.

Heston laughed. "So you are calling for help."

"Nope." I pushed the talk button. "Lock this place down."

Holly! Enjoy!
Best Patrick
Thomas

FAIRY
WITH A GUN

THE COLLECTED TERRORBELLE

PATRICK THOMAS

PADWOLF
PUBLISHING

WWW.PADWOLF.COM

WWW.PATTHOMAS.NET

Padwolf Publishing & logo are registered trademarks of Padwolf Publishing Inc.

FAIRY WITH A GUN:
The Collected Terrorbelle™
© 2009 Patrick Thomas.

COVER ART BY PATRICK THOMAS

BOOK EDITED BY ALYCIA J. MELLGREN

SICK DAY ORIGINALLY PUBLISHED DARK FURIES EDITED BY VINCE SNEED
ENDGAME ORIGINALLY PUBLISHED IN BAD-ASS FAIRIES EDITED BY DANIELLE ACKLEY-MCPHAIL, L. JAGI LAMPLIGHTER, LEE HILLMAN, AND JEFF LYMAN
OPEN DOOR POLICY ORIGINALLY PUBLISHED IN NIGHTCAPS
ZOMBIELICIOUS ORIGINALLY PUBLISHED IN EMPTY GRAVES
ATTACK OF THE TROUSER SNAKE ORIGINALLY PUBLISHED IN MYSTIC INVESTIGATORS

TERRORBELLE, NEMESIS & CO., MURPHY'S LORE, AFTER HOURS, BULFINCHE'S PUB, DMA, AGENT KARVER, GRAVEYARD ANGEL, HEX, THE INFINTIE JESTER, DAEMOR, MURPHY'S LORE LOGO AND ALL PROMINENT CHARACTERS ARE ™ AND © PATRICK THOMAS.

ISBN: 10 digit 1-890096-41-5 / 13 digit 978-1-890096-41-0

Printed in the USA

First Printing

This one's for Erin
Without whom I wouldn't know that
Terrorbelle's hair was supposed to be pink

CONTENTS

SICK DAY

When my apartment door was kicked in, I reacted naturally. First, I rolled off the other end of my couch, putting it between me and the intruder as cover. Before I hit the floor, my hand was already reaching out for my gun, which I had left on the coffee table. Next I slid about three feet further down so any bullets ripping through my furniture had a better chance of missing me. Of course, depending on who was bursting in my place, there might be something much more dangerous than a gun aiming at me. It had happened before, just not in my home and that made it personal.

I was going to take down this son of a goblin hard.

As I looked to take aim, I saw a slender, beautiful woman with hair the color of night and a black leather trenchcoat staring back. It was worse than I thought.

I stood up meekly and slipped the safety on. "Hi boss. What's up?"

Nemesis didn't speak, just glared, and her stares can be scary. Sometimes when I look in there, I see things that aren't meant for mortals to see. Or those of us who are somewhere between mortal and beyond.

The gig was up and I was busted. I wanted the day off so I called out, pretending to be sick. Still, there was some hope that I might be able to talk my way out of this. I started with a cough that sounded fake even to me. I did my best imitation of a stager and grabbed onto the back of the couch to steady myself.

"Sorry, all that exertion made me a little woozy. I think I better get something to drink," I said, reaching out for the nearest beverage. It might have been more convincing if it hadn't been a beer. A light beer to be exact. A girl's got to watch her figure, especially when she's half ogre.

Nemesis hadn't blinked or moved at all. I was starting to get worried when she finally spoke. "We have a case."

Then she turned and walked out. I scrambled to find my boots and get them on, but the worst part was figuring out what to do with my wings. I was wearing a tank top, cut low in back so they could hang free. Normally I have specially tailored clothes for when I actually plan to leave the apartment. Even in New York City, a woman with razor-sharp pixie wings stands out. Plus, the streets get crowded and I find it's best to not slice and dice my fellow city dwellers just because they were unfortunate enough to be too close when I made a quick turn.

Nemesis had made it clear I was on the poop list and there was no time to waste. I slipped on my holster and gun, then one of my padded trenchcoats to tuck my wings under. I choose pink for no other reason than I thought it made me look cute and figured cute would make it harder for the boss to stay mad at me.

I rushed out of the apartment and reached to close the door before I realized it was on the floor. I picked it up and pulled it into place, hoping no one would try to open it. My neighborhood used to be considered bad, but crime has dropped significantly since I moved in. I can't say for sure it's because I hung those four gangbangers—the ones who were stupid enough to have mugged old Mrs. Washington from 4B—naked from a lamppost, but I have my suspicions.

Ganieda was waiting at the elevator and smirking, which of course is odd. Not the smirking, the elevator. My building doesn't normally have one. Rudy, short for Thrud, was there standing and staring, but compared to Nemesis she was an amateur. She tended to play on her family's rep rather than building her own. Her father was Thor and her grandfather was Odin. She's a valkyrie.

"Terrorbelle, are you sure you're okay to be up and around so soon? Your message made it sound as if you were at Death's door," said Ganieda. "And knocking hard."

"Gloating doesn't become you, Gani," I said, realizing that perhaps I had been a bit over the top when I dramatized my imitation of me puking up a lung when I called in sick.

"But I'm so good at it," Gani said, throwing her snow-white hair back over her head.

"You had to be good at something I suppose," said Rudy, pulling on her vikingesque braid of red hair, which was slung forward over her shoulder and hung to her waist. She started to roll it up into a bun, a sure sign we were going to be seeing some action. Hanging loose, it made too convenient a grab-hold. Valkyries have some serious martial training and Rudy takes fighting seriously. The rest of life she takes too seriously, even her partying. It's not that she never cracks a joke. I've heard her do it twice and both times I was too shocked to laugh.

"Don't worry, Rudy. You'll find something you're good at some day. What's the deal?" I whispered to Gani, but from within the elevator Nemesis snapped her fingers once.

Gani smiled and waved me in. Rudy and Gani followed. Gani pushed the button and the doors closed. The wall had about a hundred buttons, each one labeled by hand. The one currently lit read *T-Belle's Apt.* Gani pushed another labeled *Nemesis & Co. Office.* Gani had rigged up the elevator years ago. It's great for transporting between two spots, but she has to plug in each "floor" individually by going to the spot herself, which meant we can't just use it to go anywhere we please. It's still impressive, especially when you consider that Ganieda has few magic powers of her own. She taps into those of her twin brother who hasn't used them in years. Actually can't where he's at. He's a magí, a mage that can use any kind of magic and he's pretty famous. Even in Faerie we've heard of Merlin.

When the doors opened, we were at work. Specifically the conference room, which was in war room mode. There were clearboards written on with erasable markers. From what I could see, I had a pretty good idea what we were dealing with.

"Who's missing?" I asked.

"Husband and wife," said Nemesis, slipping into her no nonsense work mode. Until we found these people, nothing would be mentioned about me playing hooky. After that, all bets were off. "Dan and Jenn Kingford. We were hired by the wife's mother."

"Why were they taken? They rich, connected, or have power?" I asked.

"None of the above, but Mrs. Kingford is eight and a half months pregnant with twins," said Nemesis.

"Damn." I really hate it when kids are involved. I tend to make things personal. Several years ago, my mother was slaughtered by soldiers in front of my eyes. I was eleven and I had to grow up fast. Between the torture, enslavement, and what the soldiers did to me, it was a very dark time. A kid, even an unborn one, in danger brings it all back to me. I was helpless back then. I'm not anymore. Unfortunately, the things a pregnant woman is kidnapped for rarely involve ransom. These days it tends to be a deadly style of babynapping. Sometimes it's worse than that. "Do we have any leads?"

Nemesis pointed to what looked like a finger bone key ring. The thing had a couple of blood red rubies, hair and what I was guessing were fingernails attached.

I moved to get a closer look. It was in a binding circle on the table.

"Don't touch it," Nemesis ordered.

"This is not my first day on the job," I said, annoyed.

"Just making sure your illness hadn't worsened your judgment even further," said Nemesis with a glint in her eye. Whether it was from amusement or anger, I couldn't tell.

I guess I was wrong when I said she wouldn't say anything until it was over.

Gani started coughing and gagging until she collapsed onto the floor gasping for air. "I'm not feeling well." Gani coughed loud and fake. "Don't worry about me. I'll be okay."

"Fine, next time I won't call out sick. I'll e-mail instead," I said. "The kidnapper is a necromancer?" That much I was able to garner from the fetish. Gani and Nemesis nodded. "There an alignment coming up?"

"There's one every few months if you know what you're looking for," said Gani. She makes up for her lack of innate power with a knowledge of magiks that I doubt even Merlin could match. "And yes, there's one today."

"Damn. For what? Demons, shadow creatures?" I asked. Despite my casual demeanor I was scared. Ready to puke up my lungs for real scared. Summonings are damn dangerous. Nemesis traditionally has three agents, going back to the Furies. There have been dozens over the centuries. The one I replaced left for reasons of her own. Rudy's only been with us a few months. She replaced a friend of mine we lost stopping a higher demon summoning. I was laid up for weeks. Gani was in a coma for seven days. Nemesis lost her right arm, but her mother Nyx was in a generous mood and grew her a new one made of night during the darkness of the next evening.

"Chaos spawn," said Gani, frowning. She was scared too, which made me feel better and worse at the same time.

"Double damn," I said, but it was more of a rasp. Creatures of Chaos ruled the worlds before the gods and angels fell. All the old myths talk about them helping create the universe, which I've been told is bunk. They were kicked out during the whole *let there be light* thing and have been trying to get back in ever since.

Chaos spawn are the offspring of Chaos, often half-breeds, but sometimes not. Not all of them are evil, but they do seem to lean that way more often than not, Nemesis' mother notwithstanding. Think Lovecraftian, only worse.

"Are we sure that's what the necro wants with them?" I asked, looking for a way out.

Gani nodded. "The fetish is to make sure he can't be tracked."

"Does it work?" I asked.

"Very well. I don't agree with the philosophy behind his use of his art, but I can't fault his craftsmanship. It normally takes sacrificing three virgins to make one of these. He used five. If a DMA..." Department of Mystic Affairs –government agency charged with dealing with mystic threats against the US. "... agent found this, I doubt they'd have a chance."

"Of course they don't have Gani," said Nemesis, smiling.

"Arthur was hard enough to work for, but bureaucrats? Forget about it. Of course, the only way I can counteract the fetish would be to sacrifice *six* virgins, which would be wrong and time consuming." Gani was joking. She always is when she talks like that. At least I hope she is. "So tracking the Kingfords is out. However, tracking the person who made the fetish is another matter."

"So we find the necro, we find the family," I said.

"Assuming he didn't contract the work out, yes," said Gani.

"And the odds of a necromancer wasting that many virgins for someone else are phenomenal."

If I knew how we'd be defying the odds, I'd have bought a lottery ticket.

Gani cast a spell on a locator globe, which was something of her own design. It was a glass globe about the size of a golf ball with a needle like a compass. Instead of being able to only point in a circle, it could aim its arrow in any direction. Helped with the up, down and diagonals. I've never been able to figure out how the fulcrum works or what it hangs on. "It's magic" has never been an entirely satisfactory answer for me.

The size of the needle indicated the distance from the target. Thin meant far, thick close. If the arrow had been me, I would be considering diet plans.

"He's still in the city," said Gani.

"Manhattan?" asked Nemesis.

Gani looked at the needle, then out the window. "I'm guessing Brooklyn."

"Let's go," said Nemesis. My three partners moved and I hesitated, Nemesis noticed. "Who are you hitching a ride with, Belle?"

"Nobody. I'll take my motorcycle and meet you there," I said.

"No time to waste. Choose," insisted Nemesis.

I hated this. I had a perfectly serviceable bike, but I rarely got to use it because it was a regular motorcycle and therefore too slow. My travel speed was too limited by things like traffic, weather, and the laws of physics.

The rest of Nemesis and Co. didn't share my limitations. Apparently, all valkyries were issued a flying winged horse. Rudy's was named Morningdour. I know it seems odd for somebody with wings, but I'm afraid of heights, at least on Earth. Back in Faerie, I could fly. Not real long or far, but I could soar through the sky. It has something to do with the difference in the amount of magic available on each world, there obviously being much more on Faerie. For someone used to being able to defy gravity, having to deal with the concept of obeying its laws takes some getting used to. Rudy knew my issues and when I had to ride with her, she took full advantage of that knowledge with aerial acrobatics that would make a pilot faint. Gani body slid, which was a way to pass through objects by temporarily making them or you not exist–

another of those "it's magic" things I've never been entirely clear on–then using natural forces to pull you from one place to another. It was easy to overshoot and every time I slid, it made me really sick. I always ended up puking my guts out. Nemesis shadow stepped, which is just what it sounds like. The boss steps into one shadow and comes out of another. Shadow stepping was far worse than body sliding. There were things that lived in the shadows. Things for which the darkness wasn't dark enough. After a jump, I'm always left with a chill in my bones that even a hot bath didn't fully get rid of.

Sighing, I said, "I'll go with Gani."

Nemesis nodded and walked into a corner of the office that was never kept lit and didn't walk out. Rudy went to the rooftop where we had a stable next to the helipad. Morningdour had an enchantment that ensured that little things like people and cameras couldn't detect her. It helped them hover undetected over battlefields in the old days.

Gani turned to me and smiled. She knew I had a weak stomach when it came to body sliding. "Who'd have thought your phone message would turn out to be prophetic."

"Ha, ha," I said.

"Try not to mess my shoes this time, will you?" Gani asked, still grinning.

"I don't see why you care. You must have thousands in your closet," I said. Gani lived in one of the apartments our job provided as part of our benefit package. I had one too, but found I needed time away from work so I had gotten my own place. Gani's apartment has only one closet, which was originally about 3 feet by 7 feet. Gani warped the space so you could park tractor-trailers in there and most of the space is filled with shoes. It seemed like overkill to me. I have maybe a dozen pairs of footwear and three of them are boots, and two sneakers, yet I managed to get along just fine.

"But these are new. Got them for half price," Gani said.

"Well, I hope you saved the receipt, cause I'm not promising anything," I said.

Gani reached out and took my hand in hers. "I'll try and be gentle."

A moment later, the world became streaks and blurs. A moment after that we came to a screeching halt in Bedford-Stuyvesant. I tried to hold my insides together. I really did, but I ended up staggering into a nearby alley and vomiting.

Unfortunately, as my stomach started to empty out through my mouth, Nemesis stepped out of the shadow I was puking into.

I wiped my mouth. "Sorry about the boots, boss."

Nemesis looked down and rubbed my back, then handed me a handkerchief to wipe my mouth off with. "It's okay, Belle."

Then she stuck her black leather calf high boots back into the shadow. Unlike my stomach contents which had pooled on the concrete of the alley, her boot seemed to vanish. When she took it back out, it was spotless and shiny.

"Ever think about going into the shoe shine business?" I asked, as she repeated the process with her other boot, with the same shiny result.

"Not recently," said Nemesis. She smiled.

"Gani could keep you in business for years," I said, and spit up what I hoped was the last of my stomach's contents.

"You going to be all right?" Nemesis asked.

"Yeah," I nodded, offering her back the soiled handkerchief.

"Keep it," she said. I dropped it in a dumpster.

Rudy came in for a landing in the alley and stepped off the red winged horse. Red was a very rare color for winged horses, but Rudy had played the daddy and grandpa cards until she got one that matched her hair. Normally people would call her a princess, only in her case it was technically true.

The valkyrie dismounted and went to step in the puddle I had left there.

"Rudy..." I started to warn her, but was too late. She stepped right in it.

"What?" she asked.

"Never mind," I said. The three of us went to join Gani on the street. I looked back at Morningdour and almost lost my lunch again when I saw her lapping up the same puddle her mistress had stepped in.

"Whoever made that fetish is in this building," she said, holding the locator globe up. The arrow practically filled the entire hemisphere it was pointing in.

"Rudy, you watch from the air in case he tries to make a run for it," said Nemesis. The valkyrie nodded and mounted her horse, who had finished her alley side snack. "Gani, you lock down the building so he can't get out magically."

"I'm on it," she said, handing the globe to Nemesis.

"T-Belle, you're with me," Nemesis said.

I nodded. When we got to the vestibule door, it was locked.

"Smash it," Nemesis said.

"Boss, in this neighborhood..." I started.

"The residents need that lock. Good point. I guess I'm letting this get to me. Did I ever tell you that Gary and I had just decided to try to have kids the week before he was killed?"

"No," I answered. Nemesis had spent some time living as a mortal because of induced amnesia. Gary was the love of her exceedingly long life. He was killed in a mugging in front of her. The trauma brought back her memories and the muggers paid with their lives and using her connections as enforcer for the Council of Thrones, she made sure they would pay with part of their afterlives.

"I tend to have twins. I always imagined Gary and I would have had twins," Nemesis said. Jenn Kingford was pregnant with twins. It wasn't hard to draw the conclusion.

"We'll save them," I said.

"I know," Nemesis replied, but neither one of us was entirely convinced. We *would* do our best, but sometimes that's just not enough, even with the firepower this group packs.

We started ringing all the bells, assuming someone would buzz us in and it worked.   Following the globe, we ended up in the basement at the outside of an apartment that was next to the furnace. A sign next to the door said "Super". It looked like our necromancer had a day job.

Both of us were checking the place for booby traps, both mystic and mundane.

"I got nothing," I whispered.

Nemesis nodded. "It's clear. You take the front and I'll come in from the back, unless you think he needs the lock?"

"I've got no problem smashing this one in," I said.

"Give me five seconds," said Nemesis, finding and entering a shadow.

I counted, drew my gun and kicked. The door splintered and I moved to the side, training my gun inside.

The man within was caught off-guard, but he managed to pick up a skull and what looked like a human bone. I managed to shoot the skull, smashing it into a thousand pieces. He raised the bone and pointed it at me.

That's when Nemesis pointed her gun at his head and clicked back the hammer. "Drop the arm bone or I spatter your gray matter."

The man took a second and decided to listen. The bone fell to the floor.

"Yeah, there's nothing humerus about this," I punned. The necromancer stared at me and Nemesis groaned.

"You've been hanging out with Gani and Murphy too long," said Nemesis, pulling his wallet out of his back pocket and looking at the driver's license. "Okay, Greg, where are the Kingfords?"

"I don't know what you're talking about. And you can't break in here like this. Cops got to follow rules."

"Who said we were cops?" asked Nemesis.

"I know I didn't," I said, planting myself on his couch and putting my feet up on his coffee table.

"Then who are you?" asked Greg.

"Doesn't matter. All you need to do is tell me where you've stashed the Kingfords," said Nemesis.

"I don't know who the Kingfords are," said Greg.

Nemesis' hand shot out and tweaked the brachial plexus in Greg's right shoulder. The necromancer screamed and collapsed to the floor.

"You bitch, I can't move my arm," screamed Greg.

Nemesis smiled her dark smile. Not a good sign for Greg. She hit the same spot again. "Now you can't move it and it hurts like hell. You're a little old, but I'll try to teach you manners. One, don't call people names that aren't nice. Two, don't lie to a woman who has a gun to your head."

"But I'm not lying," said Greg.

I started to flip through a week old newspaper. "Greg, does

sacrificing five virgins ring a bell?"

"I..." Greg started to deny it, but when Nemesis started to reach for his other shoulder, he thought better of it. "I may have done that, but I don't know anything about these Kingfords."

"Yeah, like you're going to make something that powerful and just give it away," I said.

Greg started to look sheepish and embarrassed.

"Why would you..." Then Nemesis and I looked around the apartment. It was filled with pictures of a blonde woman. There were literally hundreds of photos. A tiny Polaroid picture of him with her filled a place of honor above the TV. "Obsess much?"

"Who's the woman?" asked Nemesis.

"What woman?" responded Greg, trying to act innocent. Very difficult for a necromancer to pull off under the best of circumstances. Simply put, Greg wasn't up to the task.

I got up and went over to the TV and pulled the Polaroid down.

"You can't touch that," he growled.

"You obviously have a poor grasp of what the word *can't* means," I said.

"Can't is not a word. It's a contraction," corrected Greg, sounding like a bratty kid.

I wanted to hit him, but instead pretended to rip the picture, even adding tearing sound effects.

"No!" Greg screamed, louder than he had when Nemesis disabled his arm.

I held the intact picture up. "Start behaving then. Why did you give the fetish to Sandra?"

"How'd you know her name and that I gave it to her?" Greg asked.

"We know a lot," I said. The truth was I read her name on the back of the photo and took a guess. "Where is Sandra now?"

"How should I know?" Greg said.

"The alignment is in just over an hour. We don't have time for this," Nemesis said and grabbed Greg, dragging him into the shadow. Several seconds later they reappeared out of the shadow in the hallway.

Greg was trembling and babbling, rocking himself back and forth in the fetal position. The reaction was a bit on the extreme side.

"Didn't do well in the shadows?" I asked.

"We... went the long way. And I left him on his own for about a second," said Nemesis.

"Only a second?" I asked.

"Any more and he wouldn't be able to tell us anything," said Nemesis. "Sandra is where?"

"Botanical Gardens," he said.

Nemesis pulled out a tiny camcorder and pointed it at Greg. "Now I want a list of the names of your victims and what you did with the bodies, starting with the most recent five."

"Why?"

"So their loved ones can know what happened and stop living in doubt," said Nemesis.

"But I'll go to jail," said Greg.

"Prison is the least of your worries right now. Either start talking or we go back into the shadows."

Greg started talking and didn't stop for ten minutes. There were dozens of victims.

"Is that all of them?"

"Yes," said Greg. He was too terrified to lie.

"Let's go. We have a lot of ground to cover to find them," said Nemesis, tearing down four large pictures of Sandra from the wall. She handed me one.

"What do we do with him?" I asked, pointing my thumb at Greg.

"We bring him. We can't risk him warning her," said Nemesis.

We went outside and Nemesis passed out the pictures.

"Gani, you take the necromancer with you," said Nemesis. "He'd be useless after another shadow step and we may need something from him to find his girlfriend."

"You think Sandra's my girlfriend?" he said with a goofy grin. Nemesis put him in handcuffs. "Finally somebody sees the truth."

Greg obviously wasn't the sharpest sword in the armory. We ignored him as he seemed to be gloating.

"Sorry, T-Belle, I can't take you," Gani said.

"I've seen you body slide two people before," I said.

"I need my other hand to keep this loser in line," said Gani.

That left the flying horse or shadow stepping. One look at

how the necro was still trembling was enough to make up my mind. "I guess I'm riding with you, Rudy."

"Yea," she said deadpan.

"Gani, you start from the north. I'll start from the south. Rudy and T-Belle, you go east-west from above," said Nemesis, putting on her earpiece communicator. The rest of us did likewise. "Keep in constant communication. The moment anyone finds anything, tell the rest of us. We have fifty-eight minutes to complete this find and rescue. Questions?"

We had none. Nemesis walked back into the shadow in the alley. Gani looked like she was on a hyper-conveyer belt for a spilt second before she and the necromancer vanished.

I walked up to Morningdour and wished I knew about this earlier. I always tried to bring an apple or burger for her–valkyrie mounts are omnivores–to make nice.

Today I had nothing. I petted her neck and whispered, "I don't care what Thrud tells you, take it easy, okay?"

The horse tried to lick my face, but I pulled back. I knew where that tongue had been and I didn't need any gastric acid, especially my own, on my face.

I had a disgusting thought. She might still be hungry and want to make the next meal herself. Mystic animals have higher intelligence than their mundane variety. "My stomach is empty, so no matter what you do, nothing else is coming up. Besides, we have no time for play. We have to save those people and their children, okay?"

The horse nodded and I climbed on her back. Rudy got on in front of me. "You know how to get to these gardens?"

"Don't you think you should have mentioned you needed directions before they left?" I said.

"I figured you knew the way," she said, prodding Morningdour. The horse flapped her wings and we were airborne. I put a death grip on the saddle.

"But what if I don't?" I said, looking straight ahead, anywhere but down.

"Which way?" Rudy asked, ignoring my question.

I pointed and we shot off in that direction. "How can you live in New York and not bother to learn your way around?"

"Asgard I know like the back of my hand. New York is noisy, crowded and confusing. Manhattan at least makes sense, but the boroughs..."

I started to focus, to push back my fear and tried to find a happy place. It turned out to be my weekly lunch with a friend of mine named Murphy. "That's the gardens down there," I said, actually managing to look down. "Start a search grid at the north end, east to west and work our way south?"

"Works for me," said Rudy.

We checked in every five minutes and for the better part of the hour we all came up empty.

"Why is this happening during the day?" Rudy asked. "I thought these alignments happened at night."

"Most do, but the stars are still there in the day time," I said. I caught a glint of metal in the sunlight. "Rudy, there!" I said pointing.

We flew closer. In a grove of trees that shielded the scene from anyone on the ground, a woman stood over a man and a pregnant woman. The Kingfords were tied in a summoning circle in a V formation.

"We found them!" I said into our communicator and gave approximate directions.

Rudy tried to guide Morningdour toward the ritual, but as we got closer the horse whined and bucked in the air. The woman on the ground was so intent on her chanting that she hadn't noticed us yet, mainly because she hadn't bothered to look up. That could change any second.

"What's happening?" I said.

"Foul, dark magik is at work. It's spooked Morningdour. She won't go any closer," said Rudy.

Damn. There wasn't time for this. Sandra had raised the ritual blade out to her side. I had seen enough of these to know when it went up over her head it was almost time for the killing stroke.

"Rudy, take us higher," I said.

"*You* want to go higher?" Rudy said, shocked.

"Just do it," I said.

The valkyrie did as I asked. "Stop here. Join me as soon as you can," I said, taking off my coat and letting my wings unfurl as I stood up slowly on the hind end of the horse.

"I thought you couldn't fly on Earth," Rudy said.

"I can't," I said, diving head first toward the ground. I may not be able to fly, but I could glide and somewhat control my descent. I can hover. In fact, hovering is part of my daily workout, much like a swimmer might tread water using only their legs.

I wanted to scream, but that would let Sandra know I was coming and I wasn't willing to give up the element of surprise. Instead I channeled all my fear and adrenaline into making sure I glided like a dive-bomber instead of plummeting like a rock. The ground was approaching awful fast and I wasn't sure if I was going to make it when an updraft caught me and I leveled out. I found out later that the wind had been courtesy of Rudy. While she had nowhere near the skill or power of her father when it came to weather control, she could manage strong breezes and the occasional hailstorm.

I managed to plow right into Sandra's midsection with the skill of a linebacker and the grace of a speeding pickup truck, knocking the female necromancer down. I got to my feet quickly, despite the fact that I had gotten the wind knocked out of me. I ran to Jenn and Dan Kingford and sliced open the ropes binding them very carefully with my wings. In a summoning, even a drop of blood can start bad things happening.

They appeared too drugged to walk so I carried them and ran, yelling into my mike. "Gani, Gani, Gani." While she wasn't a goddess, Gani had used a spell that let her be summoned if her name was spoken three times, was listening, and decided to allow it. It didn't always work, but using the mike focused the spell. Gani, with Greg in tow, body slid to where we were.

"Get them out of here," I shouted.

Gani let go of the necromancer and grabbed hold of the couple, then slid them away to safety. Greg ran straight to Sandra's side, his hands still cuffed behind his back.

A second later, Gani was on the mike. "We're still in the park. The slide induced labor. I can't move Jenn right now. I'm going to have to deliver these babies."

Nemesis stepped out of a shadow on the far end of the clearing and started running toward the summoning circle and Sandra. I turned and rushed back too, but Greg got to her first.

"Are you okay, darling?" he said.

Sandra stood up and smacked him across the face. "You idiot! You brought them here?"

The insult seemed to hurt Greg more than the blow. "I had no choice, but I'm here to help you now.

Sandra smiled an evil grin and picked up the blade, then pushed Greg to the edge of the circle. "I guess you deserve something for that. How about a kiss?"

"Our first kiss?" gushed Greg.

Sandra nodded. "Just close your eyes and you will get a big surprise."

Greg actually waited with puckered lips. The blond necromancer finished the words of the ritual and brought the knife over her head and down into Greg's chest.

"Psych," mocked Sandra as his blood spattered on her face, then poured down her blade and his arm. Greg opened his eyes and they were filled with betrayal.

A wormhole appeared in the center of the circle. Both Nemesis and I started shooting at Sandra, but the wormhole sucked the magic and mundane bullets in. What could be best described as tentacles were swatting at the edges of the wormhole. Sandra reached down for her backup plan–a sack. The blond necromancer pulled out two puppies, undoubtedly twins. She slit their throats and let the blood flow into the circle.

There was a burst of light and something came though the wormhole and took corporal form.

Nemesis grabbed Sandra in a headlock, covered her mouth and put the muzzle of one of her guns at the base of the necromancer's skull. If Sandra couldn't speak, she couldn't give the Chaos spawn orders.

That left it up to me to face off against the thing in the circle. When the dust cleared, I was facing what was probably the ugliest dog on the planet. The Chaos spawn had taken the form of the second part of the sacrifice. The blood from Greg had opened the portal, the blood from the first puppy brought it through and gave it form. The blood of the puppy twin bound it to Sandra's will.

With the spell's summoner unable to speak, the creature was

on its own. So far it had done nothing more than stare at me. When I stared back, something happened. Gani later explained that the first person who should have looked in its eyes was the summoner, not me. Normally the summoner has something prepared in her mind to further bind the creature to her will, but all I had was me. When our eyes met, so did our minds. For a moment we each lived the other's life. I knew all about it and it me, down to each of our darkest shame and most hidden secrets. Maybe it was a trick, but I knew it didn't want to hurt anybody. Simultaneously, it reached a paw for my face and I moved my hand toward his muzzle. We touched gently and our foreheads pressed one against the other like old friends.

"Belle, kill Rover," ordered Nemesis. "Before it's too late."

"No. Rover's not evil," I shouted. Not that it couldn't change. Its world was a dark and desolate place, almost devoid of compassion, but only almost. "He's just a kid—a scared kid." Just like I was once.

"Well that kid could destroy half of Brooklyn if we don't kill it first," said Nemesis.

The wormhole was shrinking, but still there. "We can send him back."

"But we need a sacrifice..." started Nemesis, then made a decision. She shot Sandra in the shoulder and let her fall into the summoning circle. The wormhole got larger as the blood flowed onto the ground. "Everything here needs to go in there before the wormhole collapses.

"Hell, no," said Sandra, crawling away, but she made the mistake of climbing over Greg's corpse.

"Leaving so soon?" said his corpse. The sicko must have cast a spell on himself to come back as a zombie if he was ever killed. He pulled apart the handcuffs as if they were made of paper. "You aren't going anywhere before I get my kiss," said Greg as he wrapped his dead arms around her shoulders.

Sandra screamed and Greg giggled and gurgled, as blood sprinkled from his mouth from the effort of both. As his lips touched hers, Nemesis grabbed the pair and tossed them into the wormhole, where something reached out and pulled them in. The screaming stopped.

In my mind, I showed Rover the way home and what would happen to him if he stayed, careful to make sure my thoughts showed him being killed instead of the possibility of his slaughtering thousands before we could stop him. His paw again touched my face and his tongue licked my cheek. Rover nodded and leapt into the wormhole. It had shrunk, but hadn't closed.

Nemesis picked up the dead puppies and saw the look on my face. I loved animals and sometimes had a harder time dealing with them getting hurt than I did with people. "They're just meat now."

I nodded and she flung them through. An instant later, the rip in space mended and closed.

We left the area, but not before Nemesis razed the area with a grenade, destroying any vestige of the ritual. The plants would grow back, the dark magik wouldn't.

"You did good," Nemesis said, wrapping her arm around my shoulder.

"Thanks," I said, sadder than I should have been.

"What happened back there?" she asked.

I explained how we bonded. "He really wasn't that different than me a few years back."

"So when he licked you, he wasn't tasting you..."

I shook my head. "He was kissing me goodbye." I let out a sigh. "Why is it that the only guy that's been interested in me in months turns out to be a monster?"

"I'm one person who you shouldn't be asking for love life advice from. It sounds like the only monsters back there were Greg and Sandra. C'mon, let's go check on Gani and the Kingfords," said Nemesis.

Gani had managed to deliver two beautiful identical girls, whose parents were so grateful they named the first Ganieda Terrorbelle and the second Nemesis Thrud. We took them to the nearest hospital, where mother and daughters did fine. Dad didn't leave their sides for a week.

Mission accomplished, we headed back to the office, each in our own way. Nemesis shadow stepped, Gani body slid, and Rudy flew on Morningdour. Me? I took the bus and I decided to call out the next day, minus the theatrics. If Nemesis had a problem with it, tough. I still had to fix my door.

ENDGAME

Life is but a dream, only the butt I was facing was nothing short of a nightmare. Of course the fact that it wasn't human had something to do with it.

I fight monsters. It's what I do. Part of it, anyway. I'm big and strong, especially for a woman, plus I like to hit stuff. Sometimes I shoot things, but I'm not as crazy about that. I'm a damn good shot. Usually when I have to shoot, it's not an easy situation. That means things like flesh wounds are rarely an option.

I'd never admit it, but I can be a real softie. Hard to believe with a name like Terrorbelle, but it's true. Killing anything bothers me, even a monster. Maybe it's because if some people knew where I came from or could see the razor-sharp wings that I keep hidden, then they might think I'm a monster, too.

That doesn't mean I won't kill if I need to, just that it bothers me. In the end, if it's a choice between saving my skin and ending a monster, human or otherwise, the world will be less one bad guy.

That left me the problem of how to deal with Badass here. Sadly, that was her name. Maybe it wasn't the one she was given at birth, but it's what I call her. And it fit.

Badass was shorter than my six feet by the better half of a foot. Badass wasn't ugly, though her face wasn't going to be winning any beauty contests, but who was I to talk? She had a tiny hourglass figure with most of the sand up top, which tended to more than make up for any other shortcomings with a lot of men. Trust me, I know. I have half a beach worth up there.

Badass had the requisite number of eyes, arms and such to pass unnoticed on a New York City street. As long as she covered up her fanny.

I'm a butt woman. I like them round and firm and I don't mind bouncing quarters off them when the mood strikes me. I've never been interested in my own fair gender, although I can still appreciate well-formed buttocks on another woman. Usually I tend toward the jealous side. My own butt is muscular and well shaped from my pixie heritage, but it is large–especially when compared to a human's–thanks to the ogre half of my parentage. But Badass' posterior....

Let's just say it could chew up other butts and spit them out.

I first encountered her over two weeks ago and I hate to admit it, but Badass pulled a con job on me.

It was late enough to be early and I was walking home from having a drink with a friend. In Manhattan, the streets are never truly deserted, but they were quiet…until I heard the shouting.

My reaction was perhaps a little different than some of my fellow New Yorkers. I ran toward the screams. I turned the corner into an alley and saw three men and one woman. One of the men was bent over and holding his crotch like it had been kicked hard. As soon as the woman saw me, she started crying.

"They were trying to rape me," she mumbled between sobs. Whether she knew it or not, that was the right button to push. I had been eleven when soldiers had… let's say it wasn't good. Something like that stays with you always. It colors your perceptions.

I pulled my gun. That was the cue for the other two to make a run for it, which left me torn between giving chase or aide.

The woman made my decision for me. "I'm okay now. Please don't let them get away."

The man on the ground wasn't moving, but it could be a feign. A groin shot isn't always crippling. "I already called the cops. They'll be here any second," I lied. I figured that would keep him from getting any bad ideas and gave chase. I was a soldier in Faerie, one of the Daemor, an elite group of women who would make Special Forces look like amateurs. You wouldn't know it from my large girlish figure, but I never stopped my exercise regimen. Skipped it because of a rare hangover or a better offer, sure, but I never gave it up. I was able to catch up to the pair without having to resort to taking off my padded pink trench coat and using wing power. I can't fly in magic-poor environments, but by using the wings to lessen the weight I'm carrying, I can keep pace on foot with a horse in the short term.

They weren't bright enough to split up, so I followed them down into the subway. They leapt over the turnstiles and I did the same. The booth attendant was so busy chatting away on her cell phone that she either didn't notice us or didn't think we were important enough to stop her conversation.

The two jumped down on the tracks with plans of crossing to the other side until faced with the reality of crossing over the third rail.

I nabbed them before they could make the effort. "Where do you think you're going?" I clamped a hand around the back of each one's neck so their feet hung off the ground.

"The freak'll kill us!"

A shove brought them to their knees. "A girl you were about to rape has every right to kill you." A push landed their faces inches from sparking on the third rail. One wet himself.

"Please don't." They begged and groveled, neither one realizing that I couldn't touch them to the rail without riding the lightning myself. Of course, throwing them was an option.

"I bet she said the same thing to you. Why should my answer to you be any different than yours to her?"

"We never tried to rape her. She came on to us in the club and invited us to party in the alley. When we got outside, she started talking dirty and hiked up her skirt just a little bit. Stan went first and then she attacked him," said one of them.

"Why should I believe you?" I said.

"She went Lorena Bobbit on him. Didn't you see *it* lying there?"

I felt my stomach sink. "No. How'd she do it?" I asked, helping them back to their feet.

"You'll never believe me," he said.

I didn't, but there was an easy way to check. We went back to the alley. Stan was lying on the ground. Blood was spurting out of the stub of a formerly hose-like appendage, which was a good sign. If the blood wasn't flowing, it meant he was dead.

Badass was nowhere to be found.

Stan was moaning. He had lost a lot of blood and there was an excellent chance it was enough to kill him. I moved to his side and yanked one of the shoelaces out of his sneaker. I pulled a pair of surgical gloves out of my trench coat–don't ask–and tied a tourniquet around what remained of his manhood.

"What are you doing?" one of the others asked.

"Stopping him from bleeding to death," I said, tossing him

my cell. "Dial 911." I turned to the other one. "Run inside the club and get a bag of ice. Lots of it."

"Why?" he asked.

I pointed to the severed piece of Stan lying nearby. His eyes widened in understanding and he ran off.

Stan opened his eyes briefly. "Thank you."

I felt ashamed that I'd screwed up, but wouldn't look away. I owed him at least that much. "It's only a little first aid."

"No, you scared her off. She thought the cops were coming. If you hadn't...."

I heard ambulance sirens in the distance. "Help is on the way."

Stan wasn't hearing me anymore. He shivered from equal parts shock and terror. "Teeth. All those teeth."

I rode with Stan in the ambulance. The ER surgeons were able to reattach his severed member, but as to whether it would ever be functional again, only time would tell. And time tends to be on the close-mouthed side.

I found the other two men in the waiting room. Their names were Mannie and Joe. A cop interviewing them seemed to have a problem with what he was hearing. "So you want me to believe that this woman bit him on the ass?"

"No," said Joe, waving his hands. "Her ass bit *it* off."

"I'm going to need you both to submit to a drug test," said the cop.

"Excuse me, Officer, but I'd like to hear more of what they have to say," I said.

"Who are you and why exactly should I care what you'd like?" he said.

"She's the one that scared her off," said Mannie.

The cop got a lot more interested. "You got a carry permit for the gun you pulled?"

"All that and more. My name's Terrorbelle. I'm with Nemesis & Co." I handed him my card, the one with the shiny gold logo on it.

"And that should matter to me why?" asked the cop.

"Because it matters to your boss," I countered.

"What does my sergeant have to do with this?" he said.

"I meant the mayor." My boss has a lot of pull.

"Yeah, right," he said sarcastically, thinking I was a nutcase.

"We can call him if you like," I said, pulling out my cell.

The cop laughed. "At 2:00 AM? Nobody could reach him unless there was a major emergency. You've got to be kidding me."

I gave him a hard smile. "Actually, I'm not. His honor will be pissed, but he won't be taking it out on me. Or you can call One Police Plaza and give them the code on the back of that card. They will tell you to extend all due cooperation to me."

"You're serious?" he asked.

"Very," I said.

"If this is a scam, I'm going to run you in on principle alone," he said.

"You can try," I muttered under my breath. The cop got on his radio to check me out. I turned to the two men. "Tell me more."

Joe looked sheepish. "She wouldn't take her skirt off. She told us it was in case anyone walked by, she didn't want to be naked. She said she was embarrassed by how she looked without her clothes, so Stan went in without looking. It didn't seem weird at the time. Things were okay for a couple seconds, then Stan started screaming and fell to the ground grabbing his crotch. Her skirt got hiked above her waist, which is when we saw the teeth. Then she... spit it out."

That explains why a guy would risk his favorite anatomical possession. Cheap, tawdry sex. "Where were the teeth?"

"All along her butt crack. Some were sharp and pointed, others flat and huge," said Mannie. "Maybe it was some sort of conjoined twin?"

"No way. I don't know what it was, but it wasn't human," said Joe.

"Is there anything else you can tell me? Did she say what her name was, where she lived?"

"No, not really. We tried to find out, but she asked us if it really mattered. It didn't," Joe said.

"You guys are real romantics, aren't you?"

"We're the victims here. If you hadn't chased us, maybe we could have done more for Stan," said Mannie.

I got up in his face. "You're trying to blame me? I wasn't the one so hard up for some cheap sex that I lost my common sense and tried to get down and dirty with something that would bite off whatever you stuck in it. Then you ran off, leaving your wounded friend behind. Where I come from, running away is a clear sign of guilt." Although this bunch looked more guilty of stupidity and shallowness than rape. "You didn't try to explain to me what happened. If you had, I would have went after her, so don't even try to shift any of your blame on me." I had enough of my own. I felt bad enough that I made the wrong call. Not entirely my fault, but doesn't exactly chase the guilt away.

The cop came back over with a brand new attitude. "I'm sorry if I caused you any inconvenience, Ms. Terrorbelle."

I tried not to chuckle. Nemesis visits every new mayor and explains her working situation to them. Gods are afraid of her, so most mayors cave pretty quick. Makes it easier for her to work. I don't abuse it, but at times like this it saves time.

"They told you to apologize, didn't they?" I said.

The cop nodded nervously. "They told me to make sure I did nothing to upset anyone with your agency."

"Relax. I'm not planning to make any trouble for you."

The cop relaxed visibly. "What do you make of this?"

"Monster bad guy," I said.

The cop bit back a comment and instead said, "Seriously?" I nodded. "Are there monster good guys?"

I nodded. "And gals."

He didn't get it and I didn't feel like explaining, so I left.

Badass' spree of violence continued for weeks. Neither the cops nor I were able to track her down. There were at least ten victims, most of which had been butchered the same way as Stan. Three died from blood loss. Another victim was a subway pervert who was grinding himself uninvited against her in a crowded car. When she lifted up her skirt, I imagine he must have been thrilled, until she took a bite out of crime. Things were so mangled that less than half of the others were able to be made whole again. Badass spit each time. Another was missing his hands, lost trying to protect himself. He survived, but they never found the hands. The last guy died. They haven't been able to identify him yet. His face had been torn off and shredded.

The unknown victim would hopefully prove to be Badass' undoing. She left something behind in his jaw. A tooth broke off and lodged itself in his gum line right down to the bone. NYPD's

CSU wasn't able to identify what it came from, but my boss was able to get it on loan for Ganieda to look at.

Gani's the twin sister of Merlin. She has relatively minor powers of her own, but she can tap into those of her magí brother. She says he doesn't mind. After all, he is indisposed waiting for Britain's hour of greatest need. While he may exceed her in power, I have no doubt Gani exceeds him in skill. She's had hundreds of years to study while he rests.

We met in her lab. I've been in other mage's labs and they tend toward the classic stone look or something equally dramatic. Gani's looked like a scientific lab, with tables, drawers, and cabinets. She tended toward the organized, until she got knee deep in a project. Then things got messy. The lab was spotless, so she probably didn't have a side project going.

"Gani, what can you tell me about the tooth?" I asked.

"For one thing, it's human," she said, brushing her snow-white hair out of her eyes.

"How? That thing is as big and pointed as a shark's tooth," I said.

"Symbiotic possession," she said. "Reshapes the existing tissue to emulate its natural shape, but is still essentially human flesh."

"You mean this thing's natural shape is a mouth?"   "In its home dimension, pretty much. I've seen this before. It's called a Dark Maw. It's an Ancient, born of Chaos."

Crap. I was thinking demon. They tend to be easier because they're bound by more rules. "God-level power?"

"Naw. Dark Maws are strictly low-level servants, but they can be nastier than their masters, just not as powerful. If you'll pardon the pun, they tend to be mouthpieces."

"They can talk?" I said. That thought was rather disturbing.

"Usually, but in every other case I've heard of they attach at the abdomen or chest. That way they can tap into the airflow from the lungs easier," said Gani.

"Charming. You got a way to track her?" I asked.

"Have I ever let you down?"

"Other than that time you took me shoe shopping and promised me that they'd have my size?" I said. My feet are like the rest of me. Big. Fortunately, Manhattan sports several trendy transvestite shoe shops that carry my size. "No."

"It was an honest mistake," said Gani, handing me what looked like a couple of petri dishes fused together. The tooth floated in some sort of gel inside. "Follow the pointed end. Got a similarity spell on it, so unless there is more than one in the city, it'll lead us to Badass."

I stopped short at the *us* comment. "Gani, this one's mine."

"You sure?" she asked. Gani knew what had happened and how guilty I felt for letting Badass get away. If I'd been on the ball, three men would still be alive and seven more wouldn't be maimed.

"I gotta do this myself," I said.

Gani nodded. "Female macho pride aside, you need help, you call. Understand?"

"Yeah," I said, but we both knew I probably wouldn't. My personal code of honor makes me stubborn and stupid that way. "Any chance Badass is a victim in this?"

I'm a sucker for the downtrodden. I didn't want innocent blood on my hands if it came to that.

"None. The spell to do the joining has to be entered into willingly, without coercion or it won't work. Badass did this to herself. She's probably more than a little psychopathic," said Gani. "One more thing. All the attacks have taken place at night because the Maw are creatures of darkness. They hate light, especially sunlight. It'll seriously hurt them. It'll be inactive and resting during the day. The tracker won't be any good until it's awake and on the move."

"Good to know. Thanks," I said. I took a nap until a half hour before sunset.

Tracking Badass wasn't too hard. Sure, using Gani's tracker felt like cheating on some level, but in the long run I didn't care. Badass wasn't going to maim or kill anyone else if I could help it.

She was having dinner with a distinguished, gray-haired gentleman at a Park Avenue restaurant. It was the type of place where they insist on trendy dresses for the ladies and a jacket and tie for the men. A large woman in jeans, t-shirt, and a neon pink trench coat wasn't going to get past the maitre d' without getting physical. While I had no problem making a scene, I didn't want to give Badass a chance to get away, so I waited outside.

There had to be a way to take her out without anyone, including her date, getting hurt. I managed to sweet talk the maitre d' over the phone into telling me the date's name. It was John Smyth, believe it or not. Next I called my office to run a DMV check to find out what Smyth drove. Turns out the guy had fifteen cars registered, but twelve were classic makes and not likely to be taken out.

One was a limo. I got the license plate number and checked the area. It was around the corner with a uniformed driver behind the wheel. Strolling up, I knocked on the window. The tinted glass rolled halfway down.

"Can I help you?" asked the driver.

"Would you consider taking a hundred bucks to take the next couple of hours off?" I asked.

Driver man seemed offended. "Absolutely not."

"How about if I promised you a night of incredible passion," I said, batting my eyelashes.

That left him stammering. I was probably far more woman than he was used to. He finally managed to stutter out, "No, thanks." Not that I was serious, but it might have gotten him out of the car.

"Well, I tried the nice ways." I sprayed him with a lipstick-sized container of knockout gas that looked like a breath freshening spray, barely managing to catch his head before it hit the horn. I reached in the open window, unlocked the door and slid the driver over to the passenger seat. I put his hat on my head and whispered in his ear. "Smart, not choosing the night of passion. Not that I'd really put out on the first date, but if I did, I'd probably break you in two. Of course, if you took me out to dinner and a show first, you might have gotten a goodnight kiss."

A soft groan was my only answer.

Now I could wait in comfort. An hour and a half later, the driver's cell phone played "Somewhere Over The Rainbow." I'm not one to judge. Besides, that's where one of my favorite bars is.

I answered it with a deep "Yes?"

"James, bring the car around," said Smyth. "I'll get the door for my lovely date."

That was fine with me. I hadn't thought about having to get out to open the door. That would ruin the whole element of surprise thing.

"Yes sir," I answered and did as instructed.

Smyth and Badass came out of the restaurant. She wore a slinky dress and a red wig. He held the door for her and rushed ahead to beat her to the limo to repeat the process. Badass climbed in. I pushed the driver out of the passenger door, holding his jacket to make sure he landed softly and pealed out fast enough for both doors to slam shut. It was easier than explaining that when Badass told Smyth she'd eat him for dessert, it had an entirely different meaning than the one he was hoping for. Sliding into traffic, I saw Smyth in the side-view mirror, ranting and waving his arms, but couldn't hear a thing. Quality workmanship.

"What's going on?" demanded Badass.

I thrust my gun toward the backseat and pointed it at her face. "Sit back and be quiet. If I even think your butt is going to come off that seat, you're going to have some extra ventilation in your head."

She stared at the rearview. "I know you. You're the one who chased off two thirds of my threefer."

I answered by cocking the hammer back.

"Where are you taking me?"

"To turn you in to the DMA," I said. Unlike the NYPD, they won't waste time in disbelief before locking Badass up.

"I haven't committed any federal crime, so the Department of Mystic Affairs has no jurisdiction," she said, too smugly for my tastes.

"Wrong," I said, remembering her recent victims. "You kidnapped Greg Maston and Doug Combs."

"Wasn't Greg the one with the lovely hands? They were delicious. I don't remember Doug," she said.

"Well, he remembers you," I said and we hit a pothole. The limo lurched, jostling my gun hand. Badass opened the backdoor and leapt out, running opposite traffic on the one-way street.

"Damn it," I said, braking hard. The cab behind me stopped inches from the limo's rear bumper. There was no way to turn it around safely, so I flipped on the hazards and abandoned it to chase after her. I slid my gun back in my holster. Two women chasing each other in New York City was interesting to watch, but if one had a gun and no badge, it would undoubtedly warrant several 911 calls.

She had a half block on me, but like I said, I'm in good shape. I was closing the distance when she ran into a small office building. It was late, yet the door was unlocked and the lobby unmanned.

Badass frantically pressed elevator buttons until one door dinged, then opened. She rushed in and started hitting the close door button. I leapt across the lobby and managed to wedge one hand between the doors. I pushed; the elevator slid open slowly.

"Didn't you hear me say hold the door?" I quipped.

Less than amused, Badass tackled me. Her strength took me by surprise, but it shouldn't have. Gani said the Maw strengthened the host. I guess I've gotten so used to being the strongest gal on the block that I got sloppy.

Badass straddled me. I felt the Maw start to open its mouth on my stomach. I kicked both legs up to catch her neck between my ankles and flip her over. Her dress hiked up in the process. It was a sight that I could have happily lived without. She either hadn't been wearing any underwear or the Maw had chewed through it.

The cleft between her lower cheeks was hinged and lined with more teeth than a great white. Badass lunged backwards, the Maw's jaws snapping. I kicked out at her knee, but she moved. The Maw had some way of sensing attacks and moving its host body. Great.

Then the Maw did something really disgusting. It let loose with the evil mother of all farts. It was actually visible, a gray murky mist.

I covered my mouth and nose with my sleeve, but my eyes were burning. I had been tear-gassed before. This was worse. While I struggled to not pass out, Badass' leg came up, surprising me with a roundhouse kick. It caught me in the gut, slamming me against the wall. Badass jumped for the door, but I managed to dive and grab her foot. I tossed her like a rag doll into the back wall of the elevator. I stuck my head out and took a deep breath, then used my trench coat like a fan to get some of the gas out. I ripped the bottom of my t-shirt and tied it around my face for some measure of protection.

The doors shut. I hit the emergency stop button and the klaxon of the alarm started. "You weren't planning on leaving so soon, I hope."

"You're a woman. Why stop me from punishing men?"

"Because you're hurting innocents," I said.

"Nobody with a penis is innocent. That alone marks them for death. I've suffered at their hands."

"Get to the end of the line. Did any of your victims ever hurt you?" Revenge I can understand, although this was extreme.

"I was just getting them before they got me."

"You don't have the right to maim men," I said.

"The Maw gives me the right. Let me show you as I eat you alive," promised Badass, lunging fanny first at me.

"I guess you aren't used to food that fights back," I said, rethinking the wisdom of locking her in such a confined space with me. Sure, she couldn't run away, but I didn't have a lot of room to maneuver either. I barely managed to leap over her. I was so woozy from the gas that I smashed my head on the ceiling and landed even more disoriented with my back to her. Before I knew what was happening, teeth were tearing through my trench coat. I guess I should have worn the one with body armor, but it just doesn't look as good on me.

Vanity, thy name is Terrorbelle.

Luckily, that was the safest place for me to be attacked. My wings are not only razor-sharp, they're tough as hell. Small caliber bullets only bruise them, so even a deadly Chaos creature's teeth can't bite through them, at least on the first try. Instinct and training kicked in and my wings buzzed at a speed that would make chainsaws rust in envy. Badass screamed as I sliced pieces of flesh out of her hide. I did a half turn, smashing my elbow into her face. Badass crumbled like week-old cake.

The Maw was still conscious and trying to move Badass' legs without much luck. Being all mouth, limbs were still a foreign concept to it. I couldn't safely walk her to the DMA office and I wasn't about to call for help, so I switched to Plan B. Flipping Badass on her back, I cuffed her hands and feet in a reverse hogtie and shut off the stop button. The annoying alarm ended. I pressed the top floor button and got off there. Carrying Badass carefully so the Maw was facing away from me, I headed into the stairwell and up, in hopes that it had roof access. It did… after I kicked the door open.

I undid the hogtie, putting Badass belly down. I refastened the handcuffs to pipes, pulling her straight so her hands and feet couldn't move.

The Maw took this for a good time to negotiate, which gave a whole new visual to the phrase *talking out of your ass.* "I am prepared to offer you whatever you like in exchange for my freedom."

"Not interested."

Badass twitched. She was playing possum. It didn't matter. My gun sight hadn't moved from her heart since I sat down. Safer than targeting the Maw. According to Gani, if the host is killed, the Maw dies too.

"I can offer you a position of power in the world to come," said the Maw.

"How long has it been since your kind was kicked out?" I asked.

"We left of our own accord," said the Maw.

"Right. How many eons ago was it?"

"Longer than you can imagine," it said.

"Exactly my point. If you haven't been able to stage a comeback in that long, it ain't going to happen."

The Maw was undeterred. "Be my new host and I'll leave this one."

"Hey!" screamed an angry Badass, forgetting she was pretending to be unconscious.

"Silence!" shouted the Maw. I had to chuckle at the woman who was arguing with her own fanny and losing. "I can offer you great power. You will not age. I will double your strength. Are you interested?"

"Nope," I said.

Badass decided to ignore the Maw's gag order. "You can't just leave me here. I'm an American citizen."

"Wow," I said with mock awe. "Me too." Naturalized, of course. "You…"

I cocked back the hammer on my gun again. "Having a Dark Maw fused to your butt doesn't make you bulletproof. Speak again and I'll give you a flesh wound just for fun." I was bluffing, but she bought it. The Maw started to twitch like it was going to exhale. "You even think about fouling the air again and it'll be more than a flesh wound."

Badass stayed quiet, the Maw not so much. "So what happens now?"

"We wait," I said.

"For what?" it said.

"Sunrise."

"You'll kill my host," said the Maw.

"I don't think so, but so what? She's as guilty as you. More so. Without her, you'd still be waiting in darkness." Gani was mostly sure about Badass surviving, which was good enough for me. Even without the Maw, Badass was a true monster. If the Maw remained, others would be hurt, even in prison. It was worth the risk.

Eventually, the sun came up and shined where it usually don't. The twisted flesh starting smoking. Badass and the Maw screamed in pain, each trying to outdo the other. I think it was pretty much a tie.

Badass' ass burst into flame that devoured the devourer. The tar on the roof around her melted. The Maw's protection lasted until almost the end and Badass survived. What remained below the waist wasn't pretty. I didn't feel a bit sorry for her. My pity was saved for her victims.

There was enough of my coat left to cover my wings. I lugged the unconscious Badass to the DMA NYC office where she was arrested and given medical attention for all the good it would do her. The wounds had cauterized themselves, but would never heal completely. Those kind never do. The flesh's way of reminding the host what it had betrayed.

Badass cut a deal with the Attorney General's Office. Using magic to kill can get you the death penalty, so fifty years to life seemed good by comparison, even if she had to spend it sitting on a hemorrhoid pillow.

The sentence wouldn't bring back or heal her victims. Nightmares would still haunt them, but maybe knowing she was locked up would let them sleep easier. Sometimes making it through the night without waking up screaming is the only victory we rape victims have.

OPEN DOOR POLICY

It's nights like this that make me want to ask my boss for a written job description. I'm pretty certain that it wouldn't list filling in as a bouncer for a Goth vamp club as a favor from my boss to the magi Hex.

Nemesis could have asked Rudy, but no she came to me. Rudy is the daughter of Thor and more than capable to work the door at Plasma. Rudy is even stronger than me, although she's not half the fighter I am. She's only played at soldier. I've been the real thing during my time as a Daemor in Faerie. This was a grunt job, which meant Nemesis wouldn't bother with it. Gani can handle herself in a fight, but sometimes magic's only so good up close and personal. That left Rudy and me. Nemesis knows the valkyrie princess doesn't like getting her hands dirty, so does she even ask her? Nope, she goes straight to Terrorbelle without a second thought.

It really bugs me. Did Nemesis ever even bother to consider that I might have plans? It didn't matter that I didn't. It's the principle.

I don't even like being around vampyres. By nature they're all predators, even if some of them fight it. Being in a Manhattan club full of them was like being back on the battlefield—no way to relax, always assuming an attack was coming from somewhere and trying to spot it before it guts you.

I took up my spot at the door, getting ready to open it.

"Terrorbelle, I appreciate your help filling in," said Layla. The owner of Plasma was tall, thin and beautiful, the exact opposite of me. Well, I was tall and built like a brick outhouse, but it was an oversized building. My mama was an ogre and there is only so much my daddy's pixie blood could do to counteract those genes. "Is there anything you need?"

"I'm good," I said.

"That's what Hex tells me." Nice to know the magí speaks well of me. "We don't always have problems here, but when we do, the blood really hits the fan. Usually, just the presence of Barber is enough to keep the riff raff at bay." Barber was a big, black vamp that made me look tiny, although he leaned toward the quiet side. "I call in Hex when a situation looks like it may spin out of control. Since he's the one who commandeered my head bouncer I insisted he get someone to fill it. He suggested Nemesis or you would be the best candidates for the job. I guess Nemesis was busy." Layla's smile let me know she didn't think the enforcer for the Council of Thrones was all that busy tonight either.

"I guess." I was surprised that I was personally requested for this job. True, I was the second choice after my boss, but that's pretty standard. "What do I need to know about working the door?"

"We have a strict dress code." Layla smiled as she looked at my outfit. Hex had mentioned that I should dress to impress. I wore form fitting black pants and shirt with neon pink trim, belt and holster. I topped it all off with a bright fuchsia trenchcoat. "We get a lot of black, not much hot pink. You'll stand out."

"I will anyway," I said. My shoulders would give a linebacker pause, but my bras have to be specially reinforced to do their jobs. My chest is the part of my anatomy people notice most, at least without the trenchcoat.

"It's not a bad thing. You have a unique look and a pleasing face," said Layla. I nodded to acknowledge the compliment. People always feel the need to point out how attractive ugly people are. I don't buy it from any of them, except maybe Murphy. Sadly, I'd probably buy two of anything he was selling. "Please feel free to hand the coat in the check room."

"It helps cover a few things," I said.

"No one will mind the wings here. Moni comes in often with hers unhidden," said Layla. I didn't bother to point out that the graveyard angel had beautiful black angelic wings. Mine were pixie shaped, but razor sharp and harder than steel. "Thanks, but it'll be too easy to slice someone accidentally and I get the impression that fresh blood will make my night much more difficult."

Layla laughed. "It might."

"Plus, I'd have to find another place to put my gun."

"Whatever makes you happy. The bouncer at the door sets the mood for the place. Vampyres get highest priority. Best dressed are the first in the door. That holds for both vampyres and humans. People will try to tell you anything to not have to wait in line. They will say that I said to let them in or that Barber always does." Layla handed me a small walkie-talkie and a clipboard. "If there is any question about my blessing on a customer not on that list, call. If they are lying, they don't get in. Period. Barber is not here tonight, so it's your call. I will back your play. If a vampyre looks ragged or hungry, screw the dress code. Call me and I will bring them in and make sure they get fed."

Normally that statement would trouble me, but Layla has turned bloodletting into a business. She gets the Goths, college kids, and other assorted oddballs to donate or sell their blood. She in turn sells it to the vamps. It saves on a lot of unnecessary attacks and if she happened to make a few bucks in the process, so be it.

"You need anything, you call me," said Layla.

"Will do," I said, opening the door and taking my place as the guardian of the crimson velvet rope. There was already a line about forty feet long. I had no special ability to tell a vamp from a human, but it was pretty obvious in a lot of cases who was the real deal and who were the wannabes.

One genuine vamp pushed his way to the front of the line, decked out in a black silk suit with a pair of shoes that cost more than a month's rent on my apartment. He had a human woman on each arm, a blond and a brunette. Each had large enough saline implants to raise the water at the South Street Seaport to flood levels. Sadly, they each sported bejeweled chokers, undoubtedly covering matching blood hickeys. This vamp expected to just walk past me without any problem. My hand on his chest seemed to surprise him a great deal.

"Where do you think you're going?" I said.

"Inside," he said, looking down his nose at me. "I'm expected."

"That's nice," I said, but didn't move out of his way or check the list.

"I'm going in," he said.

"Ah, but you forgot to say *May I*. You'll have to go to the back of the line," I said.

"Do you know who I am?"

"Nope, but I have a sinking feeling you're about to tell me," I said.

"I am Baron Fields."

"Sorry to hear that. Maybe the harvest will be better for you next year," I said. The blond giggled, not noticing the glare the Baron gave her.

"That is my station."

"Mine's Columbus Circle or sometimes 50th, but a Metrocard ain't getting you past me," I said.

"I will not be treated this way by a human woman!"

"Oh, you think I'm human. How sweet."

Baron Bozo took a mental step back at that one and gave me the once over. All he could tell is I wasn't a bloodsucker. Apparently not being terribly impressed he trudged on. "I'm going in there with my guests. You can either step aside or face my wrath."

I put one hand on my chin as if mulling it over. "I'll go with choice B." Baron Bozo bared his fangs. "I hope you and your wrath have a good dental plan."

Next he made eye contact. Not all vamps have the same abilities, so not all can swing mind control mojo, but Baron was trying without much success. First off, he was gearing it for a human, which I'm not. He probably didn't even know Faerie existed, which is fair because most people didn't believe in vampires. Add to that as a mixed breed, my mind has its own unique qualities. Plus I was wearing my Daemor medallion as a belt buckle. The black raven on a silver circle had several built in charms, including one to make the wearer resistant to mind control. It wasn't total protection, but with a strong will it made it very hard to take over a mind and there aren't any weak-willed Daemor—too hard to get in the all female fighting force for someone of that mental persuasion.

Still he was trying so hard to impress the ladies that I decided to play along and see where he went with it. I stared glassy eyed out in front of me. Baron Bozo smiled.

If he had just tried to walk past me, I might have been nicer, yelled boo and checked the list. Instead he laid his hands on me, attempting to hurt me. Most vamps were used to superior strength being enough and had no skills in hand-to-hand combat. I grabbed his offending extremity and twisted it behind his back. Lifting him over my head, I heaved him over the waiting people. He landed at the back of the line.

"Wow," said the blonde.

"That was wild," said the brunette.

"It's all in the wrist," I said. Now that Baron Bozo was taken care of, I noticed that the pair of bimbos were staring at my chest. I wasn't sure how to take that.

"You have the most amazing boobs I've ever seen," said the blonde.

"Thanks," I said.

"Who did them? I'm thinking of upgrading again, but that size would make me fall over forward," said the blonde.

"They're natural," I said. Ogre size and pixie tone made them hold their shape pretty well.

"No way! Can I feel them?" asked the blonde, reaching out.

Her friend was doing the same. "Me too."

I caught both of their hands. "Just take my word for it."

"You can feel mine if you want," said the blonde.

"Mine too," said the brunette.

A young man in the line said "All right!"

I looked at him and said, "Shut up." The shouter took a step back and decided looking at his shoes would be a good idea.

At the back of the line, Baron Bozo had stood and dusted himself off. Just when I thought he couldn't annoy me any more, he began motioning to the girls, snapping his fingers like they were a pair of trained cocker spaniels. They sighed, put their heads down and started to go to him.

"You two can do better," I said.

The blonde shrugged. "But vampyre sex is so hot."

Baron Bozo had vamp hearing and practically preened at the words.

"With any vamp?" I asked.

The blonde shrugged. "I'm not sure. Baron is the only one we know."

I looked at him. "And he was that good?"

Both girls looked back at him, then the blonde whispered, "He looked a lot bigger than he felt. And for all those muscles he was kind of soft." Glamours are wonderful things for looking at, but they only go so far when it comes time to get down to business.

"The biting thing was sort of hot, but these hickeys are kind of embarrassing. We're not teenagers anymore."

No, they weren't.

"So if I said you both could go in, you'd rather go to the end to keep him company?" I asked.

"You'd let us in?" they said in unison, smiles showing off all their pretty caps.

I unhooked the end of the rope. "Sure. You want in?"

"Yes!" they shrieked in bimbo unity and rushed inside. I could hear Baron's grumbling as he watched them dump him to get in the club. I smiled and winked at him, then got the line moving.

It wasn't hard. I had to frisk a few people and take away some weapons, even a cross on a gold chain. Inside that piece of jewelry would be a weapon. Everyone then went through a metal detector just to be on the safe side. My sidearm was spelled to not set them off. One of the benefits of working for Nemesis. It also shot mystic ammo. I could control which kind with a thought. It also held the equivalent of more than a dozen normal clips.

Hopefully I wouldn't have to pull it tonight.

Some of the vamps were going to Plasma to fight their addictions. I could respect that. Others were just going because it was a hot club. Layla had rules, which included no fighting inside and no hunting within a three-block radius. With Barber and Hex around it didn't have to get enforced often.

I didn't have to like any of the vamps I let in. I just had to make sure they didn't hurt anyone else, vamp or human.

A little after midnight, five vamps came strolling up the side of the line, dressed in leather pants, with black straps loosely designed to take the place of a shirt. There were four men and one woman, each of them trying to out glamour the next. Even the other vamps in line took second and third takes as they went by. Their mystically enhanced beauty wasn't what had me staring. It was the five humans crawling on all fours, dressed in rags with choker chains around their throats. Back in Faerie, Thandau and others had slaves. I spent some time in a slave camp. The Daemor fought to free them. When I saw these people, I saw slaves and it made me very angry.

Now all I was going on was my gut reaction, but it rarely steered me wrong. Still, I needed more than just that. A lot of people were into bondage, domination and the like. When they find out vampyres are real, that sort of thing turns a lot of them on. Some of them do it in hopes of one day getting turned themselves. I needed to be sure of their status before I interfered.

They seemed surprised to see me at the door instead of Barber.

"Names?" I said. The vamps told me and they were on the list. "Go on in."

They moved, leading their human pets by the chains.

"Excuse me, but what are their names?" I asked.

"They no longer have any," said the one calling himself Heston, who acted the part of leader. "They are our guests."

"Sorry, there is no plus one on the list," I lied. Heston had a plus one, but none of the others did. "They can't go in."

Heston looked me in the eye, trying to work the same mojo Baron had. Heston was better, trying to feel out my mind and shift his energy accordingly.

"You will let us all pass," he ordered.

I jabbed him in the eyes with two fingers. He yelped and grabbed his face. "No, I won't. If you try that on me again, the next time I poke you and pull away my hand, your eyeballs will be impaled on my fingertips, understood?"

"What are we supposed to do with our... *companions?*" Heston used the term as if it were a joke.

"Leave them out here," I suggested.

"Very well," he said. The five vamps brought the humans over to a parking meter and fashioned the chains around the metal bars like cowboys leaving horses outside a saloon. "You will all wait here until we return."

There was no answer from the humans, no indication they had heard, but they stayed even after Heston and the other four went inside.

A human girl dressed all in black was the saddest vamp wannabe I had seen all night. She walked past the line and to me at the front. "Hi, I'm Tashana. I'm on the list."

She was, so I frisked her and let her in.

By this time, Baron was halfway to the front. He may have ticked me off, but at least he hadn't mind mojoed either of the bimbos to make them be with him. They were both willing.

"Hey Baron," I said. As near as I could tell, he was the last real vamp in line and I didn't need any vamp looking over my shoulder during what I was about to try. There was a simple way to get rid of him.

"Yes?" he said.

"Go on in," I said, lifting the rope.

Baron brushed past me with a curt nod.

I walked over to the chained people. There were three women and two men. All of them looked almost anorexic, with blood hickeys all over their bodies. I was sick to my stomach. I tried to pull the choker collar off the nearest woman, but she reached up and pulled it back on, whimpering and curling up into a ball. One of the men looked at me and I swore his eyes were begging for help. I moved to remove his collar. He made a token effort to stop me, but I got it off.

I pulled off my Daemor medallion and took the man's hand and wrapped his fingers around it. His body shuddered as its magic broke the mind control link and he fell to his knees.

"Help me," he whispered.

That was enough to prove to me that Heston and company had enslaved these people. I put the medallion back on my belt and pulled out my cell. To call the boss I only needed to push a single button.

"What is it Belle?" asked Nemesis.

"I need you and Gani down here at Plasma now," I said.

Nemesis chuckled. "Can't handle the vampires?"

"I can handle them just fine and I'm about to handle five of them. I need Gani to EVAC five enslaved people and free their minds," I said.

A shadow in the alley twitched and out stepped my boss. Shadow stepping is pretty close to teleporting. Since she knew where I was and had been here before it was easy. Without that, it wouldn't have worked.

"What do you need me for?" asked Nemesis. She was dressed in a low cut purple t-shirt, black leather slacks and a dark as shadow trenchcoat.

"To make sure none of them sneak out and get away to do it again," I said. Bad vamps are too powerful and dangerous to let live.

My boss nodded. "You worried about offending Layla or Hex?"

"Not terribly. Hex'd do the same thing and Layla said she'd back my call," I said.

"Okay, Nobody gets out," Nemesis said. "You need anything, holler."

"Will do, but I won't," I said.

"You're a little too hard headed sometimes, Belle," said Nemesis.

"One of my best qualities." I banged on my noggin with my knuckles. "When's Gani coming for EVAC?"

"She's bringing the elevator. She'll be inside." Gani had been to Plasma before and it had been fun watching her carve invisible sigils into the wall without anyone noticing.

I turned to the enslaved humans. "Come with me." Only the man who asked for help even tried to move. I shook my head, grabbed their chains and lead them inside.

I saw the elevator door materialize on a far wall and made for it. Heston spotted what I was up to and made a beeline for us, but there were a few hundred dancing vamps and humans between us.

I hit the up button, but down would have worked as well.

"Hello, T-Belle. Heard you called for a ride," said Gani. Her snow-white trenchcoat matched her long hair. White hair tends to make most women look old, but not Gani. She'd pass for a young forty, which is impressive since she wasn't exactly a teenager when she served as a mage in Camelot.

"I did. These five are under vamp mind control." I pointed to the male who had spoken. "Already started undoing it with him using my Daemor badge."

"Any idea what kind of breed of vamp?"

"None. Is it important?" I asked.

"It'd help," said Gani, helping me get the people inside the elevator.

Heston had made it through the crowd and was rushing toward us. I pointed my thumb over my shoulder. "He's one of them."

Gani looked at him and tilted her head while she read their umbras, a fancy term for the shadow of a soul. "Hmm, probably Dubbelsuger. Tend to suck blood and energy from groups. You need any help?"

Gani could probably incinerate the lot with a fireball or lightning, but that wasn't the way this was going to go down. "No thanks, I'm good."

"What do you think you are doing with our chattel?" demanded Heston.

"After I fix them up? By the looks, I'd say hitting the food court," said Gani.

"*Come out here!*" Heston ordered triggering the mind control. Four of them started to move.

"*Be still,*" ordered Gani. The four froze. While her brother sleeps, she is able to tap into some of his power and Merlin is a magí same as Hex. They are both supposed to be in the same power category. Gani knows more than either of them, which makes her as effective, if not as powerful. The snow-haired mage waved as the doors closed. Heston charged and pounded on them. A few seconds later they glowed and vanished, but Heston was still pounding so hard he put a hole in the wall.

"Don't you hate it when someone won't hold the elevator door for you?" I said.

"You will bring our property back," shouted Heston. The dance floor had pretty much cleared by this point and his four vamp friends had moved in a semi-circle around me.

"Not going to happen," I said.

"Then you will replace them yourself," he said.

"So are all Dubbelsuckers…" I intentionally mispronounced the name assuming Gani had correctly ID'ed the breed. "Delusional or is it just you?"

"You think one lone woman can beat five Dubbelsuger vampyres?"

"You're right. It is unfair. Do you have any other friends who'd be willing to help you out?" I said.

"I'm going to enjoy feeding on you. The things I'm going to make you do will make you beg me to let you meet Death," ranted Heston.

Layla had moved to watch. I looked at her and she nodded. Heston was about to violate both the no fighting and feeding rules. I was doing this anyway, but it was nice to know I had the management's blessing.

I pulled out the two-way radio.

Heston laughed. "So you are calling for help."

"Nope." I pushed the talk button. "Lock this place down." The other bouncers did as instructed.

Heston charged me fangs first. I reached out and pushed him back by his face so hard he landed on his butt ten feet away.

"Wait a second. This coat is silk." Over the armor coating anyway. "Do you know how hard it is to get blood out of silk?"

I slid my coat off and laid it over a nearby chair. Now my wings were revealed and they gleamed in the club lights. I stretched them out to their full size. It felt good after being cooped up for hours.

"What the hell are you?" asked Heston, nervous for the first time.

"Remember when you told me I'd beg you to meet Death? You have it mixed up. You are about to meet the Reaper and I'm going to play matchmaker," I said.

"Big talk for a woman with a gun," said Heston, apparently thinking if I was talking to him, I wouldn't notice the two other vamps sneaking around behind me.

"I won't need it. Trust me."

The two vamps behind me charged. Dumb move. Behind is where I'm most dangerous. I sliced out with my upper wings and both their heads were severed. I reached out and caught them by the hair before they hit the ground.

I held the heads in front on me and spoke to them. "Slaver vamp numbers one and two, meet Death, Death meet slaver vamp numbers one and two." Heston stood his ground, but the other two vamps took a step back. "Come on, people. The Grim Reaper doesn't have all night and neither do I."

The other two attacked me from the sides. They were

assuming they were faster than me. They were, but not by much. Luckily they telegraphed their moves and I was able to smash both of them in the temples with the heads I was holding, but dropped them in the process. Blood is very slippery. While they were stunned, I bent over and grabbed each of them by an ankle, inverted and spun them hard and fast. When I stopped I flung them up so their heads smashed together somewhere above me. Luckily, Plasma had high ceilings. I followed this by smashing their heads on the floor, then above me again.

I admit I was showing off which was stupid. I also assumed none of the vamps would have any weapons, but I was wrong. I was so concerned about the human slaves that I hadn't personally searched Heston or his friends. Considering his outfit I figured the metal detector would catch any weapons, but they don't work on ceramic guns.

Heston had my head lined up between his sights. I was already moving, both trying to get me out of the way and the vamps in front of me as a shield. Even as I did it, I knew I wasn't going to be fast enough. I hoped he had bad aim or the gun would backfire and blow up in his hand.

Neither happened, but he didn't manage to shoot me thanks to the blonde that had come in with Baron. She smashed a chair over his gun hand and the shot went low into the floor. I spun and my right wing sliced him at the wrist. The hand and gun dropped to the floor.

He started to spout something, but I wasn't in the mood. I sliced the heads off the vamps I was holding, then lifted Heston up and did the same to him.

I picked up the radio and hit talk. "Cleanup." I knew from past experience that the bouncers could dispose of vamp bodies. Part of me wanted to feel worse than I did, but if I let them live they would have only hurt more people. The DMA might have gotten them to trial, but if they had good lawyers they might have gotten off. Vamps live a long time, so even thirty years wouldn't be enough. They'd just get out and do it again. This was the only sensible way.

Layla was annoyed, but she handled things with class, especially after I explained about the slaves. Layla was all about protecting people, both those with and without fangs. I apologized about letting the ceramic gun slip through.

"Don't let it happen again," Layla said.

"Again? You want me to come back?" I said, surprised.

"You did a good job and after tonight, no vamp is going to mess with you. You want an occasional part time job?"

I thought about it. "On one condition."

"Which is?" asked Layla.

"The blonde that helped me out gets put on the A list and doesn't pay for a drink."

"An alcoholic drink. For three months."

"Deal."

I excused myself and went over to talk to the blonde. I realized I didn't even know her name. That was going to change.

"I wanted to thank you," I said.

"No biggie. It was the right thing to do."

"I can't argue with that," I said, extending my hand. "I'm Terrorbelle."

"I'm Sydney."

I told her the deal I worked out with Layla on her behalf and she thanked me. I also handed her my Nemesis & Co. business card with my cell number on it. "You need anything, day or night, call me."

"Wow thanks," Sydney said and got a big smile. "You know what I'd really like to do?"

"Nope," I said. She reached for my chest. "Oh, no."

"I'm not a lesbian, unless you count that one time in college. I'm just jealous and curious," said Sydney. "Please?"

I sighed. She had saved my life. "Make it *very* quick."

She was. "They feel even better than they look."

"Thanks, I think," I said.

Sydney opened up her top and revealed a black push up bra. "You want to compare?"

"I'd rather not," I said. Sydney covered up.

"Those wings are awesome. And your arms and abs are unbelievable. You must have a mind-boggling workout program," gushed Sydney.

It was kind of intense. Just the wing hovering alone was exhausting.

"You've gotta come clubbing with me some time," said Sydney.

"I'm not really a clubbing kind of gal," I said.

"Come on, just one night," she pleaded. "It'll be fun."

"Maybe," I said. The rest of that night at Plasma was easy. My night out with Sydney, not so much.

ARRESTED DEVELOPMENT

"**Y**ou're in a lot of trouble, missy," said the sheriff.

"The story of my life," I replied.

"You think this is funny?" he growled.

"Yes. It was the spotlight in the eyes that put you over the top," I said. "I mean, who does that anymore? Are you going to break out the rubber hoses next?"

"Remember when I read you your rights? I advised you to exercise your right to remain silent," he said.

"Then how will I answer your insightful questions?" I said.

"Handcuffs not enough for you? You want leg irons too?" he asked.

"Depends if you can get a pair that matches my outfit," I said. "Now what about my phone call? Or my lawyer?" The sheriff laughed and blew cigarette smoke in my face. "And that no smoking sign?"

"You must have us mixed up with your big city police." He pronounced it poo-lice. "Once we find out what we want to, then you can have your phone call." Ignoring the no smoking sign, he blew some more smoke in my face. I blew it back.

"Seems like a serious violation of my civil rights. Makes any conviction doubtful and a good reason to get it overturned on appeal," I said, knowing damn well he was railroading me.

"If you ask me, you criminals have too many rights. Makes it harder on regular law abiding citizens," said Sheriff Railroad.

"Exactly how am I a criminal?" I said.

"To start with, you were speeding at a breakneck speed. We have children on our streets in Tarmichael County," he said.

I hardly considered twenty over the posted 20 MPH limit a dangerous speed and there wasn't a single person on the road where they pulled me over. "So give me a ticket and send me on my way."

"You'd like that wouldn't you?" he said.

"Well, duh," I replied.

"It isn't happening. We're taking your motorcycle apart now."
I doubted that. There wasn't anyone else on duty but these bozos.
"We'll find the drugs."

"What drugs?" I said.

"Don't play games with me," said Sheriff Railroad.

"I'd love to. I'd suggest chess, but I doubt you know how to
play. I'd suggest a battle of wits, but seeing as how you'd never
have played before, I'd have you at an unfair advantage," I said.

The skinny and scruffy deputy who'd been sitting next to the
sheriff in silence finally perked up. "We could play strip poker."

"Sure we could if you'd round up some men I'd like to see
naked," I replied.

Deputy Sleaze jumped up and grabbed me by the front of my
shirt, a real manly thing to do considering my hands were cuffed
behind my back so the chain went between the bars of my chair.
I know Nemesis said play nice, but she wasn't here.

I head butted Sleaze and he let go of me in favor of crying
like a baby.

"That's assault on a officer," shouted Sheriff Railroad.

"More like on a little baby," I said. "I've seen tougher Girl
Scouts."

"You hurt one of my boys," Railroad said.

"He don't look like you. Sure your wife wasn't playing around?
Of course, most women would be bright enough to go for someone
better looking, but he's even uglier than you," I said.

"You broke his damn nose!" said Railroad.

"I barely touched him," I said.

"There's blood spurting out of his face," said Railroad.

I stopped myself from laughing. I could have killed him if I
wanted to. It was barely a love tap.

"It's an improvement. And I was defending myself," I said.

"Not the way I saw it," said Railroad. "You just bought yourself
a world of trouble."

"But I ordered one of peace and love. I'd like to return the
one of trouble or get a full refund," I said. "I'm pretty sure I have
the receipt somewhere.

Sheriff Railroad backhanded me across the face. SOB didn't
hold back and it hurt. "Not so funny now, are you?"

"Don't know. Want me to try a knock-knock joke."

Two more slaps, one on each cheek, followed.

"Who's there?" I said.

"What the hell are you talking about?"

"You did the knock-knock so I went to the next stage. It's not that hard a game, although next time you can just say knock-knock instead of smacking me in the face," I said.

Railroad punched me in the gut. "Happy now?"

"Not as much as you apparently. It looks like something pitched a tent in your pants. Definitely a pup tent. Probably a miniature pinscher. Poor little guy," I said.

"That's it. I'm booking you," said Sheriff Railroad. Deputy Sleaze gave out a little rebel yell.

"On what charges?" I said.

"Drug trafficking and assaulting an officer," said Railroad.

"That's bogus," I said.

Railroad pulled out a bag of white powder from his front pants pocket. "We found this in your gas tank."

"You've both been with me the entire time, so which of you went out to my bike to get it?" I said.

"I found it while I drove it to the station," said Sleaze. They had put me in the back of their patrol car. Railroad drove while Sleaze rode my bike.

"You were able to reach into the gas tank while you were driving?" I said. Sleaze nodded. "And how come it and you don't smell like gasoline?"

"That's enough. Time for your strip search," said Railroad.

"You should have played poker. It would have been more pleasant," said Sleaze in an impressively creepy fashion.

"I doubt it," I said. "The two of you put your hands in places I'd rather they didn't return when you frisked me."

"You could have had a gun," said Sleaze.

"Not in my bra. And the first two times should have told you that."

"I like to be thorough," said Sleaze.

"And I'd like a female officer to do the search, please."

They chuckled. "We ain't got one. Just the two of us in this department."

"What if I refuse?" I said.

Railroad took his nightstick out and rubbed it on my chest and on down. "We can search whether or not you're conscious, so you ain't going to refuse. At least if you know what's good for you."

"Vegetables, milk, and daily exercise are good for me. Having either of you lay another hand on me isn't."

Railroad came up behind me and put a second pair of handcuffs on me. These didn't lock me down to the chair. Unlocking the first pair, he shoved me to my feet and dragged me to a room with a shower and a drain in the floor. I guess it helped wash away evidence.

"Guys, you don't want to do this," I said.

"Sure we do," said Railroad.

"We love doing it whenever we see a woman with out-of-state plates come through our little piece of paradise," said Sleaze. "No one knows you're here. And we know the area, so ain't nobody going to find your body."

"And being serial rapists and killers doesn't bother you?" I said.

"Not in the least," said Railroad.

"We like it," said Sleaze.

It wasn't like I had many reservations before, but I still like making sure the Council of Thrones is right before I condemn two men. Death and the Fates do so love it when I question them.

"Any last words?" said Sleaze.

"Just three. *Ganieda, Ganieda, Ganieda.*" My mage partner can be summoned by saying her name three times as long as she's listening for it.

I saw a white haired blur as she body slid through the walls right behind the pair.

"*Freeze,*" intoned Gani and both men had no choice but to obey. "You okay Terrorbelle?"

"Nothing I couldn't handle," I said, suppressing a shiver when I thought about where I had to let these scumbags touch me. Gani reached on Railroad's belt for the keys and undid my cuffs. I rubbed my wrist, then my face and gut.

A raven-haired beauty materialized out of the dark corner as my boss shadow stepped into the shower room.

"Are you satisfied now that they deserve what they are about to get?" asked Nemesis.

"Very," I said. The Council of Thrones hears cases, often from those who are killed horribly. If they decide someone needs avenging, they call in Nemesis. When it's necessary, she calls in her three agents to help her. Their last victim had used her death to call down the Thrones on these two.

I of course always get to play the bait. Normally my razor sharp pixie wings would give me away, but Gani made them invisible. It's hard magic to do and only lasts about a day, otherwise I'd have her do it all the time and I'd be able to stop wearing trenchcoats. Apparently, magically speaking it's easier to make all of me invisible than just part of me. It's a pity. Just once I'd like to walk down the street without worrying if my wings were sticking out.

Nemesis looked at Gani. "Do it."

The mage nodded and took out a vial of something gray and gooey. Putting on a pair of surgical gloves, Gani stuck a finger in the goo and made an X over the pair's mouths and something much lower.

"Glad I don't have your job this time," I said as Gani pulled her hands out of Railroad's pants. She had already marked Sleaze.

"I'd have given it to you if I could," Gani said. "Maybe next time."

"Enough talk. Take them out of status," ordered Nemesis.

Gani said something in a language I didn't understand and sparks flew from each man's mouth to his groin.

I headed toward the door.

"You don't want to watch?" asked Nemesis.

I could already hear the pair stripping down. Gani's spell would make them hump any opening, allowing just enough cellular regeneration so their manhood didn't get sliced off.

"I'm good," I said. Both the boss and I had been rape victims. I believed in making sure rapists and killers got what was coming. Nemesis was of a like mind, but took it to a whole new level. Part of why even gods are afraid of her. She's got a sadistic streak a mile wide.

I walked out the front door of the small sheriff's building. Rudy was keeping watch outside to make sure we weren't disturbed.

Rudy and I have our issues, but we were friends. She knew I still had problems dealing with what those soldiers did to me and what I had to allow Railroad and Sleaze to do to me. Still better than condemning two innocent men.

"You okay?" Rudy asked.

"Yep," I replied, almost convincing myself.

"Boss watching?" she said.

I nodded. It wasn't that Nemesis got any jollies from it, but she was the one bringing this down on Sleaze and Railroad. The boss feels if it's too horrible for her to watch, it shouldn't be done.

Nemesis walked out a few minutes later. Just because she feels she needs to watch doesn't mean she'll look on indefinitely. Gani looked a little sick to her stomach as she followed behind the boss. The look on Nemesis' face was more stony than usual if anything. That's how you can tell it bothered her. Didn't stop her from dishing out punishment, which was part of what the Thrones liked about her, along with her sadistic creativity.

"You okay?" I said to them both.

"Of course," said Nemesis.

Gani wiggled her hand in a so-so gesture. "I forgot to figure in limiting anatomical openings by size in the spell. I don't know if the deputy's nostril will ever be able to be fully surgically reconstructed."

Gani's spell had no expiration date. The pair would live out their lives with this compunction. Nemesis was a firm believer that death was too good for some people. Sadly for Sleaze and Railroad, they fell into that category. I felt sorry for them for about a second until I thought about what they had planned for me and what they did to nine innocent women who decided a shortcut through Tarmichael County was a good idea. As horrible as my ordeal with Thandau's soldiers was, I survived. And more.

The job wasn't done yet. We took up positions around the building to watch from a distance, but it was the next morning before anyone found them to trigger part two of the spell. It was a cleaning woman who asked them what they were doing. Gani's spell forced them to tell that they were being punished for raping and killing nine women.

Then they ran naked and bloody out of the station and through town, picking up followers like a conga line at a drunken New Year's Eve party. They led their neighbors to the bodies. After the first dead woman, someone had the good sense to call the State Police.

Even after they were read their Miranda rights, they lead the police to the next three corpses. The arresters became the arrestees.

Last I heard they were trying to waive their appeals for the death penalty. And argue for a cell without any apertures.

UP, UP, AND AWAY

Nothing is ever simple in my life. Sometimes that's good, others it's bad. And then there are those times that can only be described as interesting.

We had had a particularly rough month at Nemesis & Co. Not as bad as one of my first cases where we lost one of our own and a limb off the boss, but emotionally draining.

To my knowledge, Nemesis has never attended a management seminar with strategies on how to improve morale. There was no weekend retreat in the woods, no meeting to get touchy feely—not her style. The boss gives orders, the rest of us take them. In a way, it is rather corporate America. Nemesis comes across as a bit of a hard-ass, and she is, but the boss has a heart. She just prefers not to show the softer emotions. When she does, it tends to only be to those she trusts. To her, the non-tough feelings are a sign of weakness. As the enforcer for the Council of Thrones, weakness is bad. Too many folks looking for revenge for their judged ones, not to mention those who fear retribution if one of their victims figures out how to call on the Thrones. Not that summoning the Thrones is done lightly. The Fates, Death, and the rest get sort of cranky if their time is wasted and are not above punishing a petitioner who didn't have what they considered a good reason. Which is why it tends to be mostly the dead and the dying who call down judgment. They have the least to lose.

Which is why it's somewhat amazing that she ever admitted the rape and memory destruction done to her by Zeus. Of course, since she effectively exiled him from his own place of power and Earth under threat of worse than death, I doubt it would be seen by most as a sign of weakness. Especially since he has to survive on a fraction of his power.

Still, she'd jump in front of a bullet for any of us. Not that a regular bullet would do her much harm, but even if it was a magic based one, it wouldn't matter. It's how she lost her arm, saving Gani from a higher demon trying to kill her. The demon got

Nemesis' arm, but she got Gani. She truly felt it was a fair trade, even before she learned her mother Nyx could grow back the missing limb. In truth, she reminds me a bit of how Mab acted toward her Daemor. Although Nemesis is a pussycat by comparison.

So instead of a typical solution to workplace burnout, Nemesis invited us all to go to Bulfinche's Pub with her, where she would run a tab for the team. Smart move on her part as Rudy inherited her father Thor's extraordinarily high tolerance for alcohol. In a regular bar, Rudy's bar bill might be as much as the rent on my apartment. At Bulfinche's, magic is pretty much nullified, so she'll get a buzz faster and much cheaper.

Me, I'm a cheap date. I drink, but rarely get drunk—too paranoid. The first time I did it was back when I was a soldier in Mab's army and it turned messy when we were attacked. I have to have an exceptional reason to get smashed these days and work related stress didn't qualify. It usually was nightmare related and I had to have someone I trusted watch over me. Usually it fell to Gani or Murphy.

Doesn't mean I don't drink casually. Fortunately, even at Bulfinche's, it takes a lot to get me drunk because of my size.

Nemesis picked Friday because it looked like the weekend would be free. After work, I met Gani in the lobby of our building. I could have met her in the office, but Bloomingdale's had a shoe sale. If I was comfortable in my office, she'd take forever. If she knew I was standing in the lobby, it would just be a long wait.

I leaned against the wall and debated whether or not I should have hoofed it. Rudy left fifteen minutes ago on Morningdour. Nemesis has the thirteenth floor for business and the penthouse for herself. The roof has a helipad and a stable for the winged horse. As I didn't *have* to fly on the beast, I let her go without me. Nemesis of course shadow stepped, so I waited on Gani and her magic elevator.

I had taken the stairs down. There was some problem with the regular elevators as some gentleman in a suit and tie was learning. He was poking the up button with the conviction that if he pushed it enough times the out of order sign would magically change to read *Fixed*.

"Elevator's busted," I said, in case the sign wasn't enough of a clue.

"Then what are you waiting for?" he asked snidely.

"The man of my dreams and a winning lotto ticket. Sadly, neither seems in a rush to find me," I said. "Stairs will get you there quicker."

"I have a huge presentation. I had to steal this client from my boss, but it's worth it. I'm going to be a rich man," he said, his bragging meant as a put down to anyone not as successful as him, myself included. "I'm not going to show up sweaty from climbing all those stairs."

"Your boss okay with you taking his client?" I said.

He snorted. "The old fool has no idea. And the best part is it'll probably put him out of business, which means he won't have enough money to sue me for breaching my non-compete contract."

"Glad to see chivalry and ethics in business isn't dead," I said.

"I'm looking out for number one," he said.

"Smells more like number two to me," I said as the blank wall pinged and turned into elevator doors, which then opened.

"I thought you said the elevators were broken," mocked the suit, who didn't even realize it hadn't been there a moment before. "I guess lying to a stranger is okay personal ethics-wise."

"Actually this is a very private elevator," I said.

Suit snorted again, looking at my jeans, pink hair and yellow trenchcoat. "Right, like you have a private elevator," he said, pushing past me.

Gani looked up like she was about to zap the guy. "Excuse me, this is a private elevator…"

"Right," mocked the suit. "Like you own this elevator."

"Actually I…" Gani's hand started twitching like it does sometimes before a spell. I had a better idea.

"I already told him, but he's in a hurry to cheat his boss and put him out of business. Maybe we could drop him off on our way," I suggested with a wink.

"Sure," she said with a smile.

The suit made a snort that was equal parts contempt and victorious. "Seven, please."

"Sure," she said, pushing a circle that lit up.

"Look at all those buttons. Hand labeled? Not very

professional," said the suit.

"Hmm," was Gani's only reply. The doors opened. "This is your stop."

Without so much as a thank you, he stepped out into an outdoor clearing, complete with grass. "What the hell?"

"Next time, be nice to strangers. You never know who you're messing with," said Gani, hitting the close door button.

"Where'd you drop him?" I asked.

"He said seven, so I dropped him near the middle of the Seven Hills out San Francisco way," Gani replied.

"I guess he's going to miss that meeting back in Manhattan," I said.

"Guess so."

"I think I'll give his boss the heads up," I said.

Gani tilted her head sideways. "He told you where he worked?"

"Naw. I lifted his business card when he shoved me," I said. I made the call. His boss was most appreciative and was going to rush to make the meeting in the suit's place.

We couldn't take the elevator all the way to Bulfinche's Pub. Gani had tried to put her sigil on the outside of the building, but it didn't take. We ended up coming out in an alley across the street.

It didn't take us long to get to the door, where a sign read *Sorry We're Open*. Opening the door is usually an adventure and today was no exception. If you've never been to Bulfinche's Pub, I recommend it highly.

The legendary Hercules greeted us at the door. He was the bouncer. Herc said hi to me and gave Gani a small bow. He always does that, sometimes calls her Lady Ganieda—never has explained why.

Inside there was an arm wrestling match going on between Rudy and her father Thor. Rudy is stronger than me and was pushing for all she was worth. The Lord of Thunder was sipping a beer and talking animatedly with Hercules, all but ignoring his daughter who was struggling to pin his hand to the table. Even without magic, Thor was a big man while his daughter was tall and slender. Without the mystic, physics took over and she wasn't going to win. Although

I'd seen humans beat mystically strong folks here at Bulfinche's, mainly because they weren't used to effort without the magical reinforcement while regular folks used their muscles all the time.

Rudy was groaning with the effort.

"Anytime you're ready sweetie, we can start," said Thor, pretending not to notice her trying her hardest.

The valkyrie stuck her tongue out at her father who shrugged and pushed her arm down, but not without some effort.

"A good try, my daughter," he said. "But no woman could ever beat me."

"That sounds like a challenge," I said, walking over. I knew Thor from joining in Hercules workout sessions. Rudy's been invited, but is too concerned with showing up her father to go. Truth be told, I like the guy. I actually have more in common with him than his daughter.

"It could be," he said with a smile. "If there was any woman man enough to take it."

I sat down and pulled off my coat. In Bulfinche's Pub, my wings weren't going to attract much attention.

"No transvestites here, but I'm willing to show you up," I said.

"I would have assumed Nemesis screened her agents for psychotic delusions before employment," Thor teased.

"I do," said the boss from the corner of the bar where she was chatting with the magí Hex and Murphy. I waved and blew him a kiss. Murphy, not Hex. Murph jumped like he was trying to catch it and then pretended to chase it around. Paddy Moran, at the station next to him, rolled his eyes. Bulfinche's leprechaun owner made like Murphy annoyed the life out of him and sometimes it was true, but it was obvious he thought of Murph as a son. A silly, annoying son, but a son just the same. "Sometimes it's a bonus."

"Sometimes it's a side effect of the job," said Gani.

Rudy leaned in toward my ear. "You'll never beat him."

I shrugged. "I've lost before, but I prefer to go down swinging."

"I'll go easy on you," said Thor.

"Don't do me any favors," I said.

"A wager then?" Thor said.

"Sure." I knew he had been beaten before, so I had at least a shot. "What are the stakes?"

"You have to follow my goats around for a day and clean up after them," Thor said.

He had a place in upstate New York he liked to spend time away from Asgard at. The team got invited up there to spend last Thanksgiving with Rudy and her family. When I say I'd never seen a spread like that, I'm not exaggerating. And no leftovers.

I've met the animals in question. They are foul tempered little critters. Can't blame them considering Thor kills them, eats them and then brings them back to life to do it all over again. And that he's been doing it for a couple of thousand years or so.

"You realize the wings don't work so good on Earth, right?" The goats could fly and did so often. There was one nearby farmer they liked to taunt. Everyone in the town thought he was nuts when he talked about the flying goats, but he wasn't.

"I'll give you a talisman to help you with updrafts," he said.

"For something like that, I might be willing to throw the match," I said. I missed flying more than just about anything.

"I don't like to win by bribery," said Thor. That much was true. In the workout sessions I'm competing against the likes of Thor, Samson, Herc, Mista—who's Rudy's fellow valkyrie, Finn Mac Cool, Kintarô the samurai, Sir Marrak the werewolf knight of the Round Table, and on rare occasions Sun Wukong the Monkey King. It's not usual for me to lose. Actually, it's rare that I win, but testing my skills against that quality of opponent has made me sharper. Thor is the last one to get angry if he loses.

"How about I get a marker for a day of weather of my choosing and that talisman," I said.

Thor raised an eyebrow. "Either way, it'll only be good for about a day's worth of wind."

"A day of flying would be great," I said, sitting across form the god of thunder and putting my right elbow up on the table. "I'll try not to show you up too badly."

Thor's chuckle could only be described as hearty. A good challenge meant more to him than a win.

"Bring it," he said. Thor spent enough time on Earth to be well versed in popular culture. He put his hand in mine, making my fingers look dainty.

"Ready when you are," Thor said.

"One question," I said looking over his shoulder. "When did Loki get out?" Thor's brother had been getting released twice a year, once known to the rest of his pantheon, once not. He had become close to Murphy, refusing a chance at freedom because any screw up of his would have Murphy taking his place chained to a rock with a gigantic acid-spitting serpent drooling over him. Murphy was willing. Loki shocked the Norse powers that be by refusing to endanger his friend. Which is good because I prefer that I be the only one drooling over Murphy.

Suffice it to say, the thought was enough to distract the Lord of Thunder and I slammed his wrist to the table.

Thor looked back, his brow furrowed, then began to laugh uproariously. "Nicely played."

"Best two of three?" I said.

"Sure," he said. "Hey, who's Murphy kissing?"

I was half expecting him to try something to distract me, but I still almost turned. Instead of checking, I put all my effort into it. Thor had to shift position to compensation. I picked up his beer and sipped it. He smiled and pushed hard enough to make me brace. This continued for what felt like twenty minutes, when I started to literally gain the upper hand. I fought for every inch until his hand touched the tabletop.

"Excellent match," he said, rubbing his shoulder.

"Thank you and back at you," I said, wanting badly to rub my shoulder too, but I wasn't quite confident enough to show weakness in front of the Lord of Thunder and the rest of the crowd. Especially since if we were outside the null zone, he could rip my arm off and beat me over the head with it.

Thor slid a brown stone in a silver setting. "Let me know what you want the weather to be and when."

"I will," I said and held up the talisman. "And thanks for this."

"Enjoy it," he said.

"I will," I said.

I got up to go say hi to Murphy.

Rudy intercepted me. "You won!"

"Why? You want a go at me," I teased.

"No, I'm just impressed. I've never seen anyone but Magni—" One of her older brothers who's actually stronger than his father. "—beat him in a contest of strength."

"Actually, I think you might have a chance now," I said.

"Terrorbelle, I couldn't even move him before," Rudy said.

"Yes, but I just tired him out. He'll recover as slowly as a human in here," I said.

The valkyrie's eyes went wide and her entire face lit up as she turned to the Lord of Thunder. "Father, I demand a rematch."

Then she turned back and hit me on the shoulder. It was her equivalent of a thank you hug. Sadly it was on my rassling arm and it hurt far more than it should. I strolled over to Murphy's station at the bar forcing myself not to rub the soreness out.

"What can I get you, T-Belle?" he said.

"You mean after my hug?" I said, leaning over the bar to wrap my arms around him. He returned the favor, but he wasn't quite strong enough to get my feet off the floor, however his toes were dangling a bit.

"Is this man bothering ye?" asked the white haired and mustached Paddy Moran.

"Yes, he is. Any chance of you firing him and kicking him out on the street?" Murphy and most of the staff lived in apartments over the bar.

"'Tis a dream of mine, actually," said Paddy.

"It feels so good to be loved," Murphy said.

"How would ye know?" said Paddy.

"I hear things and have a good imagination," he said.

"So why do ye want Murphy canned and homeless?" asked Paddy.

"He'll need someplace to stay and some enterprising woman like myself could swoop in and get a roommate. Then if I play my cards right..." I wiggled my eyebrows. "Who knows?"

Paddy chuckled. "Terrorbelle, ye really should consider raising yer standards a wee bit."

"Of course, Murphy could come and crash with me for a while. I only have six roommates," said Hex, who was a magí like Gani's imprisoned brother Merlin. Rumor has it, Hex's power levels are on a par with Camelot's missing mage or they could be. It's not common knowledge, but the magí operates under a curse that hurts him any time he uses magic and prevents him from being able to interfere in someone else's affairs without being asked first. Even with that handicap, Hex is still a major player so Nemesis makes sure we know the score, although she has threatened us with bodily harm if we share that information elsewhere. Hex is one of her few friends outside of work. Murphy is another. "Speaking of which, Bollywog says hi."

"Give her my best," I said. Bollywog is a pixie who lives with Hex who likes me, partially because I'm one of the few people in New York who speaks fluent pixie.

"Murphy could come work for me," said Nemesis. "I'd even throw in an apartment."

"Guys, I don't need any help here," I said.

"What kind of job? One of your agents?" Murphy said.

Nemesis smiled. "You are resourceful for a man with no powers, but no."

"No powers? Ye've got to be kidding me. Have ye heard his jokes? They're so bad they can drop a man at twenty paces," said Paddy. "And it's a power even I can't make go away. And I've tried."

Murphy pointed his hand like it was a gun. "Better watch it boss. You're barely five paces. You might not survive a shot at this distance."

"I'd like to try," slurred Mosie, a drunk psychic who spends much of his free time at the bar. Drinking is the only thing that keeps his visions from overwhelming him. Nemesis actually has him on the payroll as a consultant for emergencies. Not that he needs money. Whenever he's short on cash, he goes out and buys a lotto ticket. And it's always the winning one. I've asked him to give me some winning numbers, but he refuses. Tells me that's not my destiny.

Murphy pulled out a shot glass with one hand and a bottle of whiskey with the other, tossing one to the other, flipping the bottle upside down to pour the liquor. Once it was full, Murphy slid it along the bar where it stopped in front of the psychic lush who downed it in one gulp, then did a drunken rendition of a bad actor dying.

"Well, you going to make it?" asked Murphy.

Mosie climbed up off the floor, brushing himself off. "Yep, but better fire off another shot just to make sure."

Murphy took three shot glasses and juggled them, then replaced one with the bottle of whiskey. He poured the whiskey into the glass he had put down, a little each time the bottle was in his right hand.

"You're getting better at that," I said. He'd been working at it for weeks and had to reimburse Paddy for more than one smashed glass.

"I've been training," he said, then his head turned toward the door. "And here's my juggling sensei now."

I turned to see a short man walking in the door who immediately jumped into three cartwheels, stopping inches in front of the barstools.

"Dagonet!" said Murphy.

"Murph. Hi Paddy." The man turned to me and bowed. "Terrorbelle, a pleasure. Evening Hex, Nemesis." As he realized that both Nemesis and I were present, his eyes darted around the barroom and he spotted Rudy struggling to out arm-wrestle her father. Acting more than a little nervous he scanned the rest of the room, nodded a greeting to Hercules who met his eyes with a understanding glance and pointed with his chiseled chin toward Gani.

Dagonet's eyes went soft and he got a goofy smile. Dagonet is cut from the same cloth as Murphy. Both are clowns who fight the good fight. Dagonet was a knight and the jester of the Round Table, appropriately named the Infinite Jester. Gani was one of their mages, along with her twin Merlin. I'd never actually seen the two of them in the same room at the same time. Neither talked much about the other. As Dagonet's face got an expression that made me want to cry, I figured out why.

"Oops, forgot a pressing appointment. Got to run," said Dagonet, but as soon as he turned he ran straight into Gani.

"Hello Dagonet," she whispered, her eyes equal parts joy and pain.

"My Lady Ganieda," Dagonet said with a flourish and a bow.

"It's been too long."

"It has," she agreed. "I've missed you."

"Ditto," said the knight. "You look well. Great shoes."

Gani laughed. "You always know the right thing to say to a girl."

"Not always," he replied and the two shared a moment of mutual silence.

"Can I buy you a drink?" Gani asked.

"Want to get me drunk and take advantage of me?" he said.

"I never needed to before," she said.

"No, you never did," said Dagonet. "Sad how things change, isn't it?"

"Yes." Gani nodded and turned away, trying unsuccessfully to hide her face as she wiped a tear away. She walked over to the corner to look very intently at a jukebox that held a fraction of what her 500 terabyte MP3 player did. Yes, she did tweak it a bit magically. Mine too. I have enough music on mine to play constantly for about fifty years.

"Dagonet, what's going on?" asked Murphy.

"Gani and I... we are, or rather were... Hell, Murph, she's my Elsie," said the Infinite Jester, referring to my favorite bartender's late wife. To say Murphy loved her was the understatement of my life.

"Ah," said Murphy, pouring a shot of whiskey and sliding it to the former knight. After Dagonet pounded back the shot, Murphy asked, "What happened?"

"We've had an on again, off again relationship. It's hard to keep a relationship going for centuries at a time. We've not been up to the task," said Dagonet.

"But she's right there. You can try again," said Murphy.

"Hope springs eternal in the young," said Dagonet.

"If you don't go over there, are you telling me you won't regret it?" said Murphy.

"I'd probably eventually regret it if I did too," said the former knight.

"So the thought of her apart from you won't eat you up if you left?" said Murphy.

"Murphy, did I ever tell you who made Hayden?" Dagonet has

a magic sword that is both invisible and able to elongate at the Infinite Jester's mental commands. Murphy shook his head. "Gani did. I had just been made a knight in order to defend myself against a bully knight. Even in those days, I was considered short. Agility I have along with a big mouth and a fast wit. All of that is little use against a larger opponent with a sword or a lance. Merlin was a bit of a blow hard, but had the chops to back up his arrogance. He had been going on about Excalibur being the ultimate sword and had dismissed the idea out of hand that his twin sister could ever hope to match it with a weapon of her own,

"The combination of my being in mortal danger and a chance to prove something to her brother drove Gani to create Hayden. She didn't try to match Excalibur in terms of pure power. Her brother was the magí, not her. Instead she went about it smarter, making it more practical for a man of my stature and abilities. In a lot of ways, she was smarter than Merlin—than all of us, really. She was the only woman on the King's Council, the inner circle of both the Round Table and Camelot.

"Arthur and I went way back, long before he became King. One of the reasons we were so close I think. Why else put a jester on the King's Council? When it came time to fight the bully, Arthur offered me Excalibur, something he had never done before for anyone, not even for Lancelot. I was floored. It was the ultimate honor. I took Excalibur in my hands. I could feel the power. I thought about using it, but it was big and heavy so it was harder for me to use. Still, I could have tapped into the power, but Excalibur was a weapon of war. I would have had to kill my opponent to win and with that sword, I could have. The sword would have done most of the work, but that wouldn't have proved anything, other than the King lent me his power. Reluctantly, I returned Excalibur to Arthur and announced that I would be using the sword Ganieda had made,

"Despite the respect they had for Gani, the knights still viewed her as a woman, assuming she had her position because of her twin brother, so when I made that announcement it was greeted with laughter and much shaking of heads. That stopped when I fought. I didn't try to outmuscle my opponent. It would have been impossible. I used the sword, both as a weapon and a way to move around and away from my opponent," said Dagonet.

"How'd the fight end?" I asked.

Hercules moved over and put a hand on Dagonet's shoulder. "He kicked my ass."

Murphy's jaw dropped. "Herc? You were a knight of the Round Table?" The bouncer nodded. "Which one?"

"Sir Bors. And I was a bit of a bully. Dagonet showed me the error of some of my ways that day. And he proved to the other knights that he was indeed worthy to be one of their number. And he showed Ganieda that he believed in her enough to turn down the honor of being the only knight ever offered the honor of carrying the King's blade into battle."

"And neither of you even thought to tell me Herc was a knight?" Murphy said.

"My behavior at the end of Arthur's reign is not something I'm proud of. I sided with Lancelot," said Herc.

Dagonet shrugged. "You did help raise him."

"Maybe if I had done a better job..." said Herc.

Dagonet put a hand on the larger man's arm. "We all have regrets. And Lancelot was a man, responsible for his own decisions," said Dagonet. He's never hid his distaste for Lancelot and that he blames the knight more than Mordred for the fall of Camelot.

"So there's the two of you and Marrak who are still alive. Last time I asked, you didn't give me a straight answer, Dagonet. Are there any more knights of the Round Table still alive?" said Murphy.

Dagonet smiled, but Herc spoke up. "You know another. Sir Bedevere. And there is another still around, although alive is not the right word for Sagramore. And there's..."

Dagonet slapped the big man's stomach. "You'll spoil his fun finding out."

"Wait, who's Bedevere?" said Murphy.

"Sorry, as a knight member of the King's Council, Dagonet outranks me. I have to defer to him," said Herc with a smile.

"Dagonet..."

"Not happening Murph. Suck it up," said the Infinite Jester. "But in a long winded answer to your question as to whether or not I think of her, I can say every time I use Hayden I'm reminded of Gani."

"Well she's still here, so you don't have to be reminded, you can be with her," Murphy said.

"Murph…"

My favorite bartender raised a hand. "If Elsie were still alive, nothing would keep me from her side."

Dagonet looked at me out of the corner of his eye and I realized my face was showing my feelings. It's not that I'm jealous of a dead woman. Elsie is as much a part of Murphy as his bad jokes. I just hope that one day there will be a part of him that will think of me a fraction of the way he thinks about her. Murphy has risked his life for me and vice versa. I know he does love me and I him, it's just a long way from being the romantic variety.

"So you're saying we shouldn't pass up something wonderful that is right under our noses?" asked the Infinite Jester.

"Exactly," said Murphy.

"Murphy, tell me have you ever lived in a glass house?" said Dagonet, giving me a wink.

Sweet, wonderful Murphy was oblivious as always.

Dagonet sighed. "Murphy, give me an amaretto sour."

Murphy obliged and the former knight took it over to Gani who actually stopped staring at the contents of the jukebox to look in his eyes. He must have said something funny because she laughed and took the drink. A moment later, Dagonet took out a couple of quarters and put them in the jukebox and "Swing The Mood" was blaring. Dagonet bowed and Gani returned it. The pair walked to a clear section of the bar floor and proceeded to cut a rug.

"Hey, Murphy, you want to dance?" I asked.

"Sure, let me stretch first," said Murphy, starting a series of slow bends and leg movements.

Paddy rolled his eyes. Hex and Nemesis both smiled. They'd seen us dance before.

"Hey, Nemesis, you wanna trip the light fantastic?" asked Hex.

"I don't dance," said Nemesis somberly.

"Me neither," said Hex, holding out his hand. "C'mon."

Nemesis shrugged and took his hand. They have an odd relationship. Hex used to date Nemesis' mom Nyx. Hex is more troubled in his own way than me or the boss, but he tries to enjoy himself, something Nemesis should do more of.

Murphy came out from behind the bar, his left arm out stretched. I put my right hand in his left. His right went on my waist, my left on his and we did a version of the tango that was equal parts skill and silly, marching through the room, including up and over a table and chairs and between the dancing Hex and Nemesis. The next song was also a swing tune, so we moved into our next routine. Most people have undoubtedly seen a man throw and swing his partner all around. We did that, except I played the part of the guy and swung Murphy all around, behind me and under my legs. Most guys wouldn't be secure enough to let me toss them around like a rag doll, but it doesn't faze Murph. He actually likes it, except the one time I pulled his shoulder a little too hard, thus the stretching beforehand.

Our performance must have been impressive because the Infinite Jester stopped and clapped for us.

"Excellent moves," said Dagonet.

Murphy bowed. "Thanks."

"Terrorbelle, do you mind if I cut in?" asked Dagonet.

I looked at Murphy who said, "It's up to you."

"Sure," I said, holding out my arms only to have Dagonet walk past me toward Murphy, who without missing a beat started to tango with the former knight.

Gani was rolling her eyes. "You should have seen that one coming Belle."

"I should have." I held out my hands. "Care to beat them at their own game?"

"Sure, except no throwing me around," said Gani. "I didn't have time to stretch."

"Ha," I said as we started to tango. Rudy was still struggling, but was making Thor work for it. "Follow my lead."

"Like I have a choice," said Gani.

We walked up onto a chair and the table they were arm

wrestling on. I stopped between them and dipped Gani so her long white hair fell in Thor's face. The Lord of Thunder paused to brush the hair away. The distraction was enough to let Rudy push his hand down to the table.

"I won!" she said.

We continued our tango down the other side to the floor.

"Good job, Thrud," Thor said.

Rudy beamed. "Thanks Dad."

The menfolk came toward us in a tango.

"I think they want to play chicken," I said.

"Let them try," said Gani, charging forward even faster, forcing me to pick up speed to keep up with her.

"They ain't stopping," shouted Murphy.

"Dive, dive," said Dagonet and the men squatted down to duck walk. Gani and I spread out to let them pass under our arms.

Dagonet came over and put my hand in Murphy's. "I return you to your regularly scheduled partner." He went over and took Gani's hand as a slow song came on.

I looked at Murphy, but he made no move to leave the floor so I wrapped my arms around him, lowered my wings to the position I keep them under a coat and put my head on his shoulder. He rested his cheek on my pink hair and carefully wrapped his arms around me, including my wings. It was a very intimate act, easily more so than if he put his hands on my butt. It demonstrated how comfortable I was with him and how much Murph trusted me. He knew damn well if I flexed the wrong way, he could lose a hand.

I was in heaven for the three or so minutes we swayed to the song. Sadly, it ended and Murphy had to get back to work.

There was more reveling. At the end of the night, I expected Gani to leave with Dagonet after he said his goodbyes to the bar. Instead I watched as he kissed her tenderly on the cheek and exited alone.

I walked over and put my palm on Gani's back. "You didn't leave with him?" I said, stating the obvious.

Gani turned, a single tear escaping each of her eyes. "He wanted me to. I wanted me to, but I couldn't do that to him."

Seeing the questioning look on my face, she continued. "I almost always leave him and it tears me up inside. I couldn't bring myself to break his heart again. Not after last time."

"I'm sorry," I said.

"Me too," said Gani.

"Both of you stop," said Nemesis, joining us. "You had a wonderful night. And you are alive. So are the men you love. Anything more than that is a bonus because none of us know what tomorrow brings."

"I do," shouted Mosie from the bar. Nemesis rolled her eyes and ignored the drunk psychic.

As much as the boss may have liked Hex, he was a poor substitute for her Gary. Tomorrow Murphy might wake up and decide he's in love with me. Not likely, but it could happen. Gani and Dagonet could patch up their differences and live happily together for hundreds of years. Again, not something I'd bet my life savings on, but still in the realm of possibility. Gary was dead and gone forever.

Except with Murphy, I'm not overly huggy, but I looked at the sadness in the boss's eyes. Inside Bulfinche's the darkness that is her heritage couldn't hide the pain. I picked up the boss in a hug. She started to protest then surprised us both by hugging back.

I gently put her down. "Thanks for the night out, boss."

"My pleasure. Besides the three of you more than earned it," she said.

"Then how about a raise?" I teased. "Or an extra week's vacation?"

"Don't push it," she said.

"Nemesis, did you see? I beat my dad," said Rudy. "Twice." Apparently the first time had bolstered her confidence or something, because she had won again, all on her lonesome. There was something about her that was much less uptight now.

"Yes, Thrud. Very nicely done," said Nemesis.

"Of course, I couldn't have done it without the help and advice of Terrorbelle," said Rudy. Apparently it was my night for hugs, because she wrapped her arms around me and tried to lift me. Outside she would have succeeded.

"Happy to oblige," I said.

"And you Gani, should not let your little man get away," said Rudy.

"Oh, no?" said Gani, amused.

"It is obvious the esteem he holds you in," said Rudy.

Gani gave a kind of half-hearted nod. "I suppose."

"Gani, Dagonet said you were smarter than him," I said.

The white haired mage shrugged. "Well, he is a man."

"He also said you were his Elsie," I said.

The love and devotion of Murphy to his dead wife was legendary among the patrons of Bulfinche's Pub. Murph went into several afterlives to try to find her. And he's turned down the advances of literal goddesses and one of the Fates, although it was the crone so that one probably wasn't so difficult.

"Wow. That's got to be the nicest things he's said about me in a century," said Gani. "But words aren't always enough."

"Then what is?" I asked.

"I wish I knew," Gani said.

"So what are you going to do with your wind talisman?" asked Rudy.

"I figured I'd do some flying tonight," I said.

"You're not going to save it?" said Nemesis.

"Nope. Like you said, we have now. Nobody knows what tomorrow brings," I said.

"Hello, I'm sitting right here," said Mosie from the bar.

"So you'll fly yourself home?" asked Gani.

"Myself and maybe somebody else." Murphy was due to get off in a couple of minutes.

"Go get him," said Rudy.

"Enjoy," said Gani.

"Have fun, but don't forget we have a staff meeting 8:00 AM Monday morning," said Nemesis.

"Great, I'll be in no later than nine," I said.

"Don't make me come get you," Nemesis said, but she was smiling.

"I reinforced the new door," I said. Nemesis snorted.

I made my way to the bar and sat down at Murphy's station. "Hey, handsome, you have any plans for the evening?"

"What'd you have in mind?" he asked.

I dangled my new toy. "I seem to have come into possession of a means of flying for a few hours and I was wondering if you'd like to go for a ride?"

"Sure," he said, putting his hands on his waist. "I've got a strong belt on." Murphy is friends with Moni, who's a lasa, better known as a graveyard angel. She's a little younger than me and a whole lot prettier. She's got wings, but they are huge, with beautiful black feathers. No worries about accidentally cutting somebody. He's gone flying with her a few times and she holds him from behind by holding onto his belt. I won't lie and say I wasn't jealous.

"Belt? I don't need a stinking belt," I said. I looked to Paddy for permission to walk behind the bar. I think he saw what was coming and smiled as he nodded his consent. I went around and picked up Murphy like he was a bride.

The men in the bar commenced with some serious teasing of Murphy. He just smiled and put his arms around my neck.

"You realize if we end up in Vegas, I'm going to get suspicious," he said.

"Naw, if you are going to marry me it better not be because of a drunken binge," I said. "On second thought..."

Herc laughed. "I see it now. Murphy as the bride of Terrorbelle." I stuck my tongue out at him. He's said a lot worse to me.

I carried him out the door and into the street, leaving my trenchcoat behind for once.

"You sure you trust me to go for a flight?" I asked.

"Absolutely," Murphy said. "What do we do in the event of a crash landing?"

"No worries. Air Terrorbelle comes with two great big airbags to cushion your fall."

"Will there be an in-flight meal and entertainment?"

"No food. And as far as entertainment goes, why do you think I'm bringing you?" I said.

"Care to hear my rendition of *Fly Me To The Moon*?" he said.

"Sure," I said, activating the talisman and leaping up into the night sky of New York City.

We flew until the dawn. We landed on the fire escape outside my apartment and I let us inside with my specially designed key. I was too tired to fly him home, so we sat down on my couch. I put my head on his chest and promptly fell asleep. I was exhausted. Even with the winds, flying was hard work and I wasn't used to it.

Murphy was still there when I woke in the morning, with a blanket wrapped around me and his arm still on my shoulders. I closed my eyes, truly happy.

ATTACK OF THE TROUSER SNAKE

I enjoy my job, which sets me apart from a lot of people—as if razor sharp pixie wings and naturally pink hair weren't enough to do that already. Not to mention a chest that's actually made a stripper complain to her plastic surgeon that he shortchanged her. Add to that mix shoulders wide enough for linebackers to look at me with envy and you only start to scratch the surface of understanding the joys of being equal parts ogre and pixie. I stand out even in New York City, despite the fact that I usually cover up my wings with a brightly colored trenchcoat.

My job is part semi-secret agent, with parts enforcer and investigator, plus anything else my boss decides she needs. On busier days this can include getting shot at, attacked by monsters or facing down more types of evil than I can shake a stick at. Not that stick shaking typically helps, unless it's the size of a small tree trunk and applied to vital organs. Basically, I'm hired muscle for a woman who fights back the darkness in a world that doesn't even believe in magic. Fortunately, it works for me. Fighting is all I've known since I was eleven. I need to make a living and I can't see myself at a typical nine to five. Although with the speed my wings can move at, I bet I'd made a great chef at a Japanese steakhouse.

Being one of Nemesis' three female agents keeps life from getting dull, but there are gaps between our assignments. During a job, things can get so busy that sometimes sleep isn't even an option. Makes how we spend our down time that much more important, even if we go about it differently.

Gani likes to experiment and study. You'd think the twin sister of Merlin would have learned enough about magic since the fall of Camelot, but she says there's always more to find out. And since her knowledge has saved my bacon more than once, I don't discourage her.

Rudy is a club kid, partying all night and sleeping away the day. Not exactly unexpected behavior from the daughter of Thor. I pity the idiots who get into a drinking contest with the valkyrie, thinking there's no way a woman could drink them under the table. Especially since the loser pays the winner's bar tab for the night. Rudy's not much into beer or mead, preferring mixed drinks and jello shooters, which can run upwards of fifteen dollars apiece in some clubs. It's not unheard of for her to run up a four-figure tab, but in her defense she does tend to offer to out drink entire groups. She's even done it for charity a time or two. Things aren't pretty for the fools who try to welsh on their bet—Rudy can bench press a compact car fifty times. I consider that impressive—I have trouble after ten reps.

Neither research nor club hopping thrills me, unless you count spending time at Bulfinche's Pub to hang out with Murphy. I like a little quiet time to myself. Nemesis' office is in a midtown skyscraper where she pays for about two thousand square feet, but Gani has folded over the space inside so it's got as much room as a mansion. Nemesis supplies her agents with apartments, but I only use my work residence when I can't be away from the office or I'm too exhausted to go home. Otherwise, I'm at my own place down in Hell's Kitchen. It's a third of the size of my work apartment, but it's all I can afford. And it has the added bonus of getting me away from work, which can be a godsend.

One of the benefits is I have neighbors. I've gotten to know most of them, like Mrs. Washington who treats me like one of her granddaughters. Or Mr. Rodriguez who runs the corner bodega. Ever since I stopped an armed robbery there, I can't pay for my fresh fruit if I wanted to. And they know things about me that I tend to keep secret, particularly my wings. Normally I cover up when I'm outside, but sometimes if I'm just going to the corner, I don't bother. My block is my home.

My neighbors have some vague idea what I do and tend to ask me for help when the police can't or won't help. I know it's not that the cops don't care. The truth is there are only so many officers and they can be limited by what the higher ups tell them. My neighbors aren't a particularly wealthy or influential lot, so things shy of murder can sometimes get put on the back burner. And sometimes crimes not so shy of murder.

It started with a timid knock on my door by Horace Milford who lives two floors above me. He was in the grocery when I stopped the robbery and I wasn't exactly easy on the gunman in question. After disarming him, I threw him twenty feet. He would have gone further if there hadn't been a wall in the way. Throwing a 160-pound man that far isn't too difficult. Reigning myself in so he wasn't seriously hurt was more of a challenge.

I have a peephole and a camera with infrared capabilities. I checked both. Never hurts to be careful—Nemesis has a lot of enemies and I've made a few of my own, so I never know who or what may be coming to pay me a visit. Getting into our office is akin to breaking into Fort Knox. Gani could easily make a billion in the home security industry. By way of contrast my home security system consists of a recently reinforced steel door. I've done the same to my bedroom. If someone breaks in, they have to deal with me. I'm a bit more dangerous than any alarm.

There was no one hiding behind him so I opened up.

"Ms. Belle…" My driver's license reads Terror Belle, even though it's really one word. My neighborhood is still very old world. I address all my neighbors who are significantly older than me with an honorific. Most of the older men refer to me as Ms. Belle. Despite eight plus years as a soldier and Daemor, I'm barely legal to drink in New York, so I like it. "I need your help."

"Come in, Mr. Milford," I said.

The man actually blushed. "Would you mind coming out? My being alone in an apartment with a beautiful young woman might give people the wrong idea." It said something about the man, considering there was nobody in the hall. I had already suspected that his wife wore the pants in their family, but his next statement made it clear. "And I wouldn't want to upset Mrs. Milford."

I smiled. I'd lived in parts of Faerie where sex was how some people said hello to strangers. Those places tend to get lots of visitors, however casual intimacy has never been my style. I'd both offended and intrigued people when I turned them down. I found those offended preferable to those intrigued. Too many saw it as a challenge. I find decorum truly refreshing. "Sure. What can I do for you?"

"You know I manage the Jasper Hotel?"

I nodded. It was four blocks away. It wasn't exactly a no-tell hotel, but some people used it for that. No rooms by the hour, but it wasn't uncommon for people making a romantic rendezvous to rent a room for the night and check out after a few hours. It was half the price of the midtown hotels and didn't have the sleaze factor involved with the no-tells.

"You've heard about the deaths?"

"Yes." Gossip travels fast. Five people had died there in the last few weeks.

"What else have you heard?" he asked.

"Just that the police had ruled one a suicide and the other four as natural causes." Then I stated the obvious. "You think it was something else?"

"I do. All the deaths happened in the same room, which I thought was odd, but the detectives wrote it off to coincidence. Each victim was alone for the entire night, but on nights where more than one person stayed in the room nothing happened. On the days of the deaths the door's cardkey reader shows that nobody went in or out and the windows were locked when they found the bodies. And the room is on the ninth floor. Not that that is necessarily a deterrent for everybody." He looked at my wings when he said it. I didn't bother to explain that there wasn't enough magic energy in New York City for me to fly properly. I can hover and go up a bit if I have a running start and even slow a fall, but flying up to a ninth floor window is too high for me to manage. Not that he was accusing me and he rightly suspected that there were things that could fly that high. "My wife keeps going on about it being a locked door mystery—she's a big reader, but I'm more concerned that more people will die. I want to close down that room, but the owners won't let me. They don't want to lose the business and they accept the cops saying it's a coincidence. I don't know what to do, but I thought you might."

"Nothing rings a bell, but a friend of mine is more of an expert in these kinds of things. Let me give her a call. My cell is inside." I don't bother with the expense of a landline. "You okay waiting out here?"

"Of course," he said with a small bow.

My cell was on the kitchen counter. I hit "3" on my speed dial. One was my boss, two was Murphy. Three was… "Hey Gani. It's Terrorbelle."

"Hi T-Belle. What's up?" I was on speaker. I could hear something like rain and thunder in the background. I looked out the window. The sky was blue and cloudless.

"Is it raining by you?" I asked. Manhattan wasn't big enough for us to be having such drastically different weather patterns. Gani was supposed to be in her lab all day and Nemesis would have called if there were a mission.

"You called for a weather report?" Gani asked. I could hear the grin in her voice.

"Actually, I need a favor, but it sounds like there's a monsoon in the background. You go out for the day?"

"Nope, working on my weather control. I have a storm brewing right here in my lab. The entire area is barely a foot cubed."

"Sounds impressive," I said.

"I've done thunderstorms in miniature, but today I'm working on controlling the change between rain, snow and sleet. I've been able to switch between them, but I want to have all three going at once without changing the overall room temperature," said Gani.

"Is it working?" I asked.

"So far," she said. "What do you need?"

I filled her in. "Any ideas on what it might be?"

I could hear Gani start to hum, which meant she shifted into deep thought mode. "Nothing springs to mind. Want me to meet you there to give it a once over?"

"That would be great." I gave her the hotel name and address and the background noise suddenly increased in volume and I heard things breaking. "Everything okay?"

"Not really. Thinking about your problem distracted me. It seems I forgot to figure in what the localized difference in temperatures would do to each other if I lost focus. I have a mini-tornado spinning amok. I've got to go. I'll meet you there in two hours."

"Great, but if you're going to play twister you really should do it with a cute guy," I said.

I heard her snort as she hung up.

I returned to the hall and told Mr. Milford I had called in a specialist and he thanked me profusely, kissing my hand three or four times.

I got to the Jasper a few minutes early. Gani can be very punctual, but not on days when she's playing in her lab. It wasn't so bad—she was only twenty minutes late.

Mr. Milford's pupils got a little wider when he saw Gani. Mrs. Milford probably would have slapped him for it. Gani is striking with a very regal air about her, especially when in her professional mode. She wore designer clothes I couldn't even name. Forget about her shoes. Like I've said, my apartment could fit in her shoe closet. Of course, she has shoes that are older than some countries. Gani also sports waist length white hair that makes fresh snow look dingy. It was up in a bun today and she wore a pair of glasses. Gani looked like she was in her forties, pretty good considering she was pushing sixteen hundred or so. She's kind of vague on how old she really is, like it really mattered at her age.

Mr. Milford shook her hand and thanked her for coming, then took us up to room 914. We all went in. Gani took a quick walk around the room. No fancy gestures or funny noises—the good ones don't need to bother with hooey.

"Other than the residuals left by the deaths, there's nothing overtly mystic that was left behind. However, I'm sensing some things that seem to back up your theory. It feels more like they were killed, but so many deaths in the same place in such a short time make things run together."

"So you can't do an exorcism?" asked Mr. Milford.

Gani smiled. "I could, but there's nothing here to perform one on. Best guess is something from outside is coming inside."

"But how is it getting in?" he asked.

"There are plenty of things out there that a locked room wouldn't even slow down. Fortunately, most of them are fairly rare. We'll have to do this the old fashioned way," she said.

"Which is?" he asked.

I sighed. I hated the old fashioned way. "We set a trap with living bait." Which of course was going to be me.

"You want me to do it?" she asked.

"Not really," I said, but it'd be a nice change. Despite my heritage, I'm no mage. I can use magic to fly, but it's akin to a bird using updrafts. I don't store any magic in my body and the only two magic based objects I use—my gun and Daemor badge—have excellent built-in cloaks. Any creature than manages to survive in this day and age has better than even odds of sensing Gani's power levels. A magí could cloak easily, but Gani's no magí. She just taps into Merlin's power. It takes a lot of power for her to cloak the link, which can sometimes be more of a warning than the link itself.

So Gani's no good for bait. As far as the rest of the team goes, Rudy's a goddess and Nemesis is the daughter of night. Both can show up on well-honed mystic radars. I, on the other hand, have the same ambient signature as a human. It'd take a very skilled mage to sense I was anything else as long as my wings were hidden, so I almost always get to be the bait. It's gotten to the point where I had a t-shirt made up with a worm on a hook for these occasions. Gani and Rudy laughed, but Nemesis wasn't amused. We got a dress code memo after that. That from a woman who prefers black leather pants.

Worse, at least in terms of backup, Gani couldn't even stay in the building without possibly tipping off the killer. She did the next best thing and made an invisible rune on one of the walls to make a "door" for her magic elevator to enter or leave the room, which wouldn't show up on the door log either.

"So technically, you could be our killer," I teased.

"True. Think you can take me?" she said, putting up her dukes like a boxer. As a fighter, she made a great mage.

"Without breaking a sweat," I lied. One on one, if I had the element of surprise, I'd bet on me. If she had time to plan, I might survive, but I'd have to probably kill her to do it. Thankfully she's one of the good guys.

Before we left, I asked Mr. Milford to get me a list of all the employees and to cross-reference who was working the days of the deaths. Not that a killer couldn't come in on a day off, but it was a start. I also asked for copies of the bills of all the people who had stayed in the room, whether they died or not.

Gani left via her elevator. I walked home, packed a bag and returned to the Jasper, this time to check in. Mr. Milford made sure he met me at the desk, whispering he had left copies of everything I had asked for under my pillow.

I went up to 914 and everything was where he said it would be so I checked in with Gani on my cell.

"What are you wearing?" she asked.

"Gani, I didn't know you thought of me that way," I joked.

"Sorry to disappoint, but I'm just interested in your choice of attire since this is an after hours gig," she said.

I smiled. "Yes, I have my bait t-shirt on."

"Just make sure the killer ends up on the hook, not you," Gani said.

"I'll do my best," I replied, said goodbye and hung up. Pulling out folders, I tried to find a pattern in the paper trail. There was no smoking gun on the bills—some ordered room service, some didn't. There wasn't a movie that they all ordered on pay per view. Some used the hotel phone, some didn't.

Normally I'd prefer to interview the staff myself, but this wasn't an assignment for Nemesis. She's not well known in most circles, but those in power, be it mystic or political, tend to at least be aware of her reputation. This gives her some pull with the powers that be, which gives her agents some leeway when we bend the occasional rule. Since I was doing this on my private time, I knew enough not to count on that. That meant if I screwed up, it would reflect poorly on Mr. Milford and I'd hate to get him fired for trying to help.

A scan of the employee files revealed only three who were on the clock the nights of all of the deaths—a night clerk, a maintenance worker and an IT guy.

I used my cell to call Mr. Milford. I had a few questions. I wasn't sure why an IT guy worked at night, but Mr. Milford told me he went to school during the day and apparently guests got cranky if they couldn't access their e-mail and surf the web. The IT guy was typically tied to the computer system just as the night clerk had to stay in the general vicinity of the desk. The maintenance worker however could go anywhere, maybe even figure a way around the card locks. The IT guy might be able to erase the logs. The night clerk had control of the security monitors and could edit security footage. Maybe they were working together, maybe it was someone else entirely—after all it didn't have to be an employee.

"Were there any guests who were here all the nights in question?" I asked.

"Give me a moment," Mr. Milford said. I could hear the click of a keyboard. "No, not all five. Any ideas yet?"

"Lots," I said. "But nothing more solid than that."

"I normally leave in about a half hour. I could stay if you need me," said Mr. Milford. It was sweet that he was acting protective, but I could handle myself better than he could. Still the male ego is a fragile thing.

"Better to keep things normal. We don't want to alert anyone to why I'm here, but thank you," I said.

Next I checked the room over. Normally that would have been the first thing on my list, but as Gani and I had already done a check earlier I was just looking for anything non-mystical we might have missed. Despite a thorough search, I didn't find a single trap door or secret passage. Only way in, besides the door and windows, was the pipes in the bathroom. Not that those couldn't be used. To be safe, I put the toilet seat down and the stoppers in the sink and shower. It wouldn't stop anything, but the noise removing them would let me know something was coming.

The next few hours were pure boredom. I didn't talk on the phone because that might be enough to scare whatever was doing the killing off. I didn't turn the TV on because it was too much of a distraction, especially for me. We didn't have television in Faerie and I can very easily get sucked into a program. Not a good idea when I'm supposed to be keeping watch for a killer. It would make me a real target instead of just bait, so I just held a book in front of me. I can read three languages, so I made sure the book I chose wasn't written in one of them to avoid another distraction. I periodically turned a page of a French edition of the collected Three Musketeers to make it look like I was actually reading it.

I ordered room service. It came and nothing happened. It smelled good, but some poison can actually enhance the smell and taste of food. Besides my days as a Daemor made me too paranoid to eat any of it. I even examined under the cart to make sure no nasties were hiding.

Next I ripped apart my intended meal looking for anything hiding in the food. It might sound crazy but there were living creatures small enough to hide in food that could kill you. My phone rang. It was Sydney. I rolled my eyes. I liked her, but she came on about as subtle as a subway train. We had met while I was filling in as a bouncer in a vamp club, a task that fell in the "anything else my boss came up with me to do" category of my job. There was a problem and a bloodsucker got the drop on me. Sydney stepped up and hit him with a chair from behind, giving me enough time to take him down. She saved my life. The only thing she asked in return was for me to go clubbing with her–often. We'd hung out a few times, but other than a quick trip to Bulfinche's Pub, I'd been too busy to go to anything resembling a club, but Sydney called me every other day to see if I was free.

If I didn't answer, she'd just keep calling. I opened the flip top. "Hi Sydney."

"Hey Terrorbelle. Darcy got invited to a party on Park Avenue. Going to be some rich guys there. You want in?" she asked.

"Can't," I said.

"You working?" she asked.

"Not exactly," I said.

"We got a limo. We can swing buy your apartment to pick you up."

"I'm not home."

"Where are you?" she asked.

"At a hotel," I answered.

"Belle, you having a nooner?"

"It's nighttime and no, I'm not," I said.

"Is he married?"

"Who?"

"The guy you're having the affair with. I mean why else use a hotel?" she said.

"I'm not meeting a guy," I said.

"Come on, you can tell me," she said.

There was a knock at the door. I looked through the peephole.

It was Glen Baxter, the IT guy. He looked a little different from the photo on his ID badge having grown what he probably thought passed for a goatee. Maybe with a little eyeliner and some age it one day may be a real one. Not that I should talk. According to his file, he was a year older than me.

"Sydney, I have to go. There's a man at the door," I said.

"I knew it. Call later and tell me all about it. Toodles," she said.

It was easier not to argue. "Bye."

Baxter knocked again. I opened the door cautiously. "Yes?"

"Sorry to disturb you, ma'am. I work for the hotel and we've been having some problems on this floor with the wireless network. Have you noticed anything?" he asked.

"No, but I don't have my computer with me," I said.

"Do you mind if I come in and check your wireless router?" he asked.

"I don't usually let a guy do that until the second date," I said. He laughed, a little harder than the joke was worth. Normally, a woman alone in a hotel room should close the door and call the front desk to check his story, which of course would scare Baxter away if he was the killer. Still, I shouldn't appear too accepting. "Can I see some ID?"

He handed over the plastic badge on his collar and smiled, probably thinking he was being charming. Maybe he was, but since he was one of my only three suspects I had trouble seeing him as anything other than a possible serial killer.

I looked it over and smiled back, returning it to him. "I guess it'd be okay for you to come in."

"Thanks," he said, moving toward the corner by the TV. The router was a small plastic circle on the ceiling with a blinking red light. It had been green when I checked in. "Ah, here's the problem. The router is stuck in a loop. I just need to reset it."

Baxter stood on a chair then took a pen, stuck it into a pinhole, and held it for several seconds. When he took it out, the LED went off, then the green light blinked a few times before staying on.

"That should fix it. Management bought the cheapest routers they could find and sometimes this happens," he said, making no move to go.

"Well, I'm sure you have other rooms to check," I said, knowing that my router shouldn't be affecting the ones in the other rooms.

"Actually, my dinner hour just started. I have some free time," Baxter said, looking deep into my eyes, trying for seductive. He got somewhere between puppy eyes and a dog in heat.

"I'm good," I said walking to the door. "Got to wash my hair, do my nails, that sort of thing."

When I pulled on the knob, it didn't turn. I could tear it off the hinges, but I was still playing a helpless female. He might just be on the prowl for a consensual quickie, but I doubted it.

"The door's stuck," I said.

"No, it's locked. Computer thing."

I gave him one last chance. "Well, open it then."

The smile that took up residence on his face looked nothing like seductive, closer to seduced. "I think not. Your phone service is down and the button I pressed up there jams cell phones. It's just you and me."

"I can see you're very excited by the prospect." It looked like something massive had pinched a tent in Baxter's extremely baggy pants. And the tent poled was writhing. "But I'm not interested."

"Pity," he said, unzipping his fly with one hand, pulling out a washcloth soaked in some chemical I could smell five feet away with the other. "How'd you like to meet my trouser snake?"

"I doubt you'll like how the introductions will turn out," I said, pointing my gun at Baxter's groin. Something snake-like popped out and it wasn't little Baxter. It wasn't little either, easily as thick around as a litter soda bottle and about six feet long. I popped a shot off, but the thing moved too fast and the bullet ended up grazing Baxter's inner mid-thigh. The creature's accomplice fell to the ground, screeching in a high-pitched voice, while the creature itself disappeared from view. It moved too fast for me to be sure, but I think I knew what it was and it wasn't good. Not willing to take him at his word about the cell jammer I hit send on my phone and *no service* flashed on the screen

"You shot me," Baxter cried.

Moving to the bathroom, I pulled two towels down and threw them at the wounded man, then closed the door. I didn't want the creature getting away through a pipe. More people would die if it did.

"You helped that thing kill five people and planned to make me number six. Look somewhere else for sympathy."

"The first guy killed himself," Baxter whined. "The bullar was trapped in stone and convinced him to sacrifice himself. It broke the curse holding him."

Damn, I was right about what it was. I made wary circle with my gun, but it stayed hidden. "It was no curse, just a larval state. They need a human sacrifice to awaken and twelve more to transform." Probably used some sort of telepathic mind games to drive him to take his own life. This was only the second I'd seen, but Bullar become Kulshedra, which is a bigger, flying snake that breathes fire. Another hundred sacrifices turns them humanoid, looking like a hairy giant woman. It takes ten times those numbers if they kill the people themselves. Magic makes the rules, I just try to learn enough of them to keep me alive. Someone offering up a person makes it a sacrifice, which is why it was keeping Baxter here. Bullar eyes hypnotize their victims so they can put their mouths over the person's and literally suck the life out of them. It didn't matter if the intended sacrifice had a knife wound or was knocked out with chemicals on a washcloth for it to count.

"My leg hurts," Baxter complained.

He was annoying me and playing up his irritation factor, maybe figuring his snake-like partner would pop up and help by hypnotizing me. "A flesh wound is less than you deserve. Push the towels against it. It doesn't look like it got your femoral."

"How do you know that?" he whined, but did as instructed.

"You'd have lost more blood and be unconscious or dead by now," I said, taking off my coat. I may not have eyes in the back of my head, but razor sharp wings are the next best thing. I'd shred the bullar if it came at me from behind. It might not kill it, but it'd damn well hurt it.

Baxter's eyes got a little wide at the sight of my deadly appendages, but it still wasn't enough to shut him up. "I'm hurt bad. You need to get me to a doctor."

"Or put another bullet in you to put you out of my misery," I said. I'm not above killing, but I did a lot of it in my time as a soldier in Faerie. I needed a damn good reason to end a life these days and annoying me didn't quite cut it. Unfortunately. "Now be quiet."

I thought I heard something rustle. It sounded like the monster was under the bed. Now I could bend down and peak, but that would leave me vulnerable. I could use an explosive round to blow the bed up, but the blast would blind me for half a second. That's too long a window to be vulnerable when facing a fast adversary. Also, while the construction in the Jasper wasn't shoddy, it wasn't thick enough to make me confident that it could stop shrapnel from going through any walls, ceiling, or the floor. I didn't want someone from another room hurt or killed so I went with option three.

I kicked the bed across the room with one foot, flipping backwards in the process. I'm not a superior gymnast by any means, but with my muscle power I don't have to be to accomplish basic maneuvers. I get it done and don't worry about making it pretty. And I cheated by using my wings to help me hover during the spin, which also would shred the creature if it tried to attack me from behind.

Startled by the loss of its cover, the bullar leapt at me, especially impressive considering it had no legs. It sort of sprung like a coil. Magic changes the rules that way sometimes. It was too damn fast and somehow managed to change direction in mid-air toward my head. I watched its open jaws land on my face, its mouth covering mine. Years of training helped me not panic, take a deep breath and shut my mouth the moment before contact. If it managed to suck out my breath, it'd start to drain my life force. Bullar allow their victims to keep breathing in a creepy symbiotic mouth to mouth. It lengthened the death, which was more pleasurable. In a twisted way, the bullar combined feeding and sex into this one deadly act. The stolen life force allowed them to move onto the next stage in their evolution.

The serpent bit down hard to get my attention. I was angry enough I almost made the mistake of looking in its eyes. My Daemor badge, which I wore these days as a belt buckle, combined with my training gave me some resistance to mind control, but it wasn't a free pass. If it got control of me, it'd force me to breath and

I'd die.

Of course, if I didn't get it off me soon, nature will make me do the same thing and I'll die anyway.

It was too close for a safe shot, so I grabbed its tail and pulled. Its teeth sank even deeper into my face, like dozens of sharp, pointy anchors. I was pretty sure yanking it was hurting me more than it. Worse, it was trying to widen its jaws even further, opening my mouth. Once that happened, I couldn't stop it from sucking the fight right out of me.

My love life has never been much to brag about, but I have standards. Even on my worst day, I'd never let a creature like this French kiss me. It had to qualify as the second most disgusting kiss I'd ever had. Its nine sharp tongues raked against my lips, cutting as they licked. It had enough control over the little things that it was using some of the tongues to try to pry my lips apart. To add to the fun, it began to suck so the tiniest opening would let my breath escape. Its serpentine body swelled out with the effort.

The edges of my vision started to have tiny lights swirl around as the bullar's belly ballooned up even more, but it gave me an idea.

I couldn't pull it off me without tearing parts of my face, so I needed another way. Being a firm believer in the turnabout is fair play philosophy, I wrapped one massive fist around its neck and squeezed, cutting off the serpent's air supply. For good measure, I twisted its body around like a balloon animal with my gun hand to make sure the bullar couldn't breathe either. I didn't want to let go of the gun, so my grip was weaker than I would have liked, especially since it used its tail to try and pull my arms away.

Talking would literally be the death of me, but there were other ways of getting my point across. The bullar's scales were dense enough to deflect most small arms fire and its eyes were too small a target, hence my hesitation to risk a shot. I didn't want to take a ricochet or have one hit someone in another room. Instead I arched one of my upper wings until its razor edge was at the bullar's neck, just below where I squeezed. My skin was already past pink and on my way to becoming blue, but I learned long ago never to show weakness. Instead of struggling, I raised an eyebrow and held it, pointing with my eyes at my wing tip, then I nicked the serpent's skin between and under its scales. I felt flesh part and blood ooze.

I considered decapitating it without a warning, but I might not cut through on the first try and, even wounded, the bullar could still do me some damage. My face may not be the prettiest on the block, but it's the only one I've got. I had enough scars without any on my face.

The serpent made a noise that was more growl than hiss. I pushed the wing in until it cut down to muscle. If it didn't let go in the next few seconds, I'd have to try to take its head off regardless or pass out.

I won the game of chicken and the bullar let go of my face only to snap around and sink its fangs into my gun hand. I managed to hold onto my automatic, but my grip loosened enough for the bullar's tail to snake around my throat.

I had managed to take in a deep breath. The wing tip that I had threatened it with sliced out, managing to catch it partially between scales. A normal snake, even a boa constrictor, would have been sliced in half. If I had a better angle or leverage to get between its armor, the wound would have been more than an inch deep.

At the same time I smashed the fist it had wrapped its jaws around into my forehead. Hitting myself might seem like a bad idea, but I have a very hard forehead.

One night when I was dragged out clubbing by Rudy, some guy was trying to impress women by smashing walnuts into his head to open them. When I expressed that I was less than impressed, he challenged me to do better. The bar had a couple of real coconuts to make drinks from and I spilt one open on my forehead. The gentleman had been drinking and wasn't about to be undone by a woman, so he tried it himself. He came to about five minutes later.

The impact with my head hurt the bugger enough for it to open its jaws. I got my hand free for an instant before its maw opened even wider and it made a second try. Instead of pulling away, I pushed my hand down its throat, gun and all. It clamped down hard enough that my fingers started to go numb.

It hurt, but I'd learned to work through pain years ago. Physical pain was the easiest. I sprinted across the room and used my wings to hover near the ceiling. Baxter had hit a button in the router to jam my cell phone. I'm not a high tech gal, but there were simple ways of dealing with complicated gadgets. I reached up with my free hand and ripped the plastic device off the ceiling and crushed it between my fingers.

I had to let go of the bullar to wreck the tech, which it took as an invitation to wrap its tail back around my windpipe. I had managed several deep breaths and tensed my neck muscles, which where strong enough to halt the tail squeeze, at least for a bit. The longer this went on, the more the advantage would go to the serpent.

It knew this, but wasn't patient enough to wait, deciding instead to cut off my windpipe by putting the tip of its tale in my foolishly open mouth. I was distracted by my multi-tasking—I was trying to fight the creature and dial my cell phone at the same time. I bit down on the appendage as I hit "3" on my speed dial.

I obviously couldn't respond, so a few seconds later the wall morphed into elevator doors and opened. Gani looked out, ready to sling a spell. Dropping the phone, I ran toward the elevator and motioned Gani out, all the while forcibly unwinding the tail from around my throat. Maybe it was in pain from me biting its tail, maybe I had better leverage, but this time I won the tug of war and got it off, if you could call the resultant circles of bruises around my neck winning.

I mentally clicked the gun's clip to armor piercing shells and snapped my swallowed hand like it was holding a whip. Once the serpent was in the lift, I fired. There were a series of tiny bulges as the bullet ricocheted along the creature's digestive tract. I fired a second shot and this time some of the bulges were trickling blood between the scales, which fortunately didn't extend inside of the creature. Switching the clip to explosive rounds, I fired again, squeezing the serpent's neck tight behind the bullet. The blast blew half its guts out a new hole. The bullar wasn't dead, but its jaw's grip on my hand weakened.

Gani made a complicated hand motion and purple lightning jumped from her fingers to the bullar. It convulsed and fell off my hand onto the floor.

"You need to finish it?" asked Gani, stepping inside her elevator.

I looked down at my bloody hand and walked out. There were times I needed to finish a fight. Sometimes honor or revenge demanded it. This was neither. "Nah. All yours."

The bullar spoke for the first time. "Oh, mighty mage, I can offer you great power for serving me."

Gani laughed. "The only way I'm going to serve you is over rice with a garlic sauce."

"Glen Baxter, attend your master or all you are entitled to shall be lost," said the bullar as purple lightning filled the elevator, making a strobe effect in the hotel room as it filled with the aroma of cooking meat.

I'm not sure what the snake promised the geek, but it was enough to make him drag himself to his feet in an attempt to help the monster.

I was tired and hurting so I just pointed my gun and cocked it. "Take another step and you lose a kneecap."

"I don't believe you," Baxter said, pulling a switchblade from his pocket and charging me. I caught his hand and twisted it back, dropping him halfway to the floor, followed by a swift kick to the front of his leg. Baxter screamed in agony and fell the rest of the way to the floor. "You broke my knee."

"I warned you'd lose a kneecap. And it's only dislocated, not broken," I said, pulling the cheaply made knife out of his hand and snapping it in half in front of him, then putting the pieces in my pocket. Shoving him facedown on the carpet, I literally sat on Baxter to pin him as I ripped his belt off and made a tourniquet below the hip but above the gunshot wound. It wasn't too deep and had already started to clot, but was still bleeding some.

"So can I assume you'll be confessing to the cops to the murders?" I said.

"Are you crazy? You can't prove a thing and I didn't kill them," Baxter said.

"You offered them up to your trouser snake and made sure they couldn't call for help. That's the same as killing them in my book," I said.

"I'd have to be an idiot to confess," he said.

"You'd have to be an idiot not to," I said. Gani exited her elevator carrying a charred serpentine carcass and plopped it on the floor in front of Baxter's face. He whimpered as smoke rose up it and the smell of charred flesh entered his nostrils. Baxter tried to roll away, but couldn't move me off his back. "Especially once his family comes looking for him."

"Family?" he said.

"He didn't tell you? Each Bullar is part of a family of twelve. Very close. They have to team up to overpower and devour the mother, after which they go into the stony larval stage the suicide victim found him in. Once all twelve get the necessary human sacrifices, they join together to evolve to the next stage. A hydra. Now that their brother is dead, they can never move on. Your bullar at least explained to you how important evolution was to him, I assume?" Baxter nodded, his chin digging into the carpet. "That was why he did all this after all. Can you imagine how angry the other eleven are going to be that you cheated them of their chance? Can you imagine what they are going to do to you for killing their brother?"

"Me? You two killed him," he said.

"Well, that's your story. Mine is you called us and asked us to set him up. Isn't that how you remember it?" I asked Gani.

"Not so much asked as begged is how I recall it," said Gani.

"But I was loyal to him. I tried to kill you." His tone had gone up an octave. I hate to hear a grown man whine. It gives me a headache.

"Prove it," I said, taking a picture of him and the corpse with my phone. "Smile."

"Wait, don't I have to be offered as a sacrifice for them to kill me?" Baxter said.

"For the power, sure, but they'll be going after your for revenge. Besides, you're kind of puny to be split eleven ways," I said.

"I don't want to die." Baxter had tears streaming down his face.

"I imagine your victims felt the same way," I said.

"You have to protect me," he said.

"Not my job," I replied. "You'd need to be someplace safe 24/7. Bullar don't want people to know they exist. It makes their killing run smoother. If you were in jail, they probably wouldn't go after you, at least until you got out."

"And the guards would have to protect you if they did come for you," added Gani, tsking me so Baxter couldn't see.

"But that'd hardly be fair to them," I said.

"Forget about them. Someone's got to protect me," said Baxter.

"The only way they'd protect you is if you confessed to having a hand in these murders," I said.

"I'll confess," said Baxter.

And confess he did to the cop that met us in the lobby. As soon as he was taken away, Gani turned to me with a grin.

"You naughty girl, you."

"Me?" I said, with mock innocence.

"You made all of that up. Bullar and hydra have nothing to do with each other and if a bullar had family, they wouldn't care less about each other," said Gani.

"It worked, didn't it?" I said.

And it did to a point. After explaining how he doctored the computer logs, Baxter put the mention of giant magic snakes in his statement and the DA's office almost took him for a nut and let him go until my boss made a call.

The night before sentencing, Baxter called the ADA to try to withdraw his plea. After all, no snakes had shown up at Riker's to get him, so he figured he might be safe. Gani whipped up an illusion of a flock of floating snakes outside his cell and all talk of withdrawing his plea on account of insanity was forgotten.

I got invited to dinner at the Milford's by way of a thank you and had a week's worth of leftovers forced on me. And Sydney still didn't believe that I wasn't having an affair at the Jasper, especially when I explained that I had been attacked by a trouser snake.

PAYING THE PINK REAPER

I've fallen for a few men in my time. With all but one I ended up hitting the ground hard and heart first.

So when I saw the single exception in the arms of another woman, I was understandably upset. Not that it was romantic on either of their parts. Or on my parts either, sadly.

The woman had one arm around Murphy's neck, a switchblade in her other hand that was at his throat. I was most of a block away. Normally I don't pull my gun unless I have to, but it was in my hand before I even realized I had reached for it.

I'm an above average shot, but not a markswoman. At this range I could end up hitting him or the other five women around them, one of whom looked very pregnant. Instead I ran all out. With my legs, that's pretty fast at least for a sprint.

Before I got close enough to help, Murphy flipped her and took the knife out of her hand. Not too shabby for a human, but he does on occasion train with Hercules, myself, and some other legendary fighters in the parking garage at Bulfinche's Pub.

He pulled and twisted her arm, dislocating the shoulder. I was impressed. Murphy's not a soldier. He's a little too kind hearted. His fighting skills are above average, but he isn't good enough to not hurt a serious opponent. He's the type of guy to hold a door for a lady or even me. For him to hurt the woman something bad must be up.

The women all sported Grim Reaper tattoos taking up the upper part of their right arms and shoulders with a couple of variations on the traditional. Death's robes were pink and the Reaper was obviously female judging by the curves in said robes.

Two of the women pulled blades of their own and came at Murphy at different angles. He positioned himself between his attackers and the bleeding pregnant woman, which gave me a pretty good guess about what had happened.

"I'm warning you, I'm a real cut up so I'll give you this one chance to surrender now," he said.

I'm guessing having the remaining two women pull knives wasn't the response he was hoping for.

"This is Pink Reaper business. You were stupid enough to stick your nose in, so you got to pay the Reapers," said one with a nose piercing.

"And since you hurt one of us," said another with enough eyebrow rings to make her look like she had sewn tiny strips of chain mail to her face. "We gonna charge a lot."

"You take credit cards?" he said.

"Off dead bodies, sure," said Chain-brow with the smile of someone who had already killed and dismembered her opponent in her mind.

"Don't store clerks question the blood on the plastic? And the fact that you're not a man? Not that there's anything wrong with that. Some of my best friends aren't men. And some aren't even human. Go figure," he said, smiling. I swear the man would joke if he was facing down the real Grim Reaper. And come to think about it, he has. Murph was trying to make them not take him seriously. Because he went overboard on the joking, he was an easy man to underestimate. Right now he was working hard to encourage that perception as he moved into a casual defensive stance. "Wouldn't it be easier just to get a job? Or start your own business? Put all this effort into something constructive?"

"I'll show you constructive," said Chain-brow lunging. Murphy shifted his weight, caught her arm between his ribs and elbow and hit down hard with his opposite hand. I heard the pop as I got close enough. Her elbow was much wider than it should be—it happens when it gets dislocated.

"Can't do constructive unless you're in the union. Unless you can produce a union card, I'm going to have to report you," Murphy said, taking the knife from Chain-brow's limp fingers and twisting her injured forearm back until the pain drove her to her knees. He kicked her away. Not bad for defense, but he was facing multiple armed opponents. He was going to have to do more damage to get out of this mess. Or have someone do it for him.

"You gonna die funny man," said Nosering waving her knife. Murphy lifted up the one he had taken, playing the tough guy. I don't know if he could bring himself to stab someone. It's a very up close and personal thing and turns even the strongest stomach. After the first few times you harden yourself because otherwise you're the one getting cut.

"Want to bet?" I said, having finally caught up. I plowed into one with a chin stud, knocking her out, then rolled in front of Nosering letting my gun hand move back and forth pointing at each of the women. "The question is which of you gets a bullet first. Eene, meenee, mainee mo…"

"Ain't your concern, ya big bitch," said Nosering.

"It is if you're messing with him," I said. One of the others who had enough ear piercings to make the sides of her head look like they had been transplanted from a Goth robot rushed me. I did a front stomp kick and sent her flying back first into a parked car.

"Sorry T-Belle, but I seem to be running a little late for lunch," Murphy said.

"You're not blowing me off for these skanks, I hope?" I said, moving to shield him with my body. Murphy is on the short list of people I'd take a bullet or a blade for.

"Naw. None of them hold a candle to you, but they seem sadistic enough to literally consider trying it, although they'd probably lean more toward an acetylene torch. I was walking by and saw them attempt to deliver this woman's baby by C-section, starting with her palm." Which explained where the blood came from. "I asked them if they were doctors and it should come as no surprise that it turns out there's not a medical license among them. They didn't even bother to sterilize the switchblades. Very unsanitary. Not to mention evil and disturbing," said Murphy. "I'm almost positive they don't even have malpractice insurance, but you heard her trying to collect the co-pay from me."

"The baby belongs to Bándearg Anbhás," said Nosering.

"Ckuf," I cursed.

"Bad?" said Murphy.

"Yep. They serve a Pink Death," I said.

"I take it that it's not a thick and delicious dessert?" said Murphy.

"No, it's a soul feeder from Faerie. They suck the life from their followers. They try to have enough stupid people around them so their followers don't die off too quickly. It's not unheard of for them to demand the occasional sacrifice," I said. "What they do to them ain't pretty."

"It doesn't matter. They aren't getting the baby," said Murphy.

"Thank you," whispered the bleeding pregnant woman, who was cowering on cement steps.

"It is too late for that. Lucinda has pledged the child to Bándearg Anbhás," said Nosering.

"I take it back. I won't let her take my baby," said Lucinda.

"No problem. We'll take it for her. Pity, you'll have to die, but after this betrayal you were pretty much out of the gang," said Nosering, grinning from ear to ear.

"And the only way out is death," said Chain-brow.

"What, you have little skulls over the exit signs? That can't help with recruitment," said Murphy.

"You are annoying me. Shut the f…"

"Sorry to ruin your day. I advise the lot of you to run away very quickly before it gets a lot worse. Against me you barely had a shot," said Murphy. Murph is resourceful, so he would have probably figured out something. He's faced down worse than these gangbangers and always manages to survive. If he wore a hat, it'd be filled with rabbits. "But against T-Belle you better send for reinforcements. Lots of them. Go on. We'll wait."

"No need, already covered," said Nosering, looking up over our heads.

It was a dumb move. I hadn't noticed the husk diving off the ledge and without the warning never would have made the skeet shot on the tiny, animated baby-sized body. I used a concussive round, which had enough force to blow the husk off course. I shot another round at the sidewalk, knocking the Pink Reapers down and leaving a small crater. Bits of concrete cut up the Pink Reapers

"Run," I said. Murphy didn't question me and pulled Lucinda to her feet. There was a small gush of fluid.

"Oh, boy," said Murphy.

"What?" I said, already fearing the answer.

"Lucinda's water broke," he replied.

"Are you sure?" I asked.

"I'm not an expert but I have some experience," he said.

"You're a doctor?" Lucinda asked.

"No, a bartender, but I have delivered a baby." Murphy had delivered a succubus's baby while they were both trapped in a spell circle. He, baby and mother all survived and thrived. Lucinda looked more than a little freaked. Murphy looked over at me and let me see the worry on his face, but when he turned back to Lucinda he was all confidence. "They say the first time is the hardest."

"We need backup," I said, pulling out my cell and hitting "1" on my speed dial. We needed Nemesis.

"I already tried to call for help. No signal," he said.

Lucinda screamed because of what I can only assume was a contraction. "I can't walk."

"I'll carry you," I said.

"No, I'll do it," said Murphy. I looked at him. "I know you're stronger, but you're the better fighter."

"Can you manage?" I said.

"I'll have to," he said, picking her up bride style and running with me. I looked, splitting my gaze between back and up, expecting to see a Reaper or the husk. "Lucinda, try some rapid deep breathing."

"Does it help?" she asked.

"Not really, but it'll distract you," he said. "So are you hoping for a boy or a girl?"

"It's a girl," she said and screamed again.

"Excellent and the contractions are only a couple of minutes apart. We're going to see her soon," said Murphy. "We should get to Bulfinche's Pub."

It made sense. Inside the bar, no magic works without Paddy's say so. The Bándearg Anbhás would be powerless and so would the husk. There are enough heavy hitters there to handle this bunch without blinking. Problem was we were in Hell's Kitchen and Bulfinche's was across and uptown.

"I'm open for suggestions for how to get there," I said.

"Hermes could get her there in an eye blink," he said.

I looked at my cell. "The Bándearg Anbhás is still blocking the signal."

"How about land lines?" he said.

It was so obvious I hadn't even thought of it. We were still two blocks from my building. I searched the street. Most of the storefronts had large glass windows in front—not very securable. There was a tattoo parlor that had replaced most of the glass with wood, leaving a smaller window with a neon sign that announced *Rembrandt Ink* in bright letters. "In there."

I got the door and Murphy carried Lucinda inside. There were no customers. A large gentleman with a black bandanna tied around his head stood when he saw us.

"Can I help you?" he said, then looked at the sexy reaper on Lucinda's right arm. "Nice ink."

"Admire the artwork later. The lady's having a baby. We need a phone to call for help," said Murphy, putting her down on what looked like a dentist chair.

The big man looked as Lucinda who was still trying the breathing. Judging by the look on her face, it still wasn't helping the pain much.

"Sure," he said, dialing 911 before we could tell him we had better and quicker places to call. "That's weird. The phone's dead."

"Damn," I said, looking out the door.

"How about internet?" said Murphy. I was thinking the same thing. We go to the World Wide Spyder's site, have him call Paddy at Bulfinche's and he sends Hermes for EVAC.

The big man clicked on his browser. "It's down too. So's my cell."

I went to look out the small window and started barricading the door. "Pink Reapers found us. They must have some way of tracking Lucinda."

"How'd the Bándearg Anbhás work things in Faerie?" said Murphy.

"They'd mark their followers," I said. Murphy and I locked eyes, both figuring it out at the same time.

"The tattoo!" we said.

Murphy turned to the tattoo artist. "Any way you can take that tattoo off of her?"

"Why? That's beautiful work. There's a couple grand worth of ink there," he said.

"Not what he asked. Can you take it off?" I said.

"No. You'd need a dermatologist with a laser. All I could do is cover it over," he said.

"Would that work?" Murphy asked.

"We'd have to make it into something different, not cover it. That could take the Bándearg Anbhás' mark off her, maybe break her claim on the baby," I said. "Maybe."

"Do it. Do whatever you have to. Save my baby!" screamed Lucinda, alerting the Pink Reapers outside the door as to exactly where we were.

"Okay, I need you to turn that tattoo into a nice bunny or a cat or something," said Murphy.

"There's no reason to mess with something that well done. And there's no way I'm working on a pregnant woman giving birth. I'd lose my license. There's no reason to," he said.

Which is when two gunshots rang out.

"Reapers trying to shoot out the lock," I said. "There's a new one and they're all packing now."

"Okay, I only have time to explain this to you once. This young lady joined a gang, swore allegiance to an otherworldly entity who has been feeding on her soul and is going to steal her baby. To stop it, we need to change that tattoo into a damn bunny. Can we count on you or not?" asked Murphy.

Another shot shattered the tiny window with the neon sign and the big man ran out the backroom. A second later a door slammed. I followed and locked the back door. The Pink Reapers were too close for us to safely run, at least carrying Lucinda.

At least all of us. "Murphy, you run and try to get a signal."

"Not a chance," he replied, picking up the tattoo gun, checking how it worked. "Too much artwork to do."

I smiled. He didn't even have a weapon or, logically speaking, much of a chance, but he wouldn't leave either me or Lucinda. It was a stupid, self-sacrificing bone headed move and I fell in love with him all over again. Silently I hoped one day he'd do the same for me.

"I don't need magic ink or anything?" asked Murphy.

"I hope not," I said, ripping out the counter to further barricade the door. I saw a head and a hand come through the formerly neon window and took a shot. I got the hand dead on. Fortunately, a Bándearg Anbhás doesn't feed on blood or my options would be further limited.

"Sorry, this is probably going to hurt," said Murphy, putting needle to flesh.

"Not as bad as what's going on down below," she said.

They fired more gunshots. The cops would be here in minutes if the phones worked. One hand reached inside the little window with a gun. I shot it too and the gun fell inside. I picked up a desk and rammed it legs first into the wall. All four went through the sheetrock and stuck. It wouldn't be very bulletproof, but it would stop them from sticking the guns inside. It was looking like I was going to do more than shoot some hands to end this.

"That's the spirit. You have a preference for what I draw?" said Murphy.

"Kids like bunnies, right?" said Lucinda.

"Yep," said Murphy.

"Make it a bunny."

"Will do. It'd be a cartoon bunny." He moved the needle. "I'll make the eye sockets sunglasses and the hood into hair. I'll even put on a fluffy tail." Lucinda screamed. "Okay, no tail."

"Not that. I think the baby's coming," said Lucinda.

"T-belle, you're going to have to deliver the baby," said Murphy. "Sorry Lucinda, but we have to get the pants and underwear off."

"Fine," Lucinda said, complying.

Murphy looked over to inspect matters, putting down some towels that were on hand, using one to cover the important parts. "Lucinda needs you."

"I'm a little busy making sure nobody gets in," I said.

"From the looks we have a little bit, but not too long. I'll take over once I'm done here, but if it's not done you'll have to do one or the other, Belle," he said. "Sorry."

I nodded, wishing I was a better artist.

Something hit the door hard enough to make the room shake. And did it again. On the third try the door and the barricade splintered. I could shoot, but I would be firing blind, maybe hit some innocent passerby on the street. I decided to wait until I had a clear shot and the door exploded in, followed quickly by the tiny husk. My ammo includes bullets with condensed light—worked wonders with creatures of darkness, but the husk didn't qualify. I figured darkshot might work. As the daughter of night, Nemesis can actually pack concentrated light and darkness into a bullet and darkshot worked on everything *except* creatures of darkness.

The two shots caught it in the chest and the gut. The pain was enough to cause convulsions and I used the chance to stomp on it hard. I felt parts crunch, but it didn't matter. It was animated as part of the Bándearg Anbhás power, which would mend the injuries. The best way to stop something like a husk is dismemberment followed by burning. I have a permit to carry concealed in NYC but it only applies to my gun, not a battle-ax or sword. Normally, not a problem, but at times like this it makes things difficult.

I stepped back and unloaded armor piercing rounds into the husk. Regular caliber bullets wouldn't do much damage, but the slugs I used made some nice sized holes. No blood, just a pink mist. I smiled and kept firing, diving out of the way when the Pink Reapers started firing through the husk sized hole in the door. I spun, firing concussive rounds to blow out the door, then dove through the now bigger hole. I hit and kicked each of the Reapers as I passed them. They were stunned from the blast and the bits of wood that hit them and were no match for my muscles and Daemor training. Where Murphy dislocated, I broke bones and hit heads hard enough to knock the lady gangbangers unconscious.

Nosering was tougher than the rest. As I stood over her, she said, "What did you do to my baby?" Which explained where the Bándearg Anbhás got the husk. Nosering had sacrificed her own child and the Pink Death had eaten the poor thing's soul, then twisted it's tiny body as a vessel of her power. I shook my head in pity and disgust, but it explained why Lucinda was running if she realized this was the fate that awaited her daughter. "Bándearg Anbhás tells me he's a good boy. Mama's so proud of him."

I slugged her under her jaw. It was easier than asking her why she would do such a horrible thing. I knew from experience that no matter what the answer was, I wouldn't like it. I disarmed their blades and guns, then dragged them inside. I found some duct tape and secured them in the backroom.

"T-Belle, we have a little bit of a situation," Murphy shouted.

I ran to the front of the shop. The pink mists from the husk had coalesced into a vision of the Pink Death herself.

"*The child is mine!*" it shouted.

"Not unless you're a one-eared bunny it's not," said Murphy, working furiously with the needle.

"*You will not deny me what is mine!*"

"I'll deny like a politician under oath," said Murphy.

The pink vision of a voluptuous robed skeleton floated toward them. I stepped in front and pointed my gun.

"Back it off," I said, pointing my gun. She laughed. I could hear Murphy asking Lucinda questions about when she got the tattoo and I heard her mention blood.

"*You and your weapon are less than nothing.*"

"Really? Did you check out the belt buckle?"

The sight of my Daemor badge made Ms. Pink Death stop in her immaterial tracks. "*The Daemor are not what they were during the Thandau conflict. I do not fear Mab or her lackeys.*"

"So you're mean and stupid. I am also one of Nemesis' agents," I said. Sometimes name dropping can be more effective than a battle.

This time Pinky's expression changed. "*The enforcer for the Thrones? You are more formidable than you appear. Perhaps we can make an arrangement.*"

"I'm listening," I said.

"*I will allow you to have the betrayer. I will claim the infant.*" Infant humans are both a delicacy and a power source in parts of Faerie. It's why so many different races try to steal them.

"How about you relinquish your claim on both, I allow your other followers to live and I let you walk away," I said. Technically this was only part of her. If she was smart, she was anchored in Faerie so any damage to her projected form on Earth would only hurt, not destroy her.

"*I think you overreach. I have a claim of blood on mother and child and I will not be denied.*"

"Want to bet? Cause you can call me King Cleopatra," Murphy said. The king of denial allusion went over her head. Which is when I saw the knife in his hand.

"Murphy, No!" I shouted, realizing what he was going to do.

"She ain't getting the baby," Murphy said, cutting his finger and soaking the tattoo needle in his blood. He put it in Lucinda's skin and the Pink Death screamed.

"*No! I can no longer feel the infant. This cannot be! You are no mage! You cannot deny me what it rightfully mine.*"

"You just aren't getting it. You're denied," he said. "Now shuffle off."

"*I am death herself! I will destroy you!*"

"Better than you have tried. And the real Grim Reaper is a personal friend of mine. I don't think he'd be too happy with you claiming his identity and trying to steal a child," said Murphy.

The Pink Reaper bellowed and some of the pink mists that she was manipulating coalesced around the battered husk and it floated up into the air. I poured darkshot into it, but the mists put it back together as fast as I blew it apart.

Murphy had the right idea in cutting her off from Lucinda, but she was still tied in with her followers who were also feeding her power. I ran into the backroom. Pinky was too concerned with what Murphy was doing to follow me, but the husk floated through the air right behind me. Taking off my trenchcoat, I shut the door, knowing it would be about as useful as a piece of cardboard.

The Pink Reapers were awake and trying to get out of their duct tape restraints. They seemed to be withering as Pinky sucked their lives away. I went toward Nosering with the sharpest of their switchblades in my right hand. I sliced the head and chest of the tattoo right off her skin as the husk shattered the door into kindling.

I may not have had an ax, but I did have something better with me. As the husk got close I lashed out with my wings, coming over the top of my head and shoulders. I managed to detach the head and a leg. I moved on to Chain-brow and did the same to her shoulder. They were screaming and moving away. Funny when you considered that I was saving their lives by cutting them off as a food source for the Bándearg Anbhás. The pink mist was linking the head and leg to the body of the husk and the head dive-bombed me, teeth first. There was nobody in the room that I cared enough about to worry about fleshy shrapnel, so I fired an explosive round right into the husk's palate. The explosion shattered the head, but the mist held the bits of meat up in the air. Luckily the eyes were destroyed, which meant Pinky couldn't use them to see what was happening. Since she couldn't see, she made the husk's body parts fly around frantically, trying to hit me just through sheer overwhelming force.

It got close a few times, but not enough to stop me from defacing skin and ink. As I cut the next to last tattoo, pieces of the head started to fall to the floor. When I got the last, the husk dropped and shattered like old, fried dried meat.

Ignoring the screams and cries of the Pink Reapers, I rushed out to the other room. Murphy was taunting the Bándearg Anbhás. She was trying to claim the baby and Murphy and Lucinda, but it hadn't worked. Murphy kept stepping between her and the pregnant woman. Her mist enveloped Murphy, but he was smart and held both his breath and his ground. It was obviously hurting him, but he wouldn't let her pass.

"Back away from him," I ordered.

"*His blood touched my mark. He should be mine, but he resisted me and he has blocked me from Lucinda and the child. I am not going away empty-handed.*"

Pinky was right about one thing. Murphy was no mage, not that you had to be to use blood magic. I had no idea what he had done to stop her, but I wasn't going to let her hurt him.

"Forget it Bándearg Anbhás. I've destroyed your bond to your followers and your link with this place. Your power is weakened, your husk destroyed." I pulled out my phone and looked at it. "And you are no longer able to stop communications." I hit "1" on my speed dial. "Nemesis, it's me. I have a rogue Bándearg Anbhás and need back-up ASAP."

"You called the Thrones' enforcer?"

I smiled. "You're going down, Pinky."

"I'll leave, but I will not forget this. You have made an enemy." The mist backed off of Murphy. "Both of you."

"Get in line," I said.

"Yeah, cause next time we'll have a smokeless ashtray," said

Murphy.

Pinky vanished and Lucinda screamed.

Murphy spun and lifted up the towel. "The baby is crowning."

"You got it?" I asked.

"Yep," said Murphy. "Although if you called Hermes, he'd do a better job."

"I was bluffing." I looked at my cell. "We still don't have a signal. The spell was probably for a set time. Stopping her didn't affect it."

Murphy smiled appreciatively at me. "Nice." He turned his attention to the baby. "Okay, Lucinda, give me a great big push."

"I can't. It hurts too much."

I grabbed her hand. "You can and you will. You just beat the Pink Death. This is nothing. Squeeze me as hard as you want, take a deep breath and push." Lucinda did.

"One more should do it," said Murphy.

"You heard the man. One more and you can see your little girl. Push!" I said.

Lucinda tightened for all she was worth and pushed and we were all rewarded with the cries of a baby girl.

"Welcome to the world little one. You are very beautiful." Murphy cleaned her off and used some tattoo tool to clamp off the umbilical cord. "You want to cut the cord?"

"No, I don't think I could," Lucinda said, then turned to me. "Would you like to?"

"Sure," I replied. I took a switchblade that I hadn't used in a tattooectomy and poured a disinfectant that was next to the tattoo equipment. I made a cut and Murphy secured the end of it.

"Lucinda, would you like to see your baby girl?"

"Oh, yes," she said, beaming as Murphy handed her the baby.

"What are you going to name her?" he asked.

"What is your name?" she asked me.

"Terrorbelle," I said. "Seriously?" she asked. I nodded. Her face dropped. "What about you?"

"John Murphy."

It was obvious neither thrilled her.

"We were just helping. No obligation in naming her," Murphy said.

"It just I'm so grateful to you both. Without you..."

"It was our pleasure," said Murphy. I nodded and stuck my finger out into the baby's hand.

"She likes you," said Lucinda, looking at my wings. "I think I'll call her Pixie."

"I like it," said Murphy. Sure beats ogre.

"I'm a lapsed Catholic, but I want to have Pixie baptized. Would you two consider being her godparents?" asked Lucinda.

"I'd be honored," I said.

"Me too," said Murphy.

Lucinda looked into her baby's face and smiled. Then she looked back at me. "I guess that makes you her fairy godmother."

"Of course, Terrorbelle packs heat instead of a wand," said Murphy.

"Fairy with a gun," said Lucinda.

"We wouldn't have it any other way," said Murphy.

"Good," I said and picked Murphy off the ground in a hug. Some guys are intimidated by that, but not Murph. I even managed a quick smack on his lips before I reluctantly put him down. "Nice job, partner."

"Back at you," he said. "All this and still no lunch though."

I pulled him aside. "How in blazes were you able to break the binding when changing the tattoo didn't work?"

Murphy laughed. "I created a new binding." He saw my quizzical look. "I'm no mage, but I haven't worked this long at Bulfinche's Pub, not to mention hanging out with Hex, without learning a few things. I gave her a new tattoo over the old." He walked over to Lucinda and put his hand on the bandage he put over his work. "May I?" Lucinda nodded and he lifted it off. It was the shot of gold logo of a rainbow in a shot glass of Bulfinche's Pub. I've heard Gani say it is one of the most powerful sites of magic in North America. "I used my blood to bind it. I figure I'm already pretty much bound to the place and it would never hurt a person. And I figured it would trump Pinky's power."

"You constantly impress," I said.

"I'm not the one who took on all those armed assailants," he said.

"True, but my combat skills are better than yours," I said.

"I'm not that bad," he said.

"Well, we did have a term in the Daemor for someone with your level of fighting skills," I said.

"Really? What was it? Super soldier? Master warrior?" he asked.

"Nope, arrow fodder," I said.

"Fodder? Who said I'm the fodder? I just met the young lady. I demand a paternity test, but I need at least a couple of days to study," said Murphy. I shook my head and laughed.

We were able to get a signal a little bit later. Hermes came and gave mother and daughter a clean bill of health. Nemesis came and helped me out with the cops. We turned the Pink Reapers over to the DMA for prosecution. Crossing into the country with magic from Faerie and using it in the commission of a crime was the same as doing it from another county, which made it a federal offense. We got the entire lot for four counts of attempted murder and child abduction. Even got Nosering on a half dozen other charges for what she did to her baby.

Lucinda and Pixie stayed with me for a couple of weeks. Mrs. Washington looked in and helped out. She has seven kids and fifteen grandkids. What she didn't know about raising kids could fill a thimble. A rent controlled apartment upstairs opened and Murphy's boss Paddy Moran fixed things so she got it. Paddy even helped her get a job doing medical billing so she could work from home and be with her daughter. She wasn't going to get rich, but she had enough to pay the bills and put a little away. I get to visit with Pixie a lot. Truth be told, being a godmother, fairy or otherwise, is a sweet gig. Spoil the kid, play with her and then send her home.

Sadly, Pinky is still loose in Faerie. I put out some feelers back home. She'll surface someday and I'll get her then. Hopefully it'll be before she returns the favor.

ZOMBIELICIOUS

They say walking in Manhattan at night isn't safe for a woman. Of course I'm fairly certain that anyone foolish enough to mess with me on a dark street is going to get more than they bargained for.

The rest of the female population isn't always as fortunate. I live down in Hell's Kitchen. Despite the name, the neighborhood's not as bad as it once was, but it's hardly crime free. Still the sight of a woman being chased down the street by a man in a car is out of the ordinary.

I saw them pass the cross street at 47th and 11th and took off on foot after them. Being equal parts ogre and pixie, I'm more than a bit stronger than humans, but only a little bit faster without using my wings. There was no way I could outrace a car, but luckily the driver didn't realize we were racing.

The man in the car caught up with his prey, slamming the puke green sedan into her. Even as far away as I was, the sound of cracking bones made me wince. The poor lady rolled over the hood and onto the pavement. Despite her arm being broken so it bent like a second backwards elbow, the woman managed to get to her feet and limp the other way.

Not satisfied with breaking her arm, the man spun the car around. The tires screeched until he was facing the wrong direction on a one-way street. He had to swerve to avoid a yellow cab, giving his prey another few seconds lead. Not that it meant much to him as the car could make up the distance in moments, but he didn't realize his illegal U-turn was going to assure I won our race.

But stopping a couple of thousand pounds of metal isn't an easy task. I had a gun, so I could try to shoot out his tires. I'm an above average markswoman, so I'd probably hit one in three shots or less. Problem is, any bullets that miss have a tendency to keep going. I didn't want to hit any innocents.

I debated over an exploding round. One of those would stop the car no matter what part I hit, but the driver would likely end up dead. My boss and the NYPD have a tendency to overlook when a beastie gets killed, but get very upset if a human does. Truth is, so do I. Not that I didn't do my share of killing during the Thandau War. I just don't have the stomach to do it without good reason these days, so I kept my gun in its holster.

Instead, I stepped out in front of the car and put my hand up like a traffic cop. The driver didn't see a badge, uniform or anything that could hurt him, so he didn't slow down. I stood my ground until I saw the crazed look in his eyes, through the cigarette smoke filled car. I doubted five uniformed cops would have stayed him from his path. A gun might have made him change direction, but he'd just zero back in on the woman as soon as he was past if a bullet didn't put an end to him.

The idea of running down a second woman didn't faze him in the least. It seemed to excite him because he grinned and pushed the accelerator down and aimed the car at me.

Idiot. I hoped for his sake he had air bags.

It was sad. Even as I leapt into the air, my mind's ear could already hear Nemesis and Gani yelling at me for taking an unnecessary risk. Of course a speeding car would hardly bother Nemesis and Gani could just blast the thing into dust.

My jump took me just over the first story on the neighboring buildings, but not the second. It's not like I had a running start and my wings were covered up. It was times like this I really missed being able to fly, but unless New York gets a major infusion of magic, that's just the way it is. Instead I have to rely on the laws of physics. What goes up usually comes down and when I did I landed smack on the hood. I don't want to say I had the same effect as a cannonball—I'm a little sensitive about my weight and size—but the dent I made was impressive. My impact was powerful enough that the front of the car smashed down into the road for an instant, throwing the rest of the car up into the air just long enough to slam the entire vehicle to a halt.

I tucked and rolled to the side and landed safely, if not gracefully.

The airbags didn't deploy, so the guy smashed his head on the wheel. Slam man was stunned, but still in the game. His hands fell below the dash and he seemed to be frantically searching for something. My first thought was a gun so when his head ducked below the dash I pulled mine.

I wasn't working, so I wasn't wearing my armored trenchcoat. It was uncomfortable, but times like this made me rethink the wisdom of ever being without it. My ogre and pixie skin blend was tough, but nowhere near bulletproof. Neither the cops nor my boss were going to like a man with bullet holes, but that didn't mean I was going to let this schmuck put a bullet in me. Self-defense is still a damn good excuse for shooting somebody.

When the driver popped back up I aimed between his eyes, waiting to see the gun, but he didn't have one. The murderous twit had just dropped his fallen cigarette and was more worried about getting another puff than he was about the woman he had run down. He inhaled the tobacco smoke deeply. Only then did his eyes manage to focus on me and my weapon. He froze mid-puff. At this range I'd hit him in one out of one shots, but it hardly seemed fair as he was unarmed.

"Get out of the car and keep your hands were I can see them," I ordered.

"Maya is my wife. John can't have her and you won't keep us apart," he ranted as he stepped out. A rank smell assaulted my nostrils. It smelled like he'd been swimming in the New York City sewers.

I put my gun away, wishing for a clothespin for my nose. Instead I pulled out a pair of handcuffs. They were designed to hold creatures of the dark, so they should hold an irate husband.

As I moved toward him, he backed away. Part of me wanted to back away from him and his nasty scent.

"Don't make me chase you," I warned. "You must have the worst gas problem in history. I'm surprised your cigarette didn't turn the inside of your car into one big fireball."

"Not yet," he said smiling before puffing furiously on his coffin nail. He pulled the gas cap off and threw the glowing cigarette in. And for good measure threw in a lit zippo lighter behind it.

Me and my big mouth.

"Crap," I yelled as I turned and ran. Instinct took over and I was now happy I wasn't wearing my armored coat as my razor sharp pixie wings sliced through my pink trenchcoat, shredding the back. I can't really fly here, but when I leap my wings can propel me further and faster than I can jump without them. Basically, I'm a living hang glider with buzzing wings.

In movies, people always jump and the shockwave of the explosion carries them. In reality a gas tank exploding doesn't have than kind of force. Away from the center of the blast, it's the shrapnel that gets you and a piece of metal got me right in the back of the head.

Luckily my skull is a little thicker than most and I was only stunned, but I was out of it long enough for the driver to disappear.

I cursed under my breath and pulled out my cell. Nemesis was not going to be happy about this.

"Hey boss, it's Terrorbelle," I said and explained what happened. I got a little grief. The NYPD has orders from the mayor's office to give us a wide berth, but it's on a need to know basis. Most cops don't. Nemesis didn't like any of her trio of agents to make waves. As a rule, neither Gani or Rudy did, but they live in the apartments Nemesis supplies. I prefer having my own place outside the office. It helps keep my sanity and gives me a little freedom, but I also tend to find trouble more often than her other two agents. Trouble seems to have a crush on me. Pity it's the only one.

"It's not my fault. I didn't blow up the car. I just jumped on it a little." As a whole, the chewing out was minimal. "Yes, he got away, but so did the woman." Which is when I noticed a silhouette in a doorway down the block, her arm bent at a painful angle. Sirens announced the arrival of New York's bravest and an ambulance. "I think I see the woman. I've got to go. You'll call and explain things to the cops?" I hated being brought in for questioning. The cops go all tough, but they have no idea. I've lived through interrogations by Thandau's forces where torture and death were real options. Being grilled by regular police, I tend to be mouthy and cause no end of trouble. Not as bad as I was with Sleaze and Railroad, but not far off. Of course, I have used Nemesis' clout to get out of things, but she's never wild about me doing that without clearing it with her first. Thus the phone call. "Thanks Nemesis."

My boss is a little on the tough side, but she's got a good heart. Her first priority was for me to help the battered and runover wife. I wasn't the only one trying. An EMT had seen her and was trying to get her to accept some first aid. Poor guy wasn't having much luck.

"At least let me take a look at the arm, miss," he said.

"No, just leave me alone," she said, cradling the arm to her side. It was bent like a Z.

"I can't do that. Your arm is broken and you're very pale. You may have lost a lot of blood. You don't look so good."

The woman became rather indignant at that, but he was right. She was very pale, the type of pale you see in a wounded soldier who bled out before you could get to her. I looked closer and there was more to it than just her color. Her flesh looked a little worn around the edges. Also, the broken ends of the bone protruded from her skin and she wasn't bleeding. If anything, the blood oozed.

I had seen this before, sadly in my own mother.

"Let me try," I said, putting my hand on his shoulder.

"Miss, I'm trained in this..."

"So am I. I've seen worse than this on the battlefield." My first thought was I wished I had one of Mab's battle patches before I realized it wouldn't do the woman any good.

"Former soldier?" asked the EMT.

"Yes."

"Marine or Army?"

"Daemor." The EMT gave me a blank stare. "Elite special unit." In Faerie, but that was too much to expect this guy to believe. "Just back off and let me talk with her."

"I don't..."

I gently shoved him toward the curb.

"Hi, my name's Terrorbelle."

"I'm Zomb... Maya. Thanks for stepping in before."

"Happy to help."

"I don't really need any help," she said.

"Actually you do. If the arm isn't set right, the flesh will mend around it like that. You'll lose your ability to blend in."

Well, at least at night. In the day she'd stand out, unless she dressed Goth. Her makeup was put on a little heavy and bright for Goth or anything else, unless she was planning to do a play over on Broadway. "Bad idea for a zombie with a soul."

Maya's pupils got real big. "You're not afraid?"

"Nope." The fact that she was pale instead of rosy meant she hadn't eaten human flesh. A big plus in my book.

"I doubt you're strong enough to reset it, even if you are a little big," said the lady zombie.

I flexed my arm, straining the sleeves of my shredded pink trenchcoat. Big was an understatement when it came to describing me. "You'd be surprised."

Maya looked at her fractured limb and sighed. "It does look pretty bad, doesn't it?"

"Yes," I answered honestly.

"All right, go ahead. Just do it quick," Maya said.

"If you…" I pulled and twisted on the arm until there was a loud snap. "…insist."

Maya saw and heard what I did and screamed.

"What the hell are you doing?" yelled the EMT as he tried to push me aside. He was six three and a good two twenty and was very surprised when I didn't budge.

"Hands off the merchandise buddy," I said. "You want to get fresh, you should at least try to get me drunk."

"Resetting a bone is a job for the doctors at the ER. Who knows what kind of damage you did?"

Maya started flexing her arm. "Looks good to me." Then she pulled back the peeled flesh over the open areas and patted them down.

The EMT's jaw was hanging down.

"We'll be going now," I said and tried to usher Maya past the EMT.

"I don't think so. You're going to talk to the police and she's going to the ER. That was an open fracture. There could be permanent damage," he said, making the mistake of grabbing my coat collar.

"I don't take well to being touched or threatened," I said, wrapping my fingers around his shirt and lifting him off the ground. "And in case you weren't aware, a person has the right to refuse medical care. She is exercising that right."

The EMT's mouth was hanging open. At first I thought it was because his legs were dangling off of the ground and then I realized I had expanded my wings. Usually the coat would have held them down, but I had already shredded it.

I put him down and off to the side. "Bye," I said waving as I shuffled Maya down the street and around the corner.

"So you want to get a cup of coffee?" I asked.

Maya smiled like the cat that had swallowed the canary and his entire family. "Are you hitting on me?"

"No. Why would you think that?" I asked.

"I've become very popular since I came back, even with some of the ladies. You haven't heard of me? I call myself Zombielicious."

I must have made a face, because Maya laughed. "I would have reacted the same a few months ago, but there really is a market for it. There are a lot of closet necrophiliacs who are too timid to go and dig up a date. There's even a brothel with the dead in Detroit."

"Not anymore. A couple friends of mine shut it down." Moni the Graveyard Angel and my favorite bartender. I even teased Murphy that he didn't have to pay; he just could have come to me. Pity he didn't take me up on it, but I'm patient.

The dead woman and I walked in a coffee shop and took a booth. "So for money you…"

Maya waved her hands and shook her head. "Ick, no. I just strip and talk dirty. I get ten bucks a minute for the first five and five a minute after that, sometimes from up to a dozen guys at a time. For a monthly fee they can join the Zombielicious Fan Club and download pictures and old videos." The waitress came over and we ordered. I got a cup of coffee and a bagel with lox and cream cheese. She got coffee and raw hamburger. The undead need their meat raw.

"So is your website why your husband was trying to kill you?" I asked. Figured maybe she was sleeping with one of her clients.

"Naw, the site was his idea. He's trying to kill me because I'm sleeping with his brother."

Great. I got myself involved in a domestic dispute. Those are rarely pretty. "You seem a little casual about it."

Maya shrugged. "Manny is pissed, but he has good reason. He doesn't even know John and I were messing around before I died, but it's not like he can hurt me. Nothing hurts me anymore."

Made sense. Zombie nerves don't seem to transfer any pain signals. "Why'd you scream when I reset your arm then?"

"Habit I guess. I heard the noise and expected it to hurt. I have to say I'm impressed by how well you're taking it. My mother still hasn't gotten over it."

"I've had some experience with a family member, but she wasn't as fortunate as you."

"Plus, I'm guessing with those wings you're not exactly normal yourself."

"Normal isn't something I get accused of on a regular basis. How'd you get brought back?" I asked.

"The usual way."

"No such thing. There's at least a dozen ways I've heard of and there's probably more I haven't." Hex has claimed forty-seven. "I'm guessing it was done within three days of your death."

Maya's eyebrows rose up. "The same day. How'd you know that?"

"Maya…"

"Call me Zombielicious."

I couldn't bring myself to make that utterance. "You still have a soul. After three days, the body may come back, but the person doesn't."

"I didn't know that. Manny and John did some ritual their grandmother taught them when they were kids. Her old man used it to get dead folks to work his plantation. They used to play with it by killing animals and bringing them back."

"They sound charming," I said.

"Don't be judging my men. You don't know them," taunted Maya with an attitude filled bob of her head.

"Yeah, all I saw was him try to run you down with a car and then try to blow me up. I'm sure society is to blame," I said, but Maya did pick up on the sarcasm.

"You said a mouthful, sister. No one's given either of them a break. They're lucky they got me to help take care of them," she said. "They can barely get out of bed in the morning."

The waitress brought our order. "You sure you don't want that burger warmed, honey?"

"It's fine." Maya used a spoon to scoop the red ground beef into her mouth. The waitress shrugged and went on to her next customer. "Both of them are useless when it comes to making sure I have enough meat in the house. I hate putting it in the freezer or even the fridge, so I leave it out."

"I guess a little rotting meat won't hurt you at this point," I said.

"I wish Manny and John had your attitude. They're always giving me grief over the smell, even with zip lock bags."

"With the way your husband smelled when he got out of that car, I'm surprised he could even tell," I said.

"Manny doesn't smell," she said confused.

"Maybe your nose didn't come all the way back."

"John's never mentioned it, even at meals," she said.

Something clicked in my head. "You all live together?"

"Sure. We're all family," she said.

And I guess she took the idea of loving family to a whole new level.

"And neither of them mind what you do for a... living." I regretted the choice of words as soon as I said them. Murphy would never have let them pass without some crack. Maya didn't even notice.

"Naw, I think the idea of other guys getting off on me turns them both on." Having finished the extremely rare burger, she licked the spoon clean. "Sometimes they'll watch me from off camera. Although John only does it when Manny's not home obviously."

"Obliviously." I was proud of the way my tone had no twinge of sarcasm.

"And neither of them minds the money. Manny's even got me doing a blog and boy is tonight going in there. Don't even think of trying to talk me out of it," warned Maya in all seriousness.

"I wouldn't dream of it."

Maya turned her attention to the coffee, holding it in her hands and inhaling the steam. She put no cream or sugar in. It was too hot for me to do more than sip, but she downed the whole cup and motioned for another.

"I don't mind not being dead dead you know, but I'm always so cold. Coffee's just about the only thing that makes me feel warm, even if it's for a couple of minutes."

"So what are you going to do tonight?" I asked.

Maya looked at me as if I asked her if she'd be wearing slug earrings. "What do you mean?"

"You worried about going home?" I asked.

"Naw. Manny's the one who should be worried. I'm going to kick his scrawny ass."

"You're not going to really hurt him?" I asked. When a zombie kills, its craving to eat the flesh of its kill is supposed to be magnified. I wouldn't want her pale complexion to go all rosy.

"I'm going to hurt him, but he'll walk away. And he'll be sore for a week and he'll damn well never hit me with a car again."

"Fair enough, but the cops are going to want to talk to him." Me too for that matter.

"Why? I'm not going to press charges."

"And if he stopped at hitting you with the car, that might be fine, but he blew up the car on a New York City street. They don't need you to press charges," I said.

"Why, you gonna press charges 'gainst my man?" Maya started to get indignant and squeezed the table hard enough to leave indentations. I was probably stronger than her, but if we got into a fight we'd wreck the coffee shop. I got enough grief over the car. I'd never live down wrecking a restaurant.

"They don't need me either. He's going to be lucky if they don't charge him as a terrorist," I said.

"I don't see why they'd do that. Nobody got hurt and I'm the one who's making payments on that car. I still got twenty left. Manny better have sent in the insurance payment or I'm really going to get pissed."

Maya downed her third cup of hot coffee as I finished off my bagel.

"I better get going. I've got a web cast in about an hour. Already had nine guys signed up when I left," she said, standing up. "Since you asked me out, I'm assuming you're picking up the check."

"Sure. I'd be happy to walk you home in case Manny is waiting to try something again," I said.

"Even he's not that stupid. He don't want to lose all this." She emphasized her words by rubbing her hands up and down her body. "And I still ain't convinced you aren't interested, but if you think I'm going to let you get with either of my men, you got another thing coming. Thanks for the snack," said Zombielicious and she exited.

I didn't have time to wait for the check so I threw a couple of bills on the table and left soon after she did, heading in the same direction. I didn't offer to escort her just to be polite, I wanted to know where she, and thereby Manny, lived. The police had undoubtedly ran his plates and were headed out for a visit. I could call Nemesis to get the info, but figured one favor was enough for the night. I could call Jason Cervantes, an NYPD detective who's a friend, but since it wasn't his precinct it'd take him a couple hours to find out. Quickest way was to follow the zombie home.

Zombielicious headed downtown. It was the easiest tail I had in months. She didn't even bother to look behind her. I guess she rightly figured she could handle any muggers, maybe even better than me. After all, she didn't have to worry about getting stabbed or shot. It wouldn't make her any deader.

We turned a corner and suddenly I knew exactly where she lived. There was a police car outside, the bubble lights flashing and two cops in uniform running around in circles frantically screaming and hitting themselves with their nightsticks. Not that they were aiming for their arms and legs—that's just where the dead rats where crawling and biting them.

There were mace canisters near a pair of empty guns lying on the ground and almost a dozen rats with large chunks missing. Most of the rest had at least small chunks or clumps of hair not where they should be and none of the missing pieces slowed their attacks on the pair of New York's finest. From the looks of things, Manny hadn't stopped playing with dead animals when he was a kid. And to hazard a guess, I'd say he went into the sewers to kill the critters so he could bring them back. Animals are easier to control than people when they're brought back from the dead, so they'd follow Manny's instructions. And they probably wouldn't sleep with his brother, but without knowing more about John I'd hesitate to say for certain. After all, he sleeps with a dead girl, so who knows what else turns him on?

So far the cops had managed to keep their feet, which was good. If they fell, the zombie rats would swarm over them and tear them to pieces.

I ran toward the cops as fast I could, not bothering to pull my gun. Even with more than a dozen magically packed clips that I could pick from with a thought, the only thing that would help against these little monsters was explosive rounds. Problem is they'd take out the cops too. I debated about shooting Manny between the eyes, but I doubted he was the source of the power, so he'd be dead and the rats would still be on the attack. Plus, fresh blood only tended to fuel necromancy, so for all I knew it might make the rats stronger or bigger. I had no desire to explain how I set loose a couple hundred twenty-foot rats on the city.

First things first. I had to get the cops out of danger. One stumbled to the cruiser and was trying to open the door. Rats were swarming the car and using the extra height to leap onto him. His head disappeared under brown fur and tiny tails. I leapt over the pool of vermin, landing next to the cop. I shielded him as best I could, cursing myself yet again for not wearing the armored coat as the little critters bit into me. The ogre half of me made my skin tough, but that didn't mean that persistent rat biting couldn't make me bleed. Using my hands, I tossed as many rats off his head as I could. One wouldn't let go of his ear and I was afraid if I pulled too hard the cop's lobe would come off, so I squeezed the dead rat's little head until I crushed its skull and the jaws had nothing solid left to push against. I pried open the rat's mouth and tossed him into the lake of vermin flesh pressing against us.

Next I slammed the cop into the side of the car. There was no time to be gentle and it knocked a few loose. I covered him so my back was to the rats. When they made the mistake of jumping me there I let my wings go into hyper mode and slice the buggers into little slices. It was enough to make an opening so I grabbed the boy in blue around the waist and leapt up to the roof of the car, then pushed off toward the building. I used my wings to give me more oomph and I still barely caught the fire escape with my free arm

I was able to get my wings beating fast enough to get us both on the steel landing. The rats were trying to climb up the building, but not having much luck. They'd figure a way up eventually, but I bought this one cop some time.

"Thanks," he whispered.

"You're welcome," I said and pulled out my gun. Below us there was an entire swarm of rats without a human in its midst. I fired three explosive rounds and got covered in rat guts for my trouble. The pieces twitched, but whatever magic was fueling the undead vermin didn't have enough juice to mend that mess back together.

Now that I had some height I had more options. The second cop was a good twenty feet away and I leapt toward him. Arial maneuvers are always risky for me on Earth. A good tailwind can give me some buoyancy or send me crashing.

I got lucky. There was no wind and I had enough velocity that I was able to scoop the cop up and glide him across the street, to land on the roof of a car. I proceeded to smack the rats off him and leap up to plant him on a second fire escape. He was worse off than his partner and only managed to grab my hand before passing out. He needed an ambulance, but if I called for one the EMT's would only end up as dead rat chow.

I needed to take down Manny and I needed a plan. Most of my ideas needed at least a brief distraction. Fortunately Manny's dead wife had arrived and she was pissed and willing to share that feeling with her husband.

"Manny, what the..." The equivalent word back home was ckuf and technically meant what she was doing to both brothers when the other wasn't around. "...doing? Making zombie rats and siccing them on the cops? You must have gone loco."

"I bring you back from the dead and make you a star." Manny was a tad diluted. A couple of dozen sexually bent men and women willing to pay a few bucks to watch his dead wife degrade herself on a web cam hardly made Zombielicious a star. "And you repay me by screwing my brother? You thought I'd let you get away with disrespecting me that way?"

"Why? It ain't like anyone else ever gave you respect. Besides, it was until death do us part and in case you ain't noticed, I'm dead," Maya said.

"It don't count. You ain't really dead."

"Tell that to my fans."

"You weren't even dead for half a day. There ain't no death certificate. No death certificate means we still married, bitch," said Manny, obviously trying to woo her with sweet talk and good grammar. "Being dead ain't no excuse for being a ho."

Maya laughed. "I wasn't always dead when I did John. What do you think 'bout that?"

The zombie overplayed her hand because Manny didn't think too much of it. "Get her my rats. Get her, eat her up and crap her out!"

All the rats on the street stopped coming after us and turned toward Zombielicious.

"You think your little rats gonna hurt me? You dumber than a brick, Manny. Ain't nothing can hurt me anymore." But Zombielicious was wrong. The dead rats swarmed over her. She tried to throw them off, but there were too many and their strength was increased to the same proportion hers was. As they gnawed chunks out of her flesh, she began to scream and yell, "Not the face!"

Manny was so enthralled by the horror he had orchestrated he didn't notice me climb up the fire escape to the third floor and jump off. This time I caught a nice updraft. Manny finally got his first clue that something was wrong when he looked around for what must had sounded like a swarm of bees, but was really my wings flapping hard enough to keep me from hitting pavement. I cut the wing beats and dropped from about twelve feet up directly on his back.

"Kill this one!" he ordered the rats and they left Zombielicious to turn on me.

I had enough bleeding wounds for one day so got him in a head lock with one arm and with the other I pulled my gun, laid the barrel on the side of his forehead and cocked the trigger.

"If even one of them touches me, I'm blowing your brains all over this street. Think you'll be able to bring yourself back?"

Judging by the tears that started streaming down his cheeks I was guessing no. "Tell them to stop."

"Stop!" he said, his tough guy bravado replaced entirely by sobs. The rats all froze in place so I whacked him in the back of the head, knocking him out before he could give them new marching orders.

One of the officers had dropped his radio during the attack. I picked it up, pushed the transmitter and said, "Two officers down. Need immediate EMT." I gave the address. I heard sirens in a little over a minute. I started to move to get the officers down from their perches when I saw Zombielicious straddling her supine husband and smacking him across the face repeatedly. Not that he didn't deserve a lot worse, but I had subdued him without killing him and didn't want her to turn him into a corpse.

"Maya, stop." She didn't hear me so I changed tack. "Zombielicious…" Her hand paused mid-slap. "Think about what your fans would say. If you go to jail, who will they turn to?"

Maya turned to look at me. "You're right. What should I do? Hire a PR firm to spin this?"

Gotta be impressed by those priorities. "I think the first thing is get off him and go stand over there until the police come. They'll probably want to ask you questions."

"I ain't going to jail," she said, suddenly worried and defensive as she stood up

I had visions of Zombielicious turned to meat chunks as she went down in a hail of gunfire, trying to take some of New York's finest with her.

"No, they'll want info to send Manny away," I said.

"Oh, that's fine." She looked down at her unconscious and not badly bruised husband. "Pig!" She punctuated her insult by spitting in his face. It took four tries before she had enough saliva and even that was dusty, but she walked away.

The first EMT arrived on the scene and it was the same one from earlier. It made sense in the same neighborhood, especially as his shift hadn't ended yet. He wasn't happy to see me.

"Not you again."

I ignored him and ran across the street, leaping onto the first floor fire escape. It was a lot easier when I wasn't carrying a passenger. I picked up the still unconscious cop and stepped onto the rail. I pumped my wings hard and managed to hover as I stepped off. It was a simple matter to lower us onto the ground. I walked over and laid him on the gurney before jumping up to the other fire escape.

"Nice job," said the cop.

"Thanks," I said.

"I'm envious as hell," he said.

"Don't be. After all this I'm going to be so sore tomorrow I probably won't be able to move. Ready for the Terrorbelle Express?"

He nodded and stood up. I lifted him up into my arms.

"Damn you're strong," he said.

"You ain't seen nothing yet. I'm going to toss you up to about the third floor, jump to the ground by doing a back flip and catch you with my eyes closed," I said.

"Really?" said the cop, showing only the mildest signs of being nervous.

"No. I'll take you down the same way I did your partner."

And I did, but when I got to the ground the EMT had brought a cop over to arrest me.

"And she probably did this to them. Earlier I saw her break a woman's arm worse and then when I tried to stop her she threw me. Look at those bloody wings. She's a monster. Arrest her."

"The blood belonged to those rats," I said.

The cop looked at his brother in blue in my arms. I lowered his feet so he could stand.

"Ignore him. This beautiful lady is no monster. She saved our hides, probably the whole neighborhood."

"Did you say beautiful?" I asked. That was one thing I knew I wasn't. I'm too big and muscular for one thing. "You must be delirious from blood loss."

"Nope. I call them like I see them and for my money you are the second most beautiful in New York. And I love the pink hair."

"It's natural, but I've got to ask—did you hit your head too? Because if you didn't, I'd be happy to let you ask me out. If you did, I'd hate to take advantage of someone with a head injury," I said.

"Under other circumstances I'd love to." Yeah right. "But the one woman who ranks ahead of you is my fiancée."

"The good ones are always taken." Or hung up on their dead wives. Although I doubt even Murphy would have resorted to what Manny did, even to bring Elsie back.

This time I didn't need to call Nemesis to run interference. As I had just saved two of their own, and was wounded in the process, the NYPD treated me like I was royalty. The wings weren't even brought up and I was given a blanket to cover them. I did however call Gani for clean up. As the twin sister of the magí Merlin, she's been doing the magic thing for a long time and was able to deanimate and dispose of the rats, although she admits that a couple might have been out of earshot when Manny gave his stop order and could be on the loose.

I even got a police escort to Bellevue where they were taking care of the wounded cops. I was going to check on them, but I had to go for another reason. Besides needing to be patched up personally, the three of us had been bitten by dozens of rats, we had to start painful rabies shots. Testing the hundreds of rats would have taken weeks and they'd never be able to test the ones I blew up, so it was safest for all of us to get the injections.

Despite the popularization of zombies in film, people bitten by zombies do not necessarily become zombies, although I suppose it's not beyond the realm of possibility. Zombies are created by magic, not viruses, although it got me to wondering if any of the rats were carriers for rabies, could Manny's magic have also reanimated the virus as well? And if it did, would the vaccine work against them?

I wasn't terribly reassured when Gani put her hand over mine and with a very serious face said, "Some things it doesn't pay to worry about."

The next morning I had to give a full report to my boss. Manny was being charged and was most likely going away for a long time. They don't like attempted cop killers. He ended up with a broken jaw in three places from his soon to be ex-wife's love taps. Maya was thrilled that a tabloid had picked up the story and did a feature on her Zombielicious site. The fact that it was next to a Weasel-Boy sighting didn't faze her in the least.

Nemesis even congratulated me on a job well done, although she did ask who broke Manny's jaw. And I couldn't tell if she was pleased or disappointed when I said it wasn't me.

DEAD IN RED

The crime scene was messy. I'd seen worse in my time, but not lately. I wasn't a cop, but sometimes I get called in to help out on cases where things get weird. When the flatfoots saw me, I think they were hoping to watch me cringe. Male cops tend to think of women as less able to handle the gore that sometimes accompanies the ending of life. I don't buy it, but I've never been the frail, timid, or helpless type. It helps that I can bench press a Buick. Well, I can at least clear the wheels.

I examined the bloody corpse without changing my expression or vomiting. My time as a soldier and a Daemor in Faerie taught me that much. The girl looked like she had been pretty before she had been ripped to pieces.

The lead detective came over to me. Jason Cervantes was the one who called me in. We were drinking buddies, but I still didn't much like his partner and Andrea Walker hadn't bothered to hide the fact that the feeling was mutual.

"Thanks for coming Terrorbelle," Jas said. "Where's Nemesis?"

I fought back the urge to sigh. Nemesis was my boss and a force to be reckoned with. Add to that that I'm not terribly pretty and my boss is gorgeous and it's easy to see why I might have the tiniest of complexes. When my boss was around, most males tended to forget I existed. Nemesis was also one of the toughest people I've ever met. People, even my friends, prefer to deal with her in times of crisis. Not much stands in her way. Not for long at any rate.

"Nemesis and the rest of the crew are dealing with a matter for the Thrones," I said. Jas raised an eyebrow. The Council of Thrones was a court everyone and everything had to answer to and Nemesis was their enforcer. Her agency, Nemesis & Co., was really just a sideline that let her help out those that didn't even know the council existed.

"She didn't take you?" Jas asked.

"Nope," I said, biting my tongue. It ticked me off, but it wasn't Jason's fault. Or maybe it was a little. When his call came in, we were heading out. The job Nemesis had was bigger than one dead girl and I was the most expendable member of the team. I'm strong and tough, but other that that, I have no real powers, so I got left behind to help out the NYPD while the rest of the team headed to London.

"I guess you'll have to wing it," he said, making reference to the razor sharp pixie wings I kept hidden under my padded pink trenchcoat.

"Hey, at least I don't have to wear a skirt," I said. Jas engaged in a bit of cross-dressing in his off hours. It involved a long standing bet.

"But you're a woman," he said.

And dresses show only how huge my thighs and calves are. Sure it's all muscle, but my legs are at least twice as thick as a human female. It makes me stand out more than I already do. "What's your point?"

Jas smiled. Banter was standard. Helped us tough guys and gals get past the fact that until very recently the bits and pieces of meat nearby were a human being.

Walker came over to us, a cigar between her lips. The lady detective only smoked at the bad homicide scenes. It wasn't that she liked the stogies, but they helped mask the stench.

"Belle," she said, acknowledging my presence. We might not like each other, but there was a begrudging respect. I was exceptional at what I did and she was a good, honest cop. We didn't need to like each other to work together.

"Walker," I replied. Andrea pulled a cigar out of her pocket and offered it to me. I shook my head.

"What's your take on what did this?" Jas asked. "Person or thing?"

"Judging by the combination of precision and savagery, I'd have to say a little of both. Something with a lot of strength, but a mind and a sadistic one at that," I said.

Jas nodded. "That was our thought too. Any idea as to what?"

My brow crinkled as I thought about it. "Could be lots of things."

"Like an ogre?" said Walker. I was distracted enough by the state of the victim that I didn't spit out a reply at what I assumed was an accusation. As I looked into her eyes, I realized she was only trying to figure things out. She was still relatively new to the idea that humans weren't alone in the night or the day. Because of me she knew ogres and pixies existed and was bright enough to realize no pixie did this.

"No. An ogre would have just ripped the arms off with brute force. The wounds would be different. Whatever did this had claws that sliced everything apart." I looked at the bit of neck that lay alone on the alley pavement and pointed. "It looks like something chewed through her throat." I squatted down to get a better look. "Bite marks are too big for a vamp. Maybe a lunamorph."

Jas tightened his jaw. "A werewolf like Ted or Marrak?" Two more drinking buddies.

"A were-something," I said. "Wolves are just the most common."

"But the moon isn't full," said Walker.

"Most weres don't need the moon to change form. It just gives them more power," I said. Forensics was doing their job nearby, examining some cloth. I pointed at them. Jas nodded, indicating I could move closer. The material seemed to be a cloak and a red one at that. The parts covered with blood looked almost black in the dark. One of the techs ran the blue light over it and a very large portion of it turned purple white.

A couple of techs and officers were trying to free a dumpster where it had literally been shoved into a wall. The quartet was struggling and the hunk of metal wasn't moving.

"Need a hand?" I asked.

That got me snickers from the flatfoots. "Lady, if the four of us can't budge this thing, what makes you think you can?"

I walked over and made a hand motion for them to move. "Well, I have been working out," I said in my best southern belle drawl. I grabbed hold and yanked. Presto, it was free. I felt up the biceps of the smart mouth and shook my head. "Feels kind of flabby to me. You actually made it through the academy with those arms?"

That got some chuckles. I moved with the techs and looked behind the dumpster. There was a bloody picnic basket on the pavement. It was one of those moments when everything clicked together.

"We've got a very sick puppy on our hands, literally," I said. Jas and Walker looked at me with the universal expression for *Please unconfuse me* on their faces. "The killer seems to think he's the 'Big Bad Wolf'."

When I got back to the office, it was very quiet. The few day staff we had wouldn't be in for hours and who knew when Nemesis and the rest of the team would be back.

The NYPD had impressive resources, but Nemesis had better. We had instant access to every law enforcement database in the world and a few that were considerably further away. It took some doing, but it's hard for somebody to turn down Nemesis.

I ran a search for similar killings. It didn't take long to figure out we were definitely dealing with a serial killer. I came up with several murders in Europe, Asia, and South America over the last ten years with the same MO. All involved brutal slayings of a woman in red, and each victim was sexually assaulted. In the last seven months this was the third one in the US. The other two had been investigated by the Department of Mystic Affairs. The DMA was the federal agency that dealt with magic based crimes. The public and the media viewed them as a waste of taxpayer money until they needed them.

I could dial the DMA office in DC. If Nemesis called, they'd wake Uncle Sam himself up from a dead sleep to take the call. For me, they'd probably take a message at this hour. I didn't feel like waiting.

I logged on to a special web address. A minute later, the face of the World Wide Spyder was looking out of my screen at me. I double-checked to make sure the microphone and web cam were on. Some bad mojo transformed Spyder into an electronic entity. He can exist anywhere there is electricity, but without a way of getting external input he's deaf and blind.

"Hey gorgeous," came a voice from the speakers. His avatar today was a wizard with facial piercings.

"Hey cutie," I said.

"What can I do for you, beautiful?"

"You can stop with the phony flattery for one thing," I said. I'm not comfortable getting that kind of sweet talk as I know it's not true. I do look at my reflection every day and it has yet to change.

"I call them like I see them," he said.

"And I can see what you're looking at," I said. Spyder might be electrons instead of flesh, but he was still a teenaged boy. His eyes mimicked what his human body would have done and were looking directly into my cleavage. Like the rest of me, my frontal anatomy was of proportions not normally seen in human women and Spyder still had hormones even if they were probably made of tiny sparks.

Spyder's avatar face had the decency to turn pink. "I was looking at your eyes, honest."

I closed my eyes. "Really? Then what color are they?"

Spyder hesitated, but answered with confidence. "Blue."

I opened them. "Nice try, but they're lavender."

"Would you believe I had the camera in grayscale mode?"

"Nope, but don't worry about it," I said. I was only a few years older than him and certainly wasn't above checking out a cute butt or washboard abs. "I'm looking for details on a couple of DMA cases." While we have access to the Department's database, Sam stopped short of giving Nemesis access to their case files. Spyder was an agent, so he'd be able to get me details. I told him what I needed on the Big Bad Wolf. Spyder filled me in.

"Our forensics confirmed it was a werewolf," said Spyder.

"What else do you have on Big Bad?"

"Funny you should call him that. That's what Karver named him. He and his partner Mandi caught the second case, but the investigation hit a dead end."

"Who handled the first one?" I asked.

"Buck," he said.

"Oh," I said. Buck was a werewolf who worked for the Department until he crossed the line. He was doing time. "He probably won't be much help."

"Doubtful, which is too bad. He had the perp's scent and could link the killings together in court." There is a special division of the federal courts system for magic based crimes. A werewolf's sense of smell would be almost as reliable as an eyewitness account after a small demonstration for the jury. "Both the victims were women who were dressed in red cloaks with hoods, all from the same manufacturer."

"What happened when Karver ran the lead?"

"Dead end. Both cloaks were from the same batch, sold over ten years ago around Halloween. Karver checked some of the foreign cases and there were other cloaks of the same make. Problem is they shipped out to hundred of outlets with no way to track them so long after the sale."

"Great, so this sicko buys in bulk. Using the cloaks to link the crimes, how many women has he killed and raped?"

Spyder sighed. "Twenty four, including the one in New York."

My vision went kind of red for a second.

"T-Belle, you okay?" asked Spyder.

"Fine. Why?"

"I know your history," Spyder said. Which was true. I don't hide the fact that soldiers attacked and killed my mother, but first made her watch them rape me. All of them. I refuse to hide it because being ashamed of what they did only gives them power. However, because of it I tend to be a bit on the harsh side when it comes to dealing with rapists and this guy qualified in a big, bad way.

"And?"

Spyder's glanced down, even lower than before. "You just crushed the armrests on your chair."

I looked down. He was right. "Crap." Nemesis would make me pay to replace it.

"Anything I can do to help, let me know," he said.

I had been thinking about what happened. From the details of the crimes, the women had been wearing the red cloaks *before* they were attacked. It meant they were playing dress up before they were butchered.

"Were the women going on blind dates when they were killed?" I asked.

"Why don't I just get Karver on the line?" asked Spyder.

"It's not too late?" I asked.

"Doubtful. Karver doesn't sleep well. Nightmares."

I could relate, but our midnight terrors were for different reasons. Karver had been possessed by a demon that turned him into a serial killer.

"That'd be great," I said.

Moments later, Karver's face popped up on the corner of my screen.

"What do you need on Big Bad?" he said.

"No pleasantries, handsome?" I said.

"Nope."

I smiled. His face rarely cracked from his deadpan expression. "Did either of the women have a date the night they were killed?"

"According to friends and family, they both did. Neither of the girls had any suspects in common. Mallory Downey lived in Arizona, Jen Falan never left Maryland." I was impressed. Karver didn't have time to look at his own files, but he knew the women's names. I got the impression he never let go of a case, just put them aside until the opportunity to find the perp arose. "Neither used a dating service, online or otherwise. Neither shared where they had met the man they were going to see. Both received a package from a phony address. Our forensics determined that the boxes had contained the cloaks, a single red rose, and a picnic basket."

"Looks like he takes this fetish to the extreme," I said.

Karver just nodded. "You have any leads?"

"Not much more than what you had on the other cases," I said. "Spyder, did you check out if they had any contact with Big Bad online?"

"They did from separate anonymous e-mail accounts that were used from libraries or cafes in small towns with no video surveillance. A couple of calls to disposable cell phones. Each account was abandoned after the killing, otherwise I could have tracked him once he used it again. There was nothing to help us trace how they met him in the first place. I couldn't find any evidence in their access accounts or hard drives to indicate it was a chat room. And I spent a lot of time in fetish chat rooms looking for him."

"Like you minded looking in on the perverts," chided Karver.

"We don't all have to be dark and moody like you, Karver. Some of us can actually find ways to enjoy our jobs," said Spyder, his avatar smiling.

Karver actually chuckled, but looked at me. "You find anything, you let me know. I want in on taking down this bastard."

"No promises," I said.

"I'd consider it a personal favor," said Karver.

I nodded and signed off.

My next stop was Lara Sterling's apartment. That was the name of Big Bad's latest victim. Jas and Walker had been and gone. I could have asked them for permission, but there were quicker ways. Few doors could stand up to my shoulder, but that would be disrespectful to the departed. Lara had lived on the eleventh floor. Very few people locked their windows that high up, especially when there was no fire escape to worry about. I figured that was my way in.

While I do have wings, New York and most of Earth doesn't exactly let me fly the friendly skies and I had long ago used up Thor's wind talisman. However, I do have very strong fingers and toes. I tied my shoelaces together and put them around my neck, then used the nook and crannies in the building's exterior to scale up the wall. I had changed to a black trenchcoat. In the dark, I went unnoticed.

The window was unlocked, but it was of the safety variety that only opened halfway. It took quite a bit of squeezing and shimmying to crawl through, but I made it with neither the window or me being any worse for wear.

I spent the next few hours sorting through her things. Jas had taken her address book, computer and such, but if it was that easy to find this guy he wouldn't still be on the loose.

I found nothing. I tried to get an idea of what kind of person Lara was by sitting in her recliner. I tried to see what she saw when she looked around her living room. Lara liked to read judging by the full bookshelves. She had plenty of friends whose faces where spread around the room in picture frames. She had a decent collection of CDs and DVDs, but nothing overly pornographic or fetishistic. Nothing to indicate she'd be involved in any kink.

My head started to hurt. I needed a break. The newspaper was next to the chair and I decided to check to see if my lotto numbers had come up. I love my job, but who wouldn't like a few extra million in the bank? I opened the pages and realized it wasn't yesterday's paper. It was from a few days ago. Lara recycled and all her other papers were in a blue plastic container, including yesterday's. I started flipping pages. When I got to the personals I stopped. There was nothing circled, but there was a simple dot alongside one personal indicating someone had very subtly marked it off.

It read: *"Looking for fairy tale love? Big Bad Wolf looking for Little Red Riding Hood to share fantasies with."* It couldn't be that easy. There was a voice mailbox. I called it. It was still active.

"Hi, my name's Belle," I said into my cell phone, my voice husky enough to pull a sled. "I liked your ad and I'd love to meet you. Please give me a call."

I left my number and Lara's apartment, but this time I used the front door and the stairs. Easier on the cuticles. The sun was just coming up.

It was one in the afternoon when my cell rang. The caller ID was blocked, but it was probably a disposable track phone anyway.

"May I speak to Belle, please?

"This is Belle," I answered and asked a question I already knew the answer to. "Who's this?"

"It's the Big Bad Wolf."

I put on my best hussy act and let out a little squeal. Truth be told, I just imitated Sydney and Darcy. "I'm so glad you called."

"My pleasure. To be truthful, I was surprised to hear from you. My ad hasn't run in four days."

"I'm a bit of a workaholic. Last night I read through my last week's worth of papers. I saw your ad and put it aside. I slept on it and decided to call this morning before I went to work," I said.

"What do you do?"

"I'm in public relations," I said.

"You work for yourself?"

"No, I work for a small company, but maybe someday I'll go solo. What about you?" I asked.

"I came into some money a while back—made some good investments. I travel a lot. This is the first time I've tried the personals, believe it or not." I didn't. "But I'm happy I did. What appealed to you about my ad?"

"I've always liked fairy tales. I have a closet full of role playing outfits like Snow White, Alice in Wonderland, but my favorite is Little Red Riding Hood."

"You have your own Red Riding Hood outfit?" He was practically drooling.

"Three actually, but two aren't exactly the kind I'd wear in public or on a first date," I said.

"I should have tried the personal ads sooner," he said.

"What about you? Do you have your own wolf outfit?" I asked.

Big Bad let loose a laugh, then reigned it in. "I might be able to oblige."

I cooed.

"You do this a lot?" he asked.

"The outfits? Sure. I've had a couple of boyfriends who liked them, but it's been a while since I've been with anybody. Most guys just don't understand a working woman's commitment to her career." I couldn't tell if he was buying my story. It was time to turn it up a notch. "I've got to be honest with you. I only called because of your ad. I'm not looking for a serious relationship. Work has been making me crazy and I need some serious stress relief. Your ad made it sound like you might be the man to give it to me. So, are you up to it, Mr. Wolf? Will you blow…" I paused for effect. "Down my house."

"I'll do more than that," Big Bad promised.

"Good, because the wolf in the story does a lot more than that to Red Riding Hood. I'll be expecting the full treatment. You better come hungry," I said.

I could actually hear Big Bad licking his lips. "I will. Where would you like to meet?"

"Over the river and through the woods?" I suggested.

The bastard laughed. "I know a nice little place in the Village. It's called Oma's." He gave me directions and we agreed to meet at nine. "Will you wear your outfit? The one suitable for public viewing?"

I took a deep breath to calm the butterflies vomiting in my stomach so I didn't break character. "Sure. In the Village, who'll even notice?"

"Too true. See you then," he said.

"Count on it," I said and hung up. I had less than eight hours to find a Red Riding Hood outfit in my size.

I started to regret agreeing to the costume. I do a lot of my shopping in a shop down in the Village that specializes in outfits for transvestite men. It's the only way I can get cute outfits in my size. Most of the plus size shops for women have dowdy clothes and I only need the extra material up top and around the hips. I have washboard abs of my own, so those clothes are way too baggy around the middle.

Bruce, the owner, seemed happy for me when I told him what I needed. "You finally have a boyfriend?"

"No such luck. This is for work," I said, going in the dressing room in the back. Bruce has been tailoring my clothes for years so my wings either hang free or are covered depending on the situation. In his private viewing area I didn't have to hide my anatomical extras.

"Costume party?"

"I wish," I said, putting the costume on. I stepped out to get a better look in the triple mirrors.

Bruce put his hands over his mouth and wiped a pretend tear from his eyes. "You are a vision. If I was straight…"

"You'd have a different business," I said. It was a form fitting red number. I have to admit, it didn't look bad. I could really fill out a dress when I tried. By myself, the effect was nice. The problem was when you put me next to a man, I dwarfed him. "The skirt is too short."

"Nonsense, my dear. Do you know how many people, men and women, would kill for legs like that?"

"But they're so big," I said.

"But all muscle. Very sexy," said Bruce.

"Right," I said.

"You know you're not supposed to wear underwear with a dress like that," Bruce chided me. "It's a fashion faux pas."

I shook my head. "It's not happening."

"Then at least a thong," he said.

"I hate those things," I said.

Bruce smiled. "Then why do you own some?"

"Because sometimes panty lines are bad," I conceded. And sometimes I wanted guys to notice my butt in a way other than to comment on how big it was.

"This is one of those times. And a regular bra would be a disaster," Bruce said.

"All mine are custom made. You know that," I said.

"Because of your wings and those amazing breasts. You are the only person…" Again, he was being gender neutral on purpose, as he probably had more male customers that had breasts than women customers. "…I have ever met who has no need for a push up. Gravity just can't bring you down. And yours are natural," he gushed. "They're to die for."

My genes have some advantages. "I'm not going braless."

Bruce nodded. "True. It might be dangerous. You would stop traffic and probably cause lots of accidents. Use your strapless cups."

I reluctantly agreed and tried on the hooded cloak. Except for the color, it reminded me of home.

"Where are you going?" he asked.

"Dining at Oma's," I said. Bruce chuckled. "What's so funny?"

"That you'll be wearing that to Grandma's for dinner," Bruce said. Noticing my confused look, he decided to enlighten me. "Oma is German for grandmother." Big Bad really took his fetish to the extremes. "Hans is one of my regulars. He opened it a couple of months ago and named it in honor of the woman who taught him how to cook."

"How's the food?" I asked.

"Divine," Bruce said. "Do you need anything else?"

I nodded. "A picnic basket." I wasn't feeding further into his fetish. This outfit left very little to the imagination. I needed some place to carry my gun.

I made a phone call to Karver about my plans. Turns out Spyder had also found the personal ad and his partner Mandi had been about to make a call of her own. The DMA had checked the personals before, so it might really have been the first time Big Bad tried them. Karver wanted to take over the sting, but I refused. The only reason I got away with it was because I worked for Nemesis. I did agree to let Karver and Mandi do surveillance because I reluctantly agreed that taking on a killer werewolf without backup was stupid. If Big Bad got away, someone else would die. Since my normal backup was otherwise occupied, I compromised by allowing the

DMA agents to be nearby. They agreed not to step in unless I used a panic word or Big Bad got away from me. Besides, Karver said he'd owe me.

I got to Oma's early. I got an amazing amount of looks and whistles on my way, most of them from gay men. For some reason, gay men love me. One straight loser made an offer of what he'd like to do to me if I'd forgo the trip to Grandma's. Then he put his hand in a place it wasn't welcomed to bring home his message. I delivered a message of my own to his gut that left him curled up in a ball on the sidewalk.

Truth be told, it was my second time at the rendezvous point, so I wasn't surprised to find that the restaurant was closed on Mondays. By an entire lack of coincidence that was what tonight was. I put the hood up before I turned the corner and acted surprised when the restaurant door wouldn't open. I stood waiting, hoping that my prey would show up. I assumed Big Bad was watching, so I tried to look as harmless as possible.

My evil date showed up a few minutes later. Sadly, he was tall, dark and handsome. The evil ones tend to be, but at least in this case I knew that's what he was going in. I haven't always been that lucky.

"Hello Red Riding Hood, I'm the Big Bad Wolf," he said, taking my hand and kissing it. I smiled a little too big to hide my revulsion at his touch. "I would have said little, but that's one thing you certainly aren't. Are you a bodybuilder?"

"Not professionally," I said. "Surely my size doesn't intimidate you, Mr. Wolf?" Hating myself for it, I actually curtseyed in the very short skirt.

"Certainly not. I find it refreshing," he said. He wrinkled his nose. "Although you do seem to like your perfume."

"Sorry. I haven't had a date in a while and I was nervous. I forgot if I had put on my perfume and ended up with a little extra." That and it covered my scent. Without it, he'd realize I wasn't human and disappear instead of making our date.

"It doesn't matter because you were good enough to wear your costume. You look good enough to eat," he said.

"Thank you, but you're going to have to buy me dinner first." Big Bad laughed at my joke. "Where's your wolf suit?"

"Believe it or not, I'm wearing it," he said.

I faked the jump of logic he was expecting me to. "It's underneath your clothes," I purred. He ate it up. "Unfortunately, the restaurant's not open."

"Oh, that's too bad. Their food is excellent, but I know another place around the corner," he said. "I know a shortcut. Follow me."

And that's when he went into an alley. I had to make sure this was the guy because all I had so far was a few awful big coincidences and a hunch. Certainly not enough to have the DMA arrest him on. Not that I was going to give up at this point in the game.

"What's the name of this restaurant?" I asked.

"Grandma's, believe it or not." I went with not. Two restaurants in the village with the same name, even in different languages, was a little hard to swallow. Too much creativity in the area for that to happen. "I love the picnic basket. What's in it?"

"Protection. A girl can't be too careful these days," I said. We made a turn into an adjoining alley which I had learned earlier was a dead end.

"Too bad you forgot that," snarled Big Bad, turning back toward me. He had transformed from human to wolf monster more rapidly than I thought possible. Suddenly he was bigger, stronger, hairier and faster. Not to mention naked and excited. The morphing shredded his cloths. My hand was already in the basket reaching for my gun, but Big Bad was quicker than I anticipated. Before I could clear my weapon and shoot, the werewolf swiped my basket away. "Gun oil has such a unique smell, don't you think? Smart to carry a weapon, but you don't have any idea what you got yourself into."

"Neither do you," I said. I moved out of range of his claws. The fur ball was faster than me, and maybe even stronger, but I was ex-Daemor. Training tends to trump power when combined with planning. Then again most of my planning involved using the silver bullets in my gun, which was behind my foe at the moment.

"You're not scared," he said, sniffing the air.

"Why should I be? Because of what great big eyes you have?" I said. Big Bad wasn't sure what to make of me and was circling me warily. According to Karver, he raped the women before he butchered them. The slicing and dicing apparently happened when or as he finished.

"My eyes are the least of your worries. You should be commenting on my big claws and jaws. I mean, didn't you say you wanted to be eaten?"

"I lied. It's not high in my list of things to do. Your jaws are mighty big. Other parts are kind of sad for a shape shifter," I said, looking southward at his wolfhood.

"I'll show you how big I am as you scream for mercy," promised Big Bad, pouncing forward. He moved figuring I was human, so I sidestepped easily.

"I don't scream. And let me show you how big I am," I said flexing my wings. The razor sharp edges shredded the cloak and I tore the hood off.

"What the hell are you?"

I answered with a kick to his knee and heard a beautiful snap. "The end of your story."

Werewolves heal fast, but it's far from instant unless the moon is full. It wasn't. Big Bad had no intentions of waiting that long. With a growl he rushed me. I moved in reverse an instant after his attack, but the swipe of his claw raked the front of my dress, lowering the cleavage clear to my navel.

The sight distracted him enough for me to box one of his ears, knocking him several feet along the pavement. That effect is why Daemor armor always showed a little more flesh than I was comfortable with. Men tend to get stupid when a free show presents itself. I looked down at the tattered shreds I was now wearing and it was my turn to growl. "I liked this dress."

The werewolf leapt back to his feet and one hand lashed out toward my throat. I spun so my back, and more importantly my wings, were facing him and sliced his hand off at the wrist. My wings truly are deadly weapons, which is why I was so careful to keep them padded up.

Big Bad howled in pain, clutching his stump. I had made him scream.

"Ready to surrender and go to jail?" I asked.

Big Bad moved into hyper-speed and managed to land a roundhouse kick that launched me into the air. I did a belly flop onto a dumpster, my head smashing into its steel handle. I saw stars. Before I could right myself, Big Bad was behind me, tearing the back off my skirt.

I try to show mercy when I can, but I couldn't have done it then if I wanted to. I flashed back to the day that forever changed my life and a vow I made as I lay bloody and broken. I would slay whatever I had to in order to make sure I was never raped again. The buzzing of my wings was far faster than even a werewolf could react too and more dangerous than a tank of piranha. Big Bad's first thrust was his last. Fur, flesh and blood flew everywhere as the werewolf lost his remaining paw and his legs below the hips. Lastly, went enough tissue to make him an eunuch.

His screams lasted until he fell to the pavement. By then I had gotten the picnic basket and my gun, which I cocked and pointed between his beady eyes.

"One more sound and I put a silver round into your brain," I promised. "Besides people are trying to sleep."

"Why should I care?" he growled.

"Because a silver bullet in the head equals dead. Alive means maybe you'll heal. All the same to me," I lied. The fury had faded to anger and I wouldn't kill in cold blood. "And to think this could have all been avoided if people just remembered to spay and neuter their pets."

"You bitch," he growled.

"Too late for flattery," I said, pushing down on the transmit button on my earring. "Big Bad is ready for pickup."

Karver was already behind me with his gun drawn. When I shot him a questioning look, he shrugged. "I heard what was happening and thought you needed help."

"I would have used the panic word if I did." Which oddly enough was broccoli.

"I guess I was wrong," he said.

"No problem," I said. "Nice to know you had my back." Karver nodded.

A DMA prisoner transport backed into the alley, looking like a cross between a minibus and an armored car. Mandi supervised four men who restrained Big Bad's torso on a slab with silver shackles.

Karver moved over to get a good look at the werewolf, punctuating the action with a long whistle. "Remind me never to get you mad at me."

"If you can't remember that much, Uncle Sam should fire you," I said. That wasn't figurative. Uncle Sam was really the director of the DMA.

"You okay?" he asked, also knowing my history.

I thought about it. "Except for my clothes, yeah."

Karver took off his trenchcoat and gave it to me. I waved it off, but he insisted. "Take it. I got a dozen of them." I put it on. It was too tight in the shoulders and only barely closed at the waist, but I was covered.

"Thanks," I said.

"Your tax dollars at work," he countered, bending down to pick up Big Bad's wallet from the remnants of his pants. "Interested in the guy's name?"

"Nah. Drop him in front of a door and we could call him Mat," I said.

"Cute," Karver said, pulling out a wad of cash. "Here."

I was confused. "What?"

"You looked good tonight. Big Bad ruined your outfit. The least he can do is replace it," said Karver.

"You know, you're absolutely right," I said, folding my hand around the bills. "Although this time I think I'll get it in pink."

GIRLS KNIGHT OUT

I've faced down enemy soldiers, monsters born of nightmares, and creatures of the night. I never backed down from one of them, but a night out with Sydney was something that made me want to hide in my closet.

I've gone clubbing before. Rudy has dragged me with her more than once as her wing girl. Rudy is tall, muscled and thin. Clothes off the rack looked amazing on her. The rack would be more likely to fit me. Clubbing, whether the people involved admit it or not, is all about impressing others. Look good enough to make the other girls jealous, the guys fight over you and you'll enjoy the experience. Look like me and you'll have a quiet night or a line of guys talk to you who only have eyes for your boobs. Not to mention the catty comments from other less endowed females about how ridiculous my surgeon was to make them so big. Even if I felt inclined to speak to the catty ones, they'd never believe they were natural.

I'm more at home in a bar, but I owed Sydney. When I first met her I figured her for the bimbo type. After all, she was one of two surgically enhanced pretty girls on the arm of a second rate vampyre. I felt sorry for the pair and let them in the club. Later in that crimson midnight, Sydney had my back and saved my life.

We'd become friends since. I wasn't exactly wrong about the bimbo part, but there's more to Sydney. She's incredibly loyal and despite her demeanor, Sydney's no dummy. And truth be told, I like her. The rest of Nemesis & Co. were still on their mission, so when she asked me to go clubbing I didn't legitimately have anything else to do—I reluctantly said yes.

It was supposed to be Sydney, her friend Darcy and me. In the months I'd known her, Sydney's father had retired from the family limo business. Her brother had worked there while she went off to college. Believe it or not, she had an MBA. Her father split the business between the two, giving each forty nine percent and keeping the tie breaking two percent for himself. Although giving was the wrong word. He sold it to each of them with him holding the note. Her brother was pissed, figuring he should have gotten the whole thing because of the time he put in there. But luckily for Sydney, she was daddy's little girl and he refused to see her education go to waste.

The business had always been profitable, although nobody got rich. It looked like Sydney might have managed to change that in three short months. Her dad had done the typical limo type activities. Sydney quite frankly found it boring and was complaining to me one night when she had come over for pizza and videos. I suggested she come up with a way to fix it and we brainstormed. Turned out she partied with a couple of ladies who worked in the business offices of two of the big television networks in New York, both of which used limos to shuttle celebrities to and from the studio, hotel, and airports. Her friends gave her a little inside information and she managed to underbid the competition and got both contracts. Even with the low bid, it was very good money.

But that wasn't enough for Sydney. She had the quite brilliant idea of making deals with the hot clubs in Manhattan to deliver the celebs who were looking to hit the New York nightlife to their doors when she was able. In exchange, they comped the celebs and she got a certain number of slots of the A-list who didn't have to wait in line every night. I had gotten her on the A-list at Plasma to thank her for helping me and she loved it so much that she'd be willing to pay to maintain it so she figured others would too. What better way to impress a girl than a limo and walking to the front line of a hot club and being let in like you were somebody important? Or just a night out with the girls that was out of the ordinary.

Using her party contacts, she spread the word. Every night of the week she rented party limos for about five times what her father would have gotten, but the clients weren't just paying for the limo. They were paying for the prestige of not having to wait behind the velvet rope. She was also careful to vet her clients so they didn't embarrass her or screw her deal up. Sydney made them pay an outrageous deposit and sign a behavior contract. If they broke it, she kept the deposit. People went for it in droves. She already had a waiting list.

They had made so much money that it looked like they would be able to pay off their father in two years instead of ten. Her brother stopped complaining and gave her free reign to handle the contracts and PR ends of the business. She gets to combine work and partying. And her father is proud of her. It's win-win.

Sydney also gave me credit for giving her, as she puts it, a swift kick in the pants. She claims otherwise she never would have tried to change her daddy's business. Apparently I can have a limo and driver whenever I want. I've yet to take her up on it. I don't have a car, but I have a Harley I keep in the garage at work because a parking space in my neighborhood would cost two thirds of what I pay in rent. Besides, there's always public transportation.

I heard a musical horn and opened my apartment window. Sydney and Darcy were hanging out the moon roof and waving.

"We're here, T-Belle," shouted Sydney.

"I'll be right down," I said, closing the window.

I stopped in front of my full-length living room mirror. I had three. It wasn't because of any vanity. It allowed me to see the entire apartment while sitting on my couch. I grew up in a world at war, and was one of the enemies of the ruling power. It was either get paranoid or get killed. New York is a peaceful paradise by comparison, but old habits die hard.

I looked myself up and down. Not too bad I had to admit. Bruce had talked me out of pink and set me up with a new black dress to replace the one Big Bad destroyed and it was impressive. I was a tad uncomfortable with the amount of flesh exposed, odd considering I fought in Faerie in little more than a bikini top. Of course, in Faerie women and men worked hard to show as much flesh as possible, in the most provocative way. The club scene is pretty much the same.

In Faerie there were different races, so differences in size and shape didn't stand out as much as Manhattan. I'm big, mostly muscle, but I knew I'd dwarf most of the tiny women at the club. And oddly, I didn't care. Sydney was always telling me how amazing my body was. Others had too, but somehow coming from Sydney it was different. The girl was gorgeous and had simplicity about her. Obviously she was far from simple-minded, but she was honest, sometimes brutally so. She didn't seem capable of deception, which lent her words more credibility.

I was still worried about my wings. I had bounced a couple more times at Plasma and didn't bother to hide them, but for a regular club I wasn't quite willing to be so daring. I got a black cloak to go with the dress. Normally I prefer day glow colors. They go better with violet eyes and pink hair. I just wanted to try something different.

My last problem was my gun. I wasn't required to have it with me when I wasn't working, but trouble had a way of finding me or thumbing its nose in my general direction. I hated going out unarmed, but the dress was so tight it would show a mole. The idea of carrying a purse all night didn't much appeal to me. I was going to have to resort to the belt Bruce had sold me to go with the dress. It was a silver chain number in the front I could also hook my Daemor badge on, but had a holster that fit in the small of the back. It was Bruce's own design. He made it for a couple of vice cops who had to work in drag. The holster was molded to my back and the chain anchored it. With the cloak, nobody would notice. Since the gun is mystically designed to get through metal detectors and the like, the only way someone was going to notice it was if they did a pat down and the wings would probably take their attention off the firearm.

There was no place to put my cell phone, so I decided to leave it home. Sydney would have hers if I really needed to make a call.

I took a deep breath and went downstairs. I met Mrs. Washington in the stairwell. She was the grandmotherly type. Not my grandmother of course, but Gram was one of a kind. Mrs. W had long ago taken me under her wing, inviting me to dinner, giving me baked goods. Insisting that I should find a good man and settle down.

"Hello, Belle. How are..." she said, stopping short with her mouth hanging open, her eyes staring at my outfit.

"Hi Mrs. Washington. Are you okay?" I teased, slightly embarrassed.

"I'm just a little surprised by your outfit," she said.

"I'm going out to some clubs with friends," I said.

"Excellent. You need to make more time for fun. And if you can't find a man wearing that, all the males in New York must have gone blind or gay," she said.

"Thanks." I think.

"Belle, a word of advice if you'll humor an old woman."

"I will if I see one," I said.

"Such a sweet girl, but the men you meet tonight won't realize that. Just keep that in mind, won't you?" she said. I nodded that I would. "I'd tell you to be careful, but you are the most capable woman I've ever met, so I know you will be. Have fun dear."

"I'll try." We said our goodbyes and I went down the rest of the steps. Normally I take them three or four at a time, but I was doing one and two. I was most comfortable in sneakers or boots, but tonight I was wearing four-inch heels and felt a little like I was walking on stilts.

I went out the front door and down the stoop steps. No sooner did my feet hit sidewalk than a wolf whistle rang out. I turned to see who'd I have to have words with, surprised to see Lucinda and little Pixie.

"Damn, Terrorbelle girl, you look hot enough to burst into flame," Lucinda said.

"And here I thought Mrs. W's hot flashes were catching," I said, reaching out for my goddaughter. Pixie smiled and let me take her from her momma. "How's my favorite girl?"

Pixie cooed and so did two other, much louder females. Sydney and Darcy rushed out of the limo toward my goddaughter.

"Oh, what a cute baby," said Sydney.

"Can I hold her?" asked Darcy.

Lucinda has trust issues. Not surprising considering what she's been through. We've gotten to know each other much better and she's told me some about her past. Not a good relationship with her parents. They were the type to beat her when she was bad and beat her when she was good, just in case she was thinking of being bad. She ran away and lived on the streets for a few years, until she joined the Pink Reapers thinking they were the family she had been searching for. Let's say she's lucky not to be in jail or dead, even before she started following the Pink Death. When things with the Reapers ended as they did, she turned her focus on Pixie and keeping out of trouble. Twice I've had to get rid of illegal guns she had in her apartment. She slept so long on the streets, she's always expecting to be attacked. I can relate. I'm no shrink, but I've been helping her work through things. I'm pro-gun, just not with an infant around. She's also become attached to Murphy who takes the pair to Bulfinche's Pub, which is fast becoming Lucinda's favorite place in the world. Makes sense since her altered tattoo was changed to the Bulfinche's logo and we still hadn't figured out if Murphy's binding had done more than break Pinky's claim on her. Mrs. Washington also treats Lucinda like a daughter and Pixie like one of her own grandkids.

However seeing two strangers approach her daughter put her in street mode and she was a second from decking Darcy. I've felt that way myself when she's gotten ditzy, but they were just being enthusiastic. The pair both had boundary issues, but neither deserved to be hit for them.

I turned so Pixie was on my other side. "Easy ladies, you'll spook the baby and the momma. Lucinda, meet my friends Sydney and Darcy. Ladies, this is Lucinda and my goddaughter Pixie."

"Oh, she's so much cuter than the pictures you showed us," said Sydney.

Lucinda relaxed and started to smile. I had mentioned them to each other.

"Belle showed you pictures of Pixie?" Lucinda said.

"Only a few dozen," said Sydney. "She's proud to be her godmother."

"Fairy godmother," Lucinda corrected, then covered her mouth and looked at me.

"No worries. They know."

"Did she really help deliver the baby?" asked Darcy.

"Her and Uncle Murphy," Lucinda said. "So she's really proud of Pixie?"

"Proud? Pixie knocked Murphy off her phone wallpaper," said Sydney. That's only partially true. Pixie has the outside window. The inside wallpaper is one of Murphy holding Pixie.

Lucinda was beaming.

"Can we hold her?" asked Sydney.

Lucinda looked to me and I gave her a slight nod. "Sure."

"Me first," said Darcy, making all sorts of goo and coo noises. Pixie went to her for a couple moments before starting to squirm.

"Let me," said Sydney, picking up Pixie. "Such a pretty girl aren't you?" Pixie relaxed and Sydney sang a lullaby. She had a pretty good voice.

Lucinda was tense watching, but let Sydney keep holding her. It was a step in the right direction. Lucinda is extremely overprotective of Pixie, understandable since a monster tried to steal her away at birth. She only lets Murphy, Mrs. Washington or me baby-sit and it took my personal vouching for Mrs. W the first time.

"Where are you going all dressed up?" asked Lucinda.

"The Volcano Top Club," said Sydney. "You want to join us?"

"Yeah, you could have my spot," I said.

"Not a chance T-Belle. You're going if I have to drag you," said Sydney. I kept quiet about how that was an impossibility. "The more the merrier. Besides I'm a plus three at the door."

"I saw an article on it opening. I've never been to a place like that." Lucinda looked at me. "Would you mind?"

"Not at all," I said.

"Do you think Mrs. W would baby-sit Pixie?" Lucinda asked.

"I bet she would. She just got home," I said.

Lucinda took Pixie from Sydney. "I'll go ask. Then I have to go change. Give me ten minutes."

"No prob," said Sydney.

Lucinda ran inside explaining to Pixie that her mommy was going out and she'd be back later. A few minutes later her apartment window opened. "Belle, could you come up and help me figure out what to wear?"

"Sure," I said.

"We'll all come," said Sydney.

"Makeover party!" shouted Darcy, too loudly and sounding drunk. She wasn't—not yet anyway.

We went up and the party girls hit Lucinda like a swarm of locust. They dragged the girl into her bedroom, attacked her closet and started tossing out clothes which they sorted by style, color and some other factor known only to them.

I felt we were suddenly in some movie montage with Lucinda trying on outfit after outfit until the jury finally decided on one with squeals of delight. It was a short black skirt and a red silk shirt.

"What do you think?" Lucinda asked.

"You look good," I said. And she did.

Apparently that was enough because moments later we were down the stairs and into the limo. There was more screaming, some hanging out the moon roof with even more screaming, although Lucinda seemed to be really enjoying herself. So did Sydney and Darcy, but they seemed to always be enjoying themselves.

We got to Volcano Top and the trouble began. Sydney led us to the door, bypassing the line.

"Sydney Grady plus three," she said to the bouncer at the door with the clipboard.

Without bothering to look at his clipboard, he said, "Sorry, you're not on the list."

"You didn't even check," said Sydney.

"I don't have to. No way Ernesteno put the likes of you here. Do you know who's coming here tonight?" The bouncer dropped a box office name who had the nickname of Joe Hunk. His screen name was Joe Hannk.

"Yeah, I know. I arranged for him to come," said Sydney.

The bouncer laughed. "Sure you did."

Which is when one of Sydney's limos pulled up with said movie star who started to get out. Bouncer Boy tried to shove Sydney out of the way in order to get the celebrity. I stepped in front of him. He was six five easy to my six even, so he assumed he could push me around. He learned the errors of his way a half second after his hand touched my shoulder. I grabbed it and bent it back. Hard. Bouncer Boy dropped to one knee.

"Wow, kneeling before my beauty. Too little, too late," I said, taking the clipboard from him with my free hand. He was in such pain I don't think he cared. I lifted up the top sheet and pointed to Sydney's name. "Right here bozo."

"Sorry, just let me up. I gotta let him in," he said.

I let up on the pressure enough so Bouncer Boy could lift his head to watch Sydney give the movie star a double cheek kiss.

"My mistake. This place is lame, practically dead," said Sydney. I watched Bouncer Boy's pupils dilate. "I'll have the driver take you around to Thunder Head."

"Whatever you say," he said, then looked at me and got a huge grin on his face. He waved. I looked around to make sure the greeting was for me and waved back. "Who's that?"

"T-Belle. She's a friend of mine. We'll meet you at TH and you can buy us all drinks," said Sydney.

"Sounds good," he said, getting back into the limo. Sydney went to the driver. "I gotta make a call. Take him the long way."

I let go of Bouncer Boy and he got to his feet and screamed at Sydney. "What the hell did you do?"

"The deal with Ernesteno was, I deliver Joe Hunk, I got ten on the guest list for a month. No guest list, no star. I'll be calling Ernesteno to let him know it was your screw up. Bye." She made a quick call, wheeling and dealing with the owner of the Thunder Head. In moments, she had ten on the guest list for three months. She turned to the confused paparazzi and told them Joe Hunk would be spending tonight at Club Thunder Head. "If you hurry, you'll catch him before he gets there."

There was anger in the bouncer's eyes as the photographers and half his waiting line left in a hurry for the second club, but as I was between him and Sydney he didn't do anything about it.

"Ciao baby," she said and walked away, wiggling her hips.

"And next time you want to hold hands with a girl, try sweet talk," I said as Darcy, Lucinda, and I followed in her wake. We all climbed into our limo.

"Damn girl, that was sweet," said Lucinda. "You really know Joe Hunk?"

"I've been shuttling him around for the publicity tour for his latest movie." Sydney explained her limo service for the stars and her deals with the clubs.

"And I thought Terrorbelle moved in impressive circles," said Lucinda.

"She could move in both if she plays her cards right tonight. Joe Hunk likes what he saw," Sydney said.

"Yeah, right," I said. "He was probably just impressed by what I did to the bouncer."

"It don't matter what you do to impress a man, just that you do," said Darcy.

I bit my tongue. When I met the two of them they were a couple of blood toys to a lame blood junkie. Darcy wasn't high on the list of people I'd consider taking love life advice from. To her, money or power made a guy hot. What he looked like or behaved like took a distant second place.

"Either way, he's buying us the first round," said Sydney. "So what did you think of Joe Hunk?"

"Cute, in a pretty boy way. Almost too good looking," I said.

"Ain't no such thing," said Darcy.

"There is in my business. Magically enhanced beauty is sometimes used to suck people in. Think Baron Bozo," I said, referring to their vamp ex.

"I think Joe Hunk only has his plastic surgeon to thank," said Lucinda. "And if you don't hit that, you crazy."

"I've been called worse," I said as the limo pulled up in front of Thunder Head.

The door opened to enough camera flashes to blind someone. At first I assumed a bouncer had opened it, but it turned out to be Mr. Joe Hunk himself.

He reached in and offered me his hand. "T-Belle, I hope you don't mind me being forward, but I couldn't wait to meet you."

"The pleasure's all yours obviously," I said. He was cute, but I wasn't used to this kind of attention from someone like him. I was instantly suspicious and ticked at myself for thinking that way about someone who might not be too good to be true.

"Can I help you get out?" he asked.

"Sure, just don't hurt yourself," I said. He pulled, but I didn't want him to damage anything important so I helped.

As I leaned forward, his pupils went wide as he stared down the front of my dress. I was used to that, but his eyes kept going, first to my legs then my eyes. That I liked.

"What beautiful purple eyes. And pink hair. Almost like a fairy princess," he said.

"You're half right," I said.

"I would be honored if you and your friends would share some drinks with me," he said.

"Naw, I don't think they want to," I said. All three of them playfully hit me.

"Nonsense, we'd love to," said Sydney.

"I'm Darcy," she said, holding her hand out as if she expected it to be kissed. It was shaken.

Lucinda stepped up, grabbing the movie star's right hand with both of hers. "I'm a huge fan. I used to have your poster on my wall."

"I'm sorry to hear you took it down," he teased. "Guess I'll have to work harder. Maybe you'd like a new one?"

"You'd send me one?" Lucinda said.

"Better. You can make your own," he said, taking her phone and handing it to me. "Would you mind?"

"Sure," I said.

Lucinda giggled louder than I'd ever heard her. "Make sure the picture setting is on maximum size."

"I did," I said, holding the cell up. "Smile." Joe Hunk gave her a hug and Lucinda had a huge smile.

"Take an extra," she said.

I took two. Darcy moved in and handed me her phone. "Me next."

Joe Hunk put his arm around Darcy's shoulder. "Sydney, get in here," he said, and she went under his other arm.

"Say cheesecake," I said.

Joe Hunk and Sydney obliged, but Darcy substituted the word beefcake.

Joe Hunk looked at me. "You want one too?"

"I'm good," I said.

"I can imagine," he said, offering me his arm. "May I escort you inside?"

"Funny, I would have thought with all those movies you wouldn't have to resort to being an escort to make extra bucks." Sydney laughed, Darcy and Lucinda cringed.

Joe Hunk bantered back. "Twenty five million a picture doesn't go as far as it used to. But for you, tonight I'm free."

I took his arm and we walked inside. "I hope I'm not overpaying."

"You probably are, but I have a strict no refund policy," he said.

"After your last movie, I can understand why," I teased.

More flashes of cameras as a bouncer opened the door. Not only did we sweep past the line, but they didn't even bother to check ID's which made Lucinda's life much easier. She wasn't legal yet and was depending on an old fake ID.

We got escorted to a corner booth that had been roped off after Sydney's call. We ladies slid in. Joe Hunk put his hand on my shoulder. I didn't push it off.

"What can I get for you ladies?" he asked.

Lucinda looked up at his face like a lovesick puppy. "I'll have what Terrorbelle's having."

"Sorry, I'm a one-woman man," he said.

"Then I guess you wouldn't want to meet my identical twin? We like to share," I cooed in my best Darcy imitation.

I thought his knees would buckle. "I think you are all the woman I can handle."

It was a nice recovery and good answer. "Let's not get ahead of ourselves. We'll see how things go before there's any handling."

"Fair enough," he said, leaning in toward my ear. "You don't really have a twin, do you?"

"Nope, we're triplets," I teased.

"Lord have mercy," he said and took our orders instead of calling over a waitress. Sydney got a Bay Breeze, Darcy a Cosmo and Lucinda a Long Island Iced Tea. I got a beer with an Amaretto Sour Chaser.

Joe Hunk made his way to the bar, stopping to sign a couple of autographs.

"T-Belle, he is so into you," said Lucinda.

"Maybe," I said.

"No maybe girl. The man wants you bad," said Sydney. "And he's way cuter than Murphy."

"Don't you be trashing my baby's Uncle Murphy," said Lucinda to Sydney, before turning to me. "Although I hate to admit she's right. And he's interested romantically."   "You going to give him a tumble?" said Darcy in her usual tactful manner.

"To date? Maybe," I said. I knew as well as anybody that Murphy wasn't ready for anything more from me yet. He might never be and I don't actually plan to pine away waiting. I just don't have the best luck with men. "But no man gets into my bed on the first date."

"Bed? Who needs a bed? I'd take him in a bathroom stall or in the limo," said Darcy.

"Not in one of my limos you're not," said Sydney.

"Here you go ladies," said Joe, putting a tray of drinks on the table. "What did I miss?"

"They all think you're hot and that you like me. Darcy here would do you in the bathroom or a limo, but Sydney would kill her for messing up the limo. I told them I move a lot slower than that. In other words, no sex tonight or for a while," I said to a collected trio of gasps. "What do you think of that?"

"The bathrooms are hardly romantic and Sydney has been so nice to me, I'd hate to upset her by messing the limo. But there is only one woman I'm interested in right now, so if I have to wait to get to know her, nothing could make me happier," he said.

"Good answer," I said.

"And you got that I meant you, right?" he said smiling.

"I picked up on that, yes," I said.

"Great, so let's start now. Tell me about you. Married?"

"Would it matter?" I said.

"Yes," he said.

I nodded approval. "Never been married."

"Boyfriend?"

"Nope."

"Girlfriend?" he asked.

"Just these three, but that's been getting boring," I said.

"Hey!" shouted Sydney. "I am many things, but boring is not one of them."

"That's true," I said. "No girlfriend."

"Kids?"

"Nope, just a goddaughter," I said. "Now what about you?"

"Divorced, no girlfriend or boyfriend and no kids," he said. "What do you do for a living?"

"Hard to explain. Let's say I work for a private security firm," I said.

"As what?" he said.

"Anything my boss needs," I said.

"You do any work for the studios?" he asked.

"Not usually," I said.

"Would you like to?" he said.

"Why, are you offering me a job?" I said.

"Not at all. But I know people if you were interested in branching out," he said.

"Not at the moment," I said. "What about you? Do anything besides act?"

He shrugged. "I had an album that bombed a few years back. I did the usual things like wait tables while hoping to make it big. I finance a charity that gets wounded vets the care and equipment that they need."

That impressed me. Mab always took care of her wounded as best she could. "You a vet?"

"I did four years in the Marines, but my brother got wounded in Iraq. Lost his leg below the knee and had trouble getting the best prosthesis available. Even for the regular ones he had to drive two hundred miles and wait for months. I had the money, so I helped him, but it got me thinking about all the other soldiers who don't have rich brothers. You seem like you did a stint in the military. Are you a vet?"

"Let's say I was a soldier in an elite unit and leave it at that," I said.

His eyebrows raised. "Classified stuff?"

"For a first date, yeah," I said.

Joe laughed. "You know, I'm having a blast. So many people act different around me because I'm famous. You don't seem to care."

"You act. You're rich. You're cute. That's nice, but if that's all you got I wouldn't be impressed," I said.

"So are you impressed?" he said.

"Not yet, but the date's not over," I said.

"Would you like to dance?" he said.

The truth is I loved to dance. I dance around my apartment all the time, but in public is another matter. When I dance, I like to move all of me and that means my wings. Considering that they can be used as deadly weapons, I don't want to cut anyone else on the dance floor just cause I'm getting into the music. My cloak wasn't padded and wouldn't keep them in place, but I couldn't remember the last time a guy this handsome asked me to dance.

"I'd love to," I said, already making a conscious effort to keep my wings in place as we stood and walked to the very crowded dance floor.

The music was fast, hip-hop mixed with techno. As we danced, he rubbed up against me in a playful yet sensual way and I rubbed back, making sure I didn't let him get behind me.

"You're in good shape," I said.

"Two hours most days with a trainer. It's in my contracts. You're in phenomenal shape," he said.

"Personal program," I said.

"Maybe I should hire you as my personal trainer," he said.

"You'd never survive the workout," I said.

"But what a way to go," he said.

The song changed, but neither of us made a move to go.

I felt a gentle tap on my shoulder and heard a familiar voice say, "May I cut in?"

Joe moved forward in the way testosterone demanded. "Listen buddy, the lady's dancing with me, so just buzz off." He even started to push my want to be dance partner, but I pulled him back. The Infinite Jester may be little, but he had been a knight of the Round Table and he hasn't survived over a millennium by being a pushover.

"Dagonet's a friend," I said and turned toward the former knight. I pointed to Joe Hunk. "I don't think he wants to dance with you."

The Infinite Jester's pupils swelled up and he let out a whistle as he took in my outfit. "Wow. Murphy is an idiot."

I smiled and blushed a little at the compliment. "Thanks."

"Who's Murphy?" Joe asked.

"One of my best friends," I said.

"T-Belle, where's Gani?" Dagonet asked, his normal jovial demeanor gone.

"She's off on…" I looked over at Joe. "…business with Nemesis and Rudy."

"Why aren't you with them?" Dagonet asked.

"Jas needed help with a murder investigation, so I got left behind," I said. "Why? What's wrong?"

"I think they're in trouble," said Dagonet. "Gani came to me in a dream."

Ganieda and Dagonet go back a long way and have been an item on and off again through the centuries. Regardless of the status of their relationship, the pair love each other like few other people I've ever met.

"Why do you think they're in trouble?" I asked.

"Because she told me in the dream. I called her cell, then Nemesis's—no answer, so I tried yours. Same thing. I called Murphy to see if he knew where you were. He said you were going to Club Volcano Top. I got there and heard some pink-haired woman took down a bouncer and came here, so I followed."

"How'd you get in?" I said.

"You're kidding me right?" he said, laughing.

"You were on the list?" I said.

"No, but sneaking past a couple of bouncers wasn't exactly hard," he said.

"No problems?" I said.

"Not on the third try," he said with a grin.

"Why wouldn't Gani contact me?" I asked.

"Maybe it had to be someone who has a deeper connection to her than just friendship. Since contacting her trapped brother wouldn't do any good, she went for me," he said. "Do you know where they are?"

"I know where they went," I said. "London."

"And you haven't heard from them?" he said.

"We had no plan for them to check in and sometimes a job can takes days, weeks or longer," I said, worried myself. "You sure it wasn't an ordinary dream."

"Positive. I hate to break up this date, but I'll pay for the next one. I think we need to find them because something bad has happened," said Dagonet.

It figured. Joe had been standing by patiently listening and trying to make heads or tails out of our conversation.

"I have to go. I'm so sorry. Can we pick this up on a second date?" I said.

"Absolutely. Is their anything I can do to help? I made a couple of friends at the FBI when I was researching a part. I could call in a favor," he said.

"That's sweet, but it won't help," I said.

"T-Belle!" screamed Lucinda running over to me. Which is when she noticed the Infinite Jester. They knew each other from Bulfinche's. "Dagonet?"

"Hi Lucinda. How's little Pixie?" he said.

"Hopefully asleep with Mrs. W, but Sydney's in trouble," she said, pointing toward three men who were dragging her kicking and screaming toward the kitchen.

"What's going on?" I said.

"They grabbed her and said they were going to teach her a lesson for stealing from them," said Lucinda.

I ran, trying to push through the crowd without hurting anybody. It was a losing battle.

"Belle, toss me over everyone," said Dagonet.

It was a good idea. Dagonet was one of the best acrobats I'd ever seen. He should be with centuries of experience. I put my hands together, he put a foot in and I did an alley oop over the heads of the crowd. Fortunately, the club had high ceilings. Dagonet landed in a roll and was racing after the kidnappers. I decided to stop being polite and started lifting people out of my way.

They were all in an alley behind the club by the time I caught up. One of the men was cradling a bloody hand, his gun seemingly twirling by itself in the air, suspended on the point of the invisible extending sword Hayden. Dagonet retracted the unseen blade and the gun fell into his other hand. The others had let go of Sydney.

"What's going on here?" I demanded.

"They're from the limo company I underbid for the network contracts," said Sydney.

"Stole you mean. Now you're going to give them back," said one, pulling out a baseball bat he had obviously left in the alley. "Or we're going to take out our displeasure on that pretty face of yours."

I got between him and my friend. "I got a better idea. Go away and leave her alone."

Slugger laughed and raised his bat. This guy made Bouncer Boy look tiny. He was six seven and three fifty easy. He swung his Louisville special at my head expecting a crack. He got one all right, but it wasn't my skull. It was the bat hitting the palm of my hand. It hurt like blazes, not that I'd let him see it. I yanked the hunk of wood out of his hand and put one end in either of mine. It took a little straining but it snapped like a twig. I hit him upside the head with one piece and behind a knee with the other.

"I don't have time for this. Sydney Grady is under my protection," I said.

"Why should we care?" demanded Bloody Hand.

"That your car?" I asked, looking at the black town car with the obscured license plate that was idling in the alley.

"They were trying to get your friend in there," confirmed Dagonet.

"I'll show you why," I said. I always brag I can bench press a car, but in practice it's much harder than free weights. It's awkward to balance for one thing. Wrapping my cloak around my fist, I smashed the front and back windows, then popped the trunk. Satisfied that they didn't have another victim hidden in the car, I lifted up the back end of the car so it was standing on the front bumper. One I got it balanced, I moved so I had hold of it somewhere in the middle of the undercarriage and heaved. It took two tries but I got it over my head. I stepped forward and tossed it to the other side of the alley. I was already feeling it in my low back. I'd be sore tomorrow.

The look on the faces of the three toughs was priceless, but I wasn't done.

"Everyone behind a dumpster," I said. The three toughs got behind one on the far end, we got behind the other. I took out my gun and fired an explosive round into the gas tank.

The town car went boom. I took off my cloak and handed it to Sydney before leaping up in the air. I lowered myself as slowly as my wings could manage until I was crouched on top of the burning car. I stayed there long enough for the toughs to get a real good look at me and I leapt up and flipped so my feet were the highest part of me. I fired two concussive rounds to either side of the car. They went off almost simultaneous, lifting the car a foot off the ground. The shockwaves temporarily cut off the oxygen and the flames died.

"All three of you, strip down to your briefs." One started to say something, but I cut him off. "Now!"

The men hurried to obey. I took their suits and went through them until I found their wallets. I removed their driver's licenses and tossed them the wallets.

"I know where you live. I know who sent you. If anything happens to Sydney or any of her friends or employees or her limos, I'm coming for you and your boss. I don't care whether you had anything to do with it or not. I'll blow up his entire fleet of vehicles and then I'll start on him. Of course that will only be after I've paid all of you a visit. Have I made myself clear?" They nodded. "I'm sorry, I didn't hear that."

They all shouted yes.

"Is anything going to happen to my friend?" I asked.

"Absolutely not," assured Slugger.

"Good, cause you won't like where I'm going to put the bat if I ever see you again. Now scram," I said.

My tough gal act would have been easier to pull off without the cheerleading section of my three friends yelling a rap of "Go T-Belle", not to mention Darcy and Sydney taking cell phone pictures of the whole mess. I had to delete any pictures with me in them before I took back my cloak.

I saw someone in the door and spun to make sure it wasn't a fourth tough. It was Joe.

"I thought my movies were impressive. This is what you do for a living?" he asked.

"Sometimes," I said. "You still want a second date?"

"You won't hurt me if I say no?"

I couldn't tell if he was serious or teasing. "No."

"Then yes," he said. "Will you explain all this then?"

"Maybe if there's a third date," I said.

"There will be," he said.

"Not that this wasn't fun, but we have to go," said Dagonet.

"Sydney, can I swipe the limo?" I asked.

"It's yours," she said.

"Take mine," said Joe. "Please. I'll share with Sydney."

"Fine," I said. "You make sure the three of them get home safe."

"I will. Can I walk you to the car?" he said.

"Sure," I said. Joe escorted us to the street and the front of the building where his limo was.

"I had a good time," he said.

"Me too," I said.

"I guess this is good-bye," he said, moving closer to me.

"I guess," I said. We both stood there, being awkward, neither one making a move. I didn't have time for this. "Oh, what the heck." I grabbed him and dipped him back and planted a big kiss. He kissed back and he was pretty good. As I stood up and put him back on his feet, I realized the camera flashes were back. The paparazzi were recording my first kiss in months for prosperity and a few tabloids.

"I hope this doesn't get you in trouble with your publicist," I said.

"Even if it does, it was so worth it," he said. Dagonet and I got in the limo. Joe told the driver to take us wherever we wanted to go. "Wait. I don't have your number."

"Get it from Sydney," I said.

I told the driver to take us to the Nemesis & Co. offices.

It was late, so once again the few staff people we employed had long since gone home. It took me a few minutes to deactivate all of the security measures in order for us to get in.

The first place I checked was the armory.

"Oh, no," I said.

"What?" said Dagonet.   ·

"Gani's and Rudy's guns are here," I said.

"Why wouldn't they bring their guns on a mission?" he asked.

"They would. The guns are too powerful to fall into the wrong hands. If it looks like we're going to be captured, we can trigger them to come back here," I said.

"But I thought they were keyed to your genetic codes," said Dagonet.

"They are." No one should be able to fire the guns except Nemesis or her agents. I once made an exception and keyed my gun to Murphy. I got in a little trouble, but the second time I loaned it to him, he saved New York and probably the world, not to mention jumpstarted a brand new universe, so I was let off the hook. I also noticed the boss never unkeyed him, but Murphy is one of the few people she trusts and considers a friend. "But it could somehow be bypassed or someone could get the ammo out." Considering the various kinds, it could do some major damage, including to the boss. "If their guns are here, it means they are definitely in trouble."

I picked up small sheets of paper under each gun. Dagonet looked confused. "Gani put a locator spell on each piece of paper." I held them up to show Dagonet the numbers burned into them.

"Latitude and longitude coordinates?" he said.

"Yes." It had different markings if it was from off-world. The numbers for each gun were very close so they had been nearby each other. I plugged the one from Gani's gun into a handheld GPS. "They are still in London, England. A place called the old Blackfriars Bridge railway station."

I ran to Gani's magic elevator doors and hit the button. I knew she had a few stops marked off in London. Unfortunately, the doors didn't open, which means the door wasn't shut on the other end.

Dagonet was already on the phone to Paddy Moran. The owner of Bulfinche's Pub had the god Hermes in his employ. Our travel time to jolly ole England with his help would be measured in heartbeats.

Unfortunately, Hermes was in parts unknown. Paddy was also away, so Dagonet had gotten Murphy and put him on speaker.

"Murph, do you think Paddy'd let us borrow Baby?" asked Dagonet. It was the nickname for a flying car.

"He might, but he and the car are in the South Pacific. Vulcan's installing some new gizmo and the boss wouldn't let him take his classic caddy apart unless he was there helping," said Murphy. "There's nobody here that can get you transcontinental, but I have the keys to the trans-bike." To help out the trapped god Loki, Paddy had a duplicate of the valkyrie Mista's bike made. It also flew and crossed dimensions. "You'd make England in a couple of hours or less."

"It's quicker than flying by plane," said Dagonet.

"But not quick enough," I said. "Thanks Murphy, but we'll take my bike."

"T-Belle, you said London, England not London, Connecticut, right? Your bike is a regular Harley," said Murphy.

"I know a shortcut," I said.

"Can I help? Or make any calls to get you backup?" said Murphy.

"Thanks Murph, but I think time is of the essence. If you don't hear from me in two hours, send whoever you can get," I said and gave him the coordinates.

"Both of you be careful," he said.

"We will," I said, putting on a double holster and loading the two extra guns in it, and dumped my high heels for a pair of old sneakers that were under my desk. I also grabbed a charmed two-sided battle-ax. Normally, it wouldn't blend in, but right now that didn't matter.

"Murphy, you missed out on something special. T-Belle is all dolled up and looks great," shouted Dagonet into the phone. "Her weapons even match her dress."

"Dress?" he said. "She's wearing a dress?"

"We've got to go. Bye Murphy," I said and hung up the phone.

Dagonet gave me a wry grin. "Feeling guilty are we?"

"Maybe," I said, picking up a cushion from the waiting room couch and running to the stairs. "Not that it's any of your business."

"Fair enough," said Dagonet, trying to keep up. "I consider you a friend. Murphy is a very good friend. I don't want either of you to get hurt just because he's still grieving and too thick to see what's in front of him."

I nodded, but didn't meet the Infinite Jester's eyes.

Nemesis' office is on the 13th floor and my bike was in the garage in the building's basement, so I was taking each landing in two jumps.

I didn't need to think about my pitiful love life right now, so I went faster. I might not outrun my thoughts, but I figured I could at least outrun Dagonet.

I was three flights ahead of him and getting a little cocky. "Try and keep up, will you?"

I heard him chuckle, then suddenly he was floating down past me in the center of the stair well. He waved as he went by, using his telescoping invisible sword to slow his fall to the point where it looked like he was levitating. I debated about jumping myself and using my wings to lower me down. There'd be no wind so I might land on Dagonet and crush him like a bug.

The Infinite Jester won, but I caught up quickly.

"You want the helmet? My head's pretty thick," I said.

"Take a helmet from a lady? They'll take away my chivalrous knight union card," said Dagonet.

"You okay riding on the back?" I asked.

"I could do that, but I have a better idea," said Dagonet. He had a small backpack on and he pulled out some wheeled footwear that he had on in seconds. He also pulled out a rope with handles.

"What's that?" I said.

"The roller blades? They're the fastest personal transportation for getting around the city."

"No, the rope," I said.

Dagonet grinned. "It's a modified water skiing tow rope and handle."

"You're kidding."

"Usually, but I'm quite good. I'll hook it on the back of your bike and hold on."

"You sure?" I said.

"Absolutely," he said.

"Then at least take the helmet." Before he could argue, I put up my hand. "I'm not going to explain to Gani how you smashed your skull holding on the back of my bike."

We headed out through the Manhattan city streets. Luckily the traffic is less at night. I made one quick stop at a convenience store and then sped through traffic. Through it all, Dragonet held on. More than that, he weaved through traffic, doing acrobatics that would look at home in a water ski show.

When we got to Central Park, I ignored the barriers and went on the bike paths, going fast enough to make sure the cop on horseback who wanted to stop me couldn't catch me. I think Dagonet's blading backwards and waving at him was a little over the top. We made it all the way to the far end and the 110th Street—Central Park North Station. I took the stairs down toward the 2 and 3 lines on the bike. Dagonet leapt up so he went on the handrail in the middle of the stairs. After a quick check that there was no train, I jumped the bike onto the tracks heading toward the Bronx. Luckily I'm strong enough to yank the front up to make it work, much like a kid with a bicycle. Dagonet hopped onto the back of the bike and we sped into the tunnel. A few hundred feet in there was another tunnel that was camouflaged by magic to deter visitors.

Inside it was dark, but the headlight took care of that. Ahead there was light and what looked like a 1970's era subway token booth. Inside was a large gray gentleman. Amsterdam is notoriously cranky, even for a gate troll.

Despite popular myth, trolls are not native to either Earth or Faerie. They are from off planet. Many trolls have an ability to open rifts or bridges between dimensions or control a naturally occurring nexus. The one under Central Park was the later, one of the many rifts that connected Earth and my home world. Amsterdam has been the gatekeeper for this one for a long time. He's close enough to the magic of Faerie to have his aging slowed.

Amsterdam is not a terribly entrepreneurial individual. He's not here to make money. He just likes to be left alone, but doing it at the nexus gives him power to defend himself and have a long life.

He views people using the nexus as a bother and charges outrageous sums or barter to get through.

Fortunately, I've gotten to know him.

I pulled up in front of the booth. When he didn't even look up from his tiny television, I resisted the urge to rev the engine. The nexus was shrunk somewhere between a dime and a pinhole.

Amsterdam couldn't close it completely, but not even one of my pixie relations was going to fit through without his help.

Dagonet started to open his mouth, but I shushed him. I'm all about the wisecracks, but now wasn't a good time.

Amsterdam finally looked up. He knew we were there long before he saw us. He had closed circuit monitoring both sides of the rift. He had a matching booth on Faerie and just jumped between the two as customers showed up.

"Daemor," he said flatly by way of greeting. "Knight." That was said with more emotion, although I couldn't say if it was affection or annoyance. "What do you want?"

"Passage to Faerie," I said.

"What are you offering in payment?" Amsterdam asked. He might not have been all about the money, but no troll takes up bridge keeping without enjoying haggling.

I picked up the plastic bag from the convenience store and got off the bike. I knew folks who traded or gave things worth more than my bike for the toll. I figured I was going to get us through for about a hundred bucks and change.

"A two liter bottle of your favorite red caffeinated beverage, a family size box of chocolate cupcakes, a half dozen chili dogs, and the just released season of your favorite television show on DVD. It even has digital copies of each episode for your MP3 player." (A previous toll I paid.) As I announced each item, I placed it in the little drawer that extended from the booth.

Amsterdam nodded stone-faced. "That's good for one."

"One? Look at all this..." I started, but Dagonet put a hand on my shoulder and stepped up to the partition of the toll both. Amsterdam leaned his head so his ear was pressed up against the Plexiglas. Dagonet bent to meet him, cupping his mouth and whispering something that I couldn't hear. Amsterdam actually smiled and chuckled. It was the most emotion, other than annoyance or anger, that I had ever seen from him.

"That's good for the second," he said, waving his hand so the nexus grew big enough for us to pass through. Dagonet and I got back on the bike and rode through.

Going through a dimensional nexus is a singularly disturbing experience. Not as much as shadow stepping, but enough to make my stomach empty it's contents once we crossed over into Faerie. I emptied an explosive round into the vomit. It might seem excessive, but there are those in Faerie who could use those contents in a spell against me.

I hooked my Daemor badge onto a holder I had installed on the bike. Faerie magic tends to attack technology, but the badge had charms to protect tech. In theory, wearing it should have worked, but the bike was large enough that I didn't want to take any chances. We sped off and I quickly veered onto a Faerie path.

"I assume you know where you're going," said Dagonet, sounding nervous. Faerie paths are dangerous, able to mess you up in time and space. We could be on one a few minutes and have a century pass or be gone a year and have only seconds go by. Murphy coined the term quantum geography and it fits. Also there is a real danger of stepping off a path in the wrong place and getting lost forever. Going down an unfamiliar path is a treacherous and often stupid thing.

"Yep," I said. Tralla, one of the Daemor, was a pathmaker. That means not only could she magically sense where paths went, she could actually form new ones and alter the tracks of others. She had mapped all the paths in Faerie and drilled them into the rest of the Daemor. It was too sensitive to trust to the regular troops, even the officers. It was the functional equivalent of being able to teleport. It was one of our main advantages over Thandau and his forces. Learning it was the equivalent of memorizing an atlas of New Jersey. Still, I'd never forget it, so I knew not only how to get around Faerie, but jump from Earth to Faerie and back. Since there are only a few dozen nexi between them, it's limited as a form of travel, but when it worked, it worked well. Plus we were trained to know how to control the quantum geography factors. Less than a second would pass on Earth in the time we traveled to London.

"What'd you say to Amsterdam?" I said.

"Can't tell. Part of our deal, but it's an ongoing joke," said Dagonet.

"And I thought I got off easy on the toll," I said.

Dagonet chuckled. "If you think it's easy, you make him laugh."

"Beyond my abilities I think," I said. "We'll be coming out in an alley near St. Martin's in Ludgate Hill."

"I know it well. I was imprisoned in Ludgate prison back in the 1460's. Coincidentally so was Thomas Malory," said Dagonet.

"The guy who wrote Le Morte d'Arthur?" I said.

"Yep."

"You have anything to do with that?" I asked.

"I may have told him a few tales, but he changed them around to his liking. Not too kind to me, but he got the important ideas right," said Dagonet ruefully. He has issues with his lack of fame, but at the same time plays his importance down. "We can head over to Ludgate Circus and to Blackfriars Bridge railway station."

"I've never heard of that station," I said, hitting the brakes so I didn't skid off a sharp turn on the path.

"Been closed since 1964. Do we have a plan?" he asked.

"Not yet. They were on Thrones' business. Some guy who had been cannibalizing children. One of the kids called down the Thrones. They weren't expecting much trouble," I said.

"Which means they either underestimated the mark or there was someone or something else waiting for them," he said.

"Which means they probably have something waiting for me," I said.

"Which might be another reason Gani didn't reach out for you," Dagonet said. "Be prepared for anything."

"Easier to say than do," I said. "Here's our off ramp."

"Where?" he said as we were literally going through it. It was marked but subtly and probably hard for human eyes to see.

Going back though a nexus to Earth wasn't any more pleasant but my stomach was empty so I didn't have to stop as we sped across London.

I parked my bike under the train overpass and hooked my Daemor badge back on my waist chain. The building was mostly brick. The top was where passengers had gotten on the train. The building was underneath it. Other than the boarded up glass doors, there were no windows on the street.

"We go in from above?" said Dagonet.

"Probably best," I said. It was more than thirty feet to the roof, but less than half that to the low end of the track platform. "You need a hand to get up there."

"Two actually," said Dagonet, taking Hayden out of his wrist sheath, pointed the invisible sword down and expanded it so he was raised up. I dropped my coat on the bike, put my gun in my right hand and the ax in my left.

I got a running start and leapt to the low end of the platform, pushing off the metal overhanging the street and pushed off toward the roof. With the help of my wings I made it to the top. We passed a billboard on our way to the entrance. The doors leading down were chained and locked. Dagonet used Hayden to slice first through the chain and then the dead bolt.

Without a word we descended the stairs as quietly as we could. The building was dark except for one area that was blinding with sun lamps. Nemesis lay in the center, battered and bloody.

To the right of her Gani was in the center of a spell circle unmoving. Rudy was hung from the ceiling, each of her limbs held by metal rope of the type used to suspend bridges, only thinner and she was stripped down to the skin, parts of which had been peeled off of her.

Dagonet started to rush to Gani's side. I reached out to stop him, but he had already stopped and was scanning the abandoned terminal for whoever did this. So was I.

I was also scanning for traps. Whoever did this knew Nemesis & Co. was coming, which should have been impossible. The Thrones don't usually announce things in advance. Being a flyer I think of space differently than people reliant solely on their legs, so I always check above me. This time I was almost too late.

A man dropped from beams on the ceiling right toward me. My natural reaction was to drop and roll out of his way. In Faerie, I would have flown to meet him in the air. He was probably prepared for either of those, as well as me shooting him so I stood my ground until he was close enough for the ax. I swung, catching him in the leg. Dagonet extended his invisible sword right into his heart. Our attacker hit the ground bloody and beaten.

"That was too easy," I said.

"Agreed," said the Infinite Jester.

I pumped several rounds into his body or at least I tried, but the man was no longer there, having run to the far end of the terminal in the blink of an eye.

"That was disappointing, Terrorbelle. You didn't react at all like you were supposed to. You're ruining my plans here. First, you don't show up with the rest of your team and when you do, you bring him. Nemesis doesn't have male agents. Probably some deep-rooted issues there, but I don't like to judge. I'll give you a chance to surrender," he said.

"Why would I want to do that?" I said, trying to draw a bead on him, but he kept moving and dodging too fast, using the pillars for cover. Dagonet and I had split up to make separate targets.

"I'd consider it a personal favor. I don't want to kill you right now. I like to play with my food before I eat it. There's no meal like one you get to know first," he said.

"Well, since we are getting to know each other, I'm guessing your real name isn't really Robert Bittern," I said.

"Trying to get my name. Very commendable, but I'm not fool enough to give that up. Knowing it has made me far too powerful," he said. Every person and many things have true names which can grant them oodles of power, but it's a double-edged sword. Anyone else who learns the name can pretty much control them. From the looks, knowing his true name made Matuku pretty much unkillable, damn fast and who knows what else.

"But not as much as your daddy, I'll bet," I said. I was reaching, but the way he moved and talked marked him as part human, part something else. Blame it on being a mixed race girl myself. I was guessing it was a god, probably a minor one. And most demigods are on the father's side.

"Ooh, you're good. Much more than just hired muscle. I'll trade you the name I'm known by for the little guy's known name," he said.

"You first," said Dagonet. "And throw in a little detail."

"Sure. You can call me Matuku. I grew up in the South Pacific," he said. "My daddy was Tawhaki."

"Never heard of either of you," said Dagonet.

"I like my privacy. Makes it easier to make new friends and have them for dinner. Now follow through on your end of the bargain, short stuff," said Matuku.

"I am Sir Dagonet, jester knight of the Round Table."

"Ah, that explains it. You're here for the white haired hag," said Matuku. "You'd think she'd know better than to step into a spell circle after such a long life. Of course she was trying to save a darling little baby. Not that I blame her," Matuku said, holding up the leg of an infant and biting into it like it was chicken. "Babies always taste better if you save some for the next day."

Matuku dodged back somehow sensing that Hayden's blade had been coming right at his face. Instead of his skull, it caught the baby's limb and pulled it away when it retracted.

"That's very rude. If you're hungry, you could have asked. I might have shared. I even have some tangy curry sauce to dip in, not to mention this chardonnay that really brings out the flavor."

Dagonet cursed. Matuku laughed. "I guess I can't expect everyone to have as sophisticated a palate as me. Look, I like both of you. I'll make you a deal. Pick one of my captives, agree to leave me alone and I'll let you take her. One of three. You won't get a better offer."

"You won't do it," said Dagonet.

"You doubt my honesty?"

"That you have any? Yes. You won't release Nemesis or Ganieda because once prepared for you, either would destroy you. And Thrud would simply call in her family and the valkyries who would delight in destroying you," said Dagonet. "You just want to see us agonize over which to choose."

Matuku giggled. "You've got me there. Although I though about sparing Thrud. I asked her to be my consort. Sort of a courtesy since we are both children of thunder gods, but the bitch turned me down. Some people have no gratitude."

"Here's my offer," I said. "Let them all go right now and I'll just kill you, none of the traditional Thrones punishment that lasts for ages."

Matuku stopped with most of his body behind a pillar and stroked his chin. "Hmm, I'm doubting that. You are the soft one of the group, always opting for punishment over outright slaughter."

"Not always," I said.

"True, but you are the weakest of the group. And Sir Tiny there has a magic sword, but other than that he's human. You don't have enough power to take me down," said Matuku.

"Want to bet?" said Dagonet a second after Hayden had shot out and pierced the cannibal demigod through the chest and to the far wall. Matuku screamed. "Terrorbelle, go!"

He didn't have to ask me twice. I ran and leapt up, hovering next to Rudy, grabbing hold of her with my gun hand. With my ax, I sliced the four cords suspending her off the ground and lowered her to the ground.

"Terrorbelle, he…" Rudy started to sob and I knew what had happened.

"I'm so sorry, Rudy," I said.

"How did you…"

"One day at a time," I said, handing Rudy her gun. She took it, but seemed more concerned with covering her nakedness. Wishing I hadn't left my coat outside, I stripped out of my dress and gave it to her. She looked at me. "Take it," I said, grateful I had worn a strapless bra instead of bra cups. There was no helping the thong. "Help Dagonet. I'm going to help the boss."

I ran to Nemesis, trying not to let the fact that Matuku was pushing himself along the invisible blade in an attempt to get to Dagonet distract me.

The boss was in a heap, several large darts sticking out of her. I had no idea what was in them. I could only assume it was some mystic based poison. I pulled them all out.

"Nemesis, wake up!" I shouted. Nothing. I slapped her across the face. Nothing. Her breathing was shallow and I barely felt a pulse. She was well on her way to dying. Without knowing the poison, there could be no antidote and that would be more Gani's department anyway.

I couldn't let her die.

As the daughter of Nyx, the darkness of night could help heal her, but unfortunately it was daytime in London. Still she had an affinity for darkness and shadow. I shot out the sunlamps, but there was still some light coming through the not entirely boarded up doors. I lifted the boss up and carried her toward the darkest corner of the terminal. What I was about to try was incredibly stupid. If it worked, I might not survive, but if I didn't Nemesis definitely wouldn't.

Nemesis had once mentioned that sometimes she has to focus to not step into the shadows. I hoped that held true when she was unconscious as I stepped into the darkness carrying the daughter of night.

As soon as I felt my stomach sink, I knew it worked. We had shadow stepped. Unlike the paths of Faerie, I had no idea how to navigate. Whenever I had to travel through the darkness before, I just held onto Nemesis. Normally, it would be impossible to see here, but there are different shades of darkness and Nemesis grants her agents the ability to see in this realm. She temporarily does the same to those she brings here to scare.

Part one of my plan had worked. Part two, where the shadows healed Nemesis so she woke up and got us out of here before kicking Matuku's butt wasn't going so well. I tried to wake her again, but no luck. Worse, I could hear things scurrying in the darkness. I was trying hard not to look at them. Nemesis's mother was a creature of primordial darkness and Chaos, not that much unlike Rover the shadow dog. Unfortunately, not all of Nemesis' relations are as socially well adjusted as her mom. Many are elder things looking for a reason and a chance to destroy a world or two, many even the universe, just because they were kicked out.

I doubt the things coming for us would be as nice as Rover. There are things in the darkness that will drive people mad just for looking at them, so I only surveyed the area out of the corners of my eyes and it wasn't good. We were surrounded on all sides. Something that felt like a tentacle touched my shoulder and I went into defense mode and cut it off with a wing. There was plenty of magic here, so I took to the air. In an attempt to not get hopelessly lost, I tried to stay near where we entered. Not wanting to be eaten or worse, I curled into a ball, covering Nemesis with my body and started spinning head over toes, faster and faster. Anything trying to touch me would get cut, shredded, or worse. With any luck that would be enough.

My hopes that the rapid movement would help wake my boss soon died. I could feel things probing, trying to reach past my defenses. So far they were being diced, but I was getting dizzier and queasier the more I spun. Sooner or later, I'd slow down and something would get through. I needed help.

"Ganieda, Ganieda, Ganieda," I tried, hoping Gani was listening and the summoning could break her out of her prison. It didn't work. I tried to think of anyone I could summon that would be powerful enough to hear the call, survive the trip, kick some tentacle, and willing to help. Nobody came to mind. Then it came to me in a flash.

"Nyx, Nyx, Nyx." Nemesis's mother was the equivalent of a goddess. She didn't have to answer the summons, but this was her place of power. Nyx would at least know I was calling. Whether she showed up was up to her.

"*Be gone!*" boomed a voice that seemed to come from everywhere at once.

I heard thousands of feet, wings, tentacles, and other appendages scurry away. I slowed my spinning and tried not to throw up on my boss's mom.

"*Who summons me?*" she demanded.

For the record, she knew damn well who had called. If it was someone summoning her Earth-side she might not know, at least in the daytime. But here in her place of power? Nyx took in everything before she even bothered to show up. True we had only met the one time, but she would hardly not recognize her own daughter.

Still, one doesn't piss off angry embodiments of night. I followed protocol. "I Terrorbelle, agent of your daughter Nemesis, have called you."

"*For what purpose?*"

"Your daughter has been poisoned and is near death. I have brought her here so she might be healed," I said.

"*I told her to be careful the last time I restored her arm. My daughter needs to be taught a lesson and if death is the only way, then so be it. Besides, it will transform her and bring her into her true power so she can leave the mortal world behind.*"

"Nemesis is unable to speak for herself, so I find myself honor bound to speak in her place," I said.

"*Because my daughter has chosen you as one of her servants does not mean you are her equal or have any standing to address me. Because she is fond of you, I will return you back to Earth in a place were night yet reigns.*"

"While I appreciate your offer, first I beseech you to let me speak," I said.

"*Very well. If what you say does not please me, I may kill you myself and feed your carcass to the creatures of night.*"

"You can try," I said.

For that Nyx decided to materialize in human form in front of me. She was even more beautiful than her daughter, her skin as pale as moonlight and her hair as black as night, with stars scattered among the strands. I didn't even dare look at her eyes, but her lips were smiling.

"*You think you can stand against the living night?*"

"Probably not, but I won't go down without a fight," I said, thinking of the solid light and dark bullets in my and Gani's gun. They could hurt Nemesis. Maybe they could hurt her mom. "Neither would your daughter. Since she can't fight now, I'm just acting as her proxy."

"*Why? Because it's your job?*"

"No, because Nemesis is my friend."

There was a sound that was nothing like laughter, yet I knew that's exactly what it was.

"*I like you Terrorbelle. You stood up to me, much as Ganieda once did although she had a much better chance of survival than you do. Very well, I offer you a bargain. I will restore the health of my daughter. In exchange, I get one day of your life.*"

"You mean you want to hire me for a day?" I asked.

"*Not exactly. One day of your existence belongs to me.*"

I didn't like the sound of that. "You mean I have to do whatever you ask for a day?"

"*That and much more.*"

"You are being awfully cryptic. What does that mean exactly? What day?"

Nyx laughed and it was a cold, dark thing. "*Time is wasting and my daughter is fading into the beautiful darkness. Do you agree?*"

"You'll guarantee my safety?"

"*I will not, but I will assure nothing of the darkness will be able to hurt you easily.*"

"For the day?"

"It will last a bit longer."

"You realize I will not do anything I find morally objectionable?"

"We shall see, but I grant you the option of that possibly although it may come with a price. Do we have a deal?"

"Yes," I said with no idea of what I had gotten myself into.

Nyx knelt in front of her daughter and tenderly cradled Nemesis in her arms, kissing her once on the head. She reached a hand into Nemesis' chest and pulled out what looked like a dark fog, then shifted her hand through her daughter's body like she was panning for gold. With each motion, more of the dark fog came out.

A few moments later, Nemesis started to cough. Nyx turned her on her side and she vomited up something that was the consistency of tar.

It took her several moments to get a hold of herself, but when she did, she genuflected in front of Nyx.

"Thank you, mother."

"Do not thank me. I felt it was time for you to throw off the mortal coil and join me here. You should thank Terrorbelle. She is the one who convinced me otherwise."

"Thanks, Belle," Nemesis said.

"Just doing my job," I said.

"You are doing far more than that. I believe there are still matters of great urgency awaiting you daughter. You should deal with them."

"I shall."

"And Terrorbelle, tell Ganieda that the cannibal is his father's son."

"Okay," I agreed having no idea what that meant. "And thank you, Nyx."

"You are welcome. Do not forget our bargain."

"I won't," I said.

"What bargain?" asked Nemesis. "And what happened to your clothes?"

"Time for that later. Dagonet was holding off Matuku, but just barely," I said.

"Gani and Rudy?"

"I couldn't get Gani out of the spell circle," I said, telling her what the cannibal demigod had done to Rudy. She figured out where my clothes went without me having to explain. We'd both been there and back.

The boss was just about as angry as I had ever seen her. We shadow stepped back into the terminal.

Matuku was about ten feet from the Infinite Jester. Rudy was on the floor, curled into a ball. The cannibal was holding a red-haired Barbie-type doll. The hair looked real and was the same shade as Rudy's. It was covered in blood and patches of skin, about the same size as the bloody areas of the valkyrie's hide. The bastard had bound her against her will while she was chained and was hurting her even more now.

Nemesis shot the doll with an explosive round, destroying it and the spell. The next round went straight for Matuku's head, but somehow he managed to dodge it. The effort made Nemesis collapse. The effects of the poison were still affecting her and there was still some light in the terminal.

"Not that this hasn't been fun, Tiny, but I think it's time for me to go." With visible effort Matuku ripped his body to the side nearest the stairs, making the sword blade tear through his ribs in order to free himself. It must have hurt, because he held his side as he limped toward the stairs.

"Get him!" screamed Nemesis, too weak to do it herself. I raced after him, Dagonet not far behind me, but neither of us could match his speed. Once at the decommissioned tracks, he ran out over them, with us following. Unfortunately, with each second, his lead increased.

"Terrorbelle, stop," said Dagonet.

I obliged and Dagonet jumped up and wrapped his legs around my waist and his arms around my neck.

"Not that I'm not flattered, but do you think this is the best time? Not to mention explaining it to Gani," I teased.

Dagonet handed me Hayden. "I can control it without touching it, but I'm not strong enough to lift you. Hold it and I'll shoot us ahead."

Hayden's point was embedded in a track tie and as soon as I told him I had a good grip, the invisible sword telescoped and we shot up and over the tracks, closing the distance.

Dagonet retracted the blade as we passed over Matuku. Taking his sword, he jumped off. My momentum carried me to the other side of the cannibal and I used my wings to guide my descent and landed on my feet.

We had him between us, but at enough of an angle that I could shoot without worrying about hitting Dagonet. I hit Matuku repeatedly with a half dozen type of rounds and Dagonet was rapidly skewering him with in and out extensions and retractions of his blade.

The damage we inflicted should have reduced him to hamburger, but Matuku still somehow held it together. Worse, he was smiling.

"You both are more skilled than your more powerful betters. I think you might have caught me if I had ran the other way," said Matuku.

"No!" screamed Dagonet as the cannibal demigod jumped into the Thames River below us.

What I did next was stupid, but I was angry. Matuku was not getting away after what he did to Rudy, especially since he'd be coming after all of us anyway. I watched and realized Matuku was not coming up. Worse, from what I could make out through the murky water and the blood flow into the current, the cannibal was walking along the bottom of the river with the same ease he had run down the tracks with, albeit at a much slower pace.

I leapt off the bridge, using a nice updraft to help me catch up to him. I could hear Dagonet yelling at me to come back. He'd spent enough time in Faerie to know ogres can't swim and figured I was enough ogre for that to hold true for me. He was right. My body is too dense for me to swim well. I'm much better at sinking, but that would let me get to the bottom faster.

I had been deep breathing during my flight. Once I was over where Matuku was submerged I took as deep a breath as I could manage, tucked in my wings and pointed my body into a dive. I hit the water and kept going down. Matuku had no idea I was there until I passed him, with my wing slicing his head off. I grabbed it with my left hand and started shooting explosive rounds at his body with my right, which only slowed it down. It attacked me and I managed to cut off one of his arms and both legs as it attacked me. The remaining arm managed to grab a leg and stick it back on.

I can hold my breath for a while, but I was pushing it. I tried to get to the surface, but couldn't make it. Apparently the Thames is a tidal river, which means its depth varies with the tides. At low tide, I could have pushed off the bottom with enough force to get my head above water for a breath of air. Sadly, it was high tide.

Matuku's reassembled body could move faster than me under water, so no matter how hard I tried I couldn't get away. I was just about out of air, which he seemed to sense, his body staying just out of reach figuring he could outwait me.

As my world dimmed, I found my life flashing before my eyes—what the soldiers did to Ma and me—Gram, my papa, my time and friends as a Daemor and my time working for Nemesis. There were even visions of my neighbors, Sydney, Lucinda and little Pixie. But the last person I saw was Murphy. I wished him only the best and thought at least I'd get to meet Elsie and we could compare notes.

When all else was black, I saw his face and suddenly I felt his lips on mine. There was no tongue as in my usual fantasies, only sweet air being pushed in my mouth. He pulled me on his lap and I heard the rev of an engine and suddenly I was above the water. I looked down and realized I was laid across the front of his flying and apparently submersible motorcycle while we floated above the Thames.

I coughed and spit up water all over him, not that he seemed to care or matter. He was soaked to the bone.

"Oh, thank God," he said, hugging me.

I kissed him and he kissed back, before pulling back awkwardly. Damn, he was a good kisser, better than the movie star. And I felt something in that kiss. Maybe my maybe someday would really come.

"You forget you can't swim?" he asked.

I smiled and realized I still had a hold of Matuku's hair and head. "I didn't want to come to London and go home without a souvenir."

"That's the guy who did all this?" Murphy asked.

"Part of him, yeah," I said. "What are you doing here?"

"I had Fred cover the bar and took the bike in case you needed help," he said.

"Good call," I said.

"What happened to your clothes?" he asked.

"Had to loan them to Rudy. However, if you kiss me like that again, I promise to get rid of the rest of them," I teased.

Murphy surprised me by leaning in and giving me a gentle kiss, but this one was on the lips.

"What was that for?" I asked.

"For being you," he said.

Murphy flew us back to the railroad bridge and picked up Dagonet.

"You should have seen her tonight, Murphy," said Dagonet from the back of the bike.

"Against the bad guy?" he said.

"Naw, in the club. The girl can dance and the way she filled out that dress. Why, if I were a thousand years younger..."

"You'd still be in love with Gani," I finished.

"Pretty much," Dagonet agreed.

We touched down outside and this time I just kicked in the front door. Nemesis was waiting and I tossed her the head. She said hi to Murphy, confused as to where he had come from since we were an ocean away from his normal stomping grounds. The head was trying to glare at me, but I didn't care. Gani was free of the spell circle. She saw Dagonet and rushed toward him, stumbling. The Infinite Jester leapt forward and caught her.

"You came," Gani said.

"Was there ever any doubt?" said Dagonet.

"No," she said and she bent down to kiss him on the lips as the pair embraced.

I excused myself from the men and walked to Rudy. She handed me my dress. She was wearing the boss's leather trenchcoat. Rudy had a few inches on me so it was tight and short on her, but she wasn't swimming in it like my dress. "How are you doing?"

"Better since Nemesis blew up the voodoo doll. Still shaky though," she said. "Would you mind if I came over to your apartment tonight to... talk. Maybe crash on your couch?"

"No problem," I said.

"Thanks. For everything," Rudy said.

"I second that," said Nemesis. "What is the deal you made with my..."

"How did you get Gani out?" I said, changing the subject.

"Not a very good spell circle. If he hadn't drugged her with a dart, it wouldn't have held her. I used a light to make a shadow and jumped her out," said Nemesis. "But enough of changing the subject."

"Actually, Matuku's body is probably heading this way," I said. "I dismembered him, but he just pulled himself back together."

Nemesis stared at me. "Why didn't you just separate the parts from the torso and bring them back here?"

"Because it kind of happened underwater," I said. Nemesis' jaw actually dropped.

"Are you insane!?" she screamed. "You should have been killed. Although it explains why Murphy is all wet."

"Actually, Dagonet had these two seltzer bottles and suggested a duel and he's a bit better at it than I am," said Murphy.

"Murphy, normally I find your jokes endearing, but right now, shut up," said Nemesis. Murphy made a key locking gesture with his hand over his mouth. Dagonet reached out, pretending to steal the key and threw it far away. Nemesis ignored them both. "We have to dismember and incapacitate the body before it gets here."

"Too late," said Dagonet as the demigod's body walked in the door I kicked open. The knight stepped protectively in front of Gani and she stepped forward to return the favor. The mage let loose a mystic blast that sent the body out the door and onto the street. It picked itself up and marched toward us again.

"If I knew his true name, this would be over," said Gani, who had been brought up to speed. The head in Nemesis' hand stuck his tongue out.

"Nyx said to tell you that the cannibal was his father's son. Does that help?" I said.

"What does that mean?" she said.

I shrugged and started listing the little I knew. "His name's Matuku. His father was a thunder god from the South Pacific named Tawhaki."

Gani started humming, rolling her eyes back in her head as if she were searching for information written on the back of her eyelids. Then she smiled and snapped her fingers. "I got it," she said, muttering something that was probably a word and the body stopped short and the head got a horrified expression.

"How'd you do that?" I said.

"It was simple. I just combined the Tongan words for father, lightning, and son and mixed in his father's name. Demigod true names are often quite literal," Gani said.

"Of course," I said as if I understood everything she said.

Rudy grabbed the head from Nemesis and things got ugly. She started cursing at the cannibal rapist and pulled a knife out of the boss's coat. Rudy literally sliced off Matuku's manhood, then went at it with the intensity of a hibachi chef until it was in tiny pieces. Apparently she promised to spread them all over the world so they would never be found and reattached. Both Murphy and Dagonet involuntarily crossed their legs, but Nemesis smiled and I couldn't actually find fault with Rudy's actions. Yeah it was brutal, but no more so than what he did to her. And back when I was attacked by the soldiers I would have done worse if I could have.

We headed home. Nemesis shadow stepped my bike back to the garage at work, along with the now immobilized Matuku. I understand she took the long and scenic route through the shadows. That was only the start of his torment. Exactly what it was I don't know because Nemesis wouldn't tell me. She felt I'd sleep better that way.

Gani moved the broken vending machine Matuku had jammed in her elevator and took herself, Dagonet, and Rudy back to the office.

Of course, I had two hours of Murphy to myself on the ride back on the flying motorcycle over the Atlantic. Apparently he too loved the dress. Apparently I was going to have to start wearing more of them. Bruce was going to be thrilled.

I held onto him tight from behind the whole way. I thanked him and he brushed it off, telling me that a world without Terrorbelle in it would be a much worse place. I squeezed his chest that much tighter and told him I never wanted to be in a world without John Murphy in it.

When he dropped out of the sky in front of the stoop of my building, Rudy was waiting. And so were Lucinda, Sydney, and Darcy. I got a lot of oohs. Apparently a guy who can drop out of the sky is much more competitive with a movie star.

I ended up with an apartment full of friends for the night. At some point Mrs. W and Pixie joined us too. I made waffles and we greeted the dawn together. Except for Pixie. She slept through it all, a lot of it on Rudy's lap.

It was good for Rudy. We ended up spending a lot of time over the next week together, She coped well. Apparently cutting up the demigod's penis was extremely therapeutic. She even told the other ladies, although I thought Sydney's suggestion to have the pieces bronzed and made into necklaces for all of us was tacky and over the top. Sadly, I think Rudy liked the idea, so I was going to be looking carefully at any jewelry the valkyrie gave me.

And Rudy passed Dagonet coming out of Gani's quarters when she went home. They still weren't back together, but at least they had a night with each other. I'm sure it helped the times when they were apart.

Of course, the picture of me and Joe Hunk made the front cover of "The Post" the next day. It was small and in the upper corner, but it was still there. Another made a supermarket tabloid later in the week. This one was a quarter of the page and in color. It speculated he was dating an unnamed lady wrestler.

Sydney had the first one framed for me by lunch and the second within an hour of it hitting the stands. My first reaction was worrying if Murphy would see them and what he would think. My second reaction was to hope he did see it and it got him off the sidelines and into the game.

I did have to eventually tell Nemesis my deal with her mother. It worried her, but she promised to do whatever she could for me when the time came.

And when I joked about getting a raise and an extra week of vacation, she actually gave them to me. Made me really worry about what her mom might do, but no sense in stressing about it until Nyx came to collect.

PATRICK THOMAS is the author of over 80 published short stories and more than 17 books including the popular fantasy humor series MURPHY'S LORE™, which includes the collections EMPTY GRAVES and NIGHTCAPS in the AFTER HOURS™ series. Other books in the series include the collections BARTENDER OF THE GODS, TALES FROM BULFINCHE'S PUB and THROUGH THE DRINKING GLASS the novels REDEMPTION ROAD, SHADOW OF THE WOLF, and FOOLS' DAY.

His collection MYSTIC INVESTIGATORS is available from Dark Quest Books.

Patrick co-edited HEAR THEM ROAR and the upcoming NEW BLOOD vampire anthology. He has also edited for Fantastic Stories and Pirate Writings. Patrick has novellas in GO NOT GENTLY from Padwolf (which also includes C.J. Henderson and a World Fantasy Award winning novella from Parke Godwin) as well as one in FLESH AND IRON from the Two Backed Books imprint of Raw Dog Screaming.

His stories have sold to various magazines and anthologies including SAILS & SORCERY, CROSS-GENRE CTHULHU, HARDBOILED CTHULHU, SPACE & TIME, ABYSS & APEX, CTHULHU SEX, DREAMS OF DECADENCE, DARK FURIES, CLASH OF STEEL 3: DEMON, BREACH THE HULL, SO IT BEGINS, BAD-ASS FAIRIES, THE 2ND COMING, UNICORN 8, JIGSAW NATION, CRYPTO-CRITTERS VOL. 1 & 2, THE DEAD WALK AGAIN, TIME CAPSULE and WARFEAR.

He co-created the YA fantasy series THE WILDSIDHE CHRONICLES™ and wrote two of the first six books in the series. Patrick also pens the syndicated satirical advice column DEAR CTHULHU™. The first collection DEAR CTHULHU™: HAVE A DARK DAY will be out from Dark Quest Books later this year.

Please visit his website at www.patthomas.net

EMPTY GRAVES

PATRICK THOMAS

When Graves Empty the last one out is a rotten corpse

VOL. 2

Printed in the United States
212135BV00002B/1/P

9 781890 096410